# ALSO BY KELLEY ARMSTRONG

**A Rip Through Time** mystery ser[i]
*A Rip Through Time*
*The Poisoner's Ring*
*Cocktails & Chloroform (novella)*
*Disturbing the Dead*
*Schemes & Scandals (novella)*
*Death at a Highland Wedding*
*Kirkyards & Kindness (novella)*
*An Ordinary Sort of Evil*

**Haven's Rock** mystery series
*Murder at Haven's Rock*
*The Boy Who Cried Bear*
*Cold as Hell*
*First Sign of Danger*

**Standalone Horror**
*Hemlock Island*
*I'll Be Waiting*
*The Haunting of Paynes Hollow*

**Past Series**
**Rockton** mystery series
**A Stitch in Time** time-travel gothic series
**Cursed Luck** contemporary fantasy duology
**Cainsville** paranormal mystery series
**Otherworld** urban fantasy series
**Nadia Stafford** mystery trilogy

**Standalone Thrillers**
*The Life She Had*
*Wherever She Goes*
*Every Step She Takes*
*Known to the Victim*

**Standalone Romantic Comedy**
*Finding Mr. Write*
*Writing Mr. Wrong*

**Young Adult**
*A Deadly Inheritance*
*Someone is Always Watching*
*Aftermath*
*Missing*
*The Masked Truth*
**Otherworld: Kate & Logan** paranormal duology
**Darkest Powers/Darkness Rising** paranormal trilogies
**Age of Legends** fantasy trilogy

# PRAISE FOR THE "RIP THROUGH TIME" SERIES

"Armstrong puts a fresh, fun spin on an age-old premise. Mallory's snarky narration complements the [delightful] plot, and the vividly sketched cast is studded with charming iconoclasts. Readers will eagerly anticipate future installments."
*Publishers Weekly*

"Armstrong handles the time-traveling problems…with unusual resourcefulness and dexterity. [A] clever time-traveling thriller."
*Kirkus*

"The best time-travel tale I've read in a long time."
*The Providence Journal*

"I, for one, will absolutely be following the further adventures of this historical series."
*Mystery & Suspense Magazine*

"Pure Kelley Armstrong, featuring fabulous, likable, and diverse characters as well as gripping action and a compelling mystery or two to solve."
*Bookreporter*

"An intense, intricately plotted mystery"
*Library Journal (starred review)*

# COCKTAILS & CHLOROFORM / SCHEMES & SCANDALS

## A NOVELLA DUO

### A RIP THROUGH TIME

## KELLEY ARMSTRONG

This is a work of fiction. Names, characters, businesses, places, events and incidents are either the products of the author's imagination or used in a fictitious manner. Any resemblance to actual persons, living or dead, events, or locales is purely coincidental.

No part of this book may be reproduced in any form or by any electronic or mechanical means, including information storage and retrieval systems, without the written permission of the Author, except by a reviewer who may quote brief passages in a review.

"Cocktails & Chloroform" © 2023 K.L.A. Fricke Inc.
All rights reserved.

"Schemes & Scandals" © 2024 K.L.A. Fricke Inc.
All rights reserved.

Cover Design by The Killion Group

ISBN-13 (ebook): 978-1-989046-94-4
ISBN-13 (paperback): 978-1-989046-96-8

# COCKTAILS &
CHLOROFORM

# CHAPTER ONE

A Victorian widow, a Canadian detective, and a preteen pickpocket walk into a bar. . . . I'm sure there's a joke in there somewhere, but when we step through the door, no one's laughing. The bustling pub goes dead quiet, and the all-male patrons turn to stare. Mostly, they stare at Isla, the aforementioned widow, possibly because she's taller than most of the men there, but more likely because she's clearly a woman of quality, in her lilac-gray gown, silk gloves, and boots that are ninety-five percent horseshit free.

A few patrons leer at me, but I've learned not to take it personally. It's the body I'm wearing—that of a buxom nineteen-year-old housemaid with blond curls and the requisite big blue eyes. In real life, I'm a thirty-one-year-old cop who looks a whole lot less like a Victorian milkmaid. Three months ago, I was attacked in an Edinburgh alley at the same time as Catriona Mitchell had been, exactly a hundred and fifty years earlier. The result? A body swap across time.

I hope Catriona is not in *my* body. The poor, innocent child would be quite beside herself, lost in a strange world. Yeah, not exactly. I'm pretty sure Catriona Mitchell falls somewhere on the sociopath spectrum, which is the actual reason why I hope she's nowhere near my real body.

The third member of our educational excursion is pickpocket-turned-parlormaid, Alice, who sidles up beside Isla and whispers, "Are you sure this is a good idea, ma'am?"

"No," Isla says. "I am quite certain it is a very bad idea." She lowers her voice to a stage whisper. "Which is why we are doing it. *Someone* is rather fond of bad ideas."

Isla slants me a look.

"Me?" I say.

"It *was* your idea."

"The chemistry lesson was my idea. Buying the alcohol ourselves was not."

"It is a bad idea for a good cause," Isla whispers to Alice.

"For science," I say.

"For science," Isla echoes.

Alice sneaks a wary look at me. Unlike Isla, Alice doesn't know who I really am. She's accepted that a blow to the head changed Catriona's personality, but she's still leery, especially when I'm around Isla, in case her fellow maid is up to something. Alice bore the brunt of Catriona's darker side, and it's going to take more than a few months for Alice to accept that her bully sister-in-service is truly gone.

"If you're sure, ma'am," she says to Isla.

"I am."

Alice nods. "I won't mention it to Dr. Gray."

"Oh, my brother will learn of it. I shall tell him . . . as soon as it is too late for him to stop us."

Isla resumes her walk across the pub. We're still in the New Town, which means we're in a respectable part of Edinburgh. Honestly, though, this would have been easier in the Old Town. There, I can go into a pub, and no one bats an eye. But the women of the New Town are proper ladies, and proper ladies do not enter a house of spirits, even accompanied by their maids.

Isla doesn't slink in and duck past the well-dressed men. She strides through, chin high. The signs of visible widowhood help, allowing her a certain amount of freedom, even if—at thirty-three—she's still a relatively young woman. But that's not really what bolsters her confidence. Isla was raised to know her worth, and her worth—according to her family—was on par with that of her brothers. She's a chemist, in practice if not by trade, and she's as well educated as any man in this room.

Isla is a force of nature, and I am just an admiring observer. Also, I'm the one carrying the knife, in case anything goes wrong.

"Ma'am . . ." the bartender says carefully when Isla walks up. "Are you . . . in the right place?" His brogue is thick enough that I still struggle to follow, but I've learned to smooth it out in my head. That's easier when my own voice bears the same accent.

"Do you sell spirits?" Isla asks.

"Aye . . ."

"Then I am in the right place. I am in need of spirits for a party I am hosting this evening, and my brother was called away on business and could not fetch them. Nor could my groom, as he accompanied my brother."

The man relaxes. "All right then, ma'am. What might I be able to do for you?"

"I require the highest proof of alcohol you sell."

"Highest . . ."

"Concentration of alcohol. I require at least one hundred proof, being approximately fifty-seven percent alcohol by volume. Whisky is somewhat low for what I require. I was thinking absinthe. The strongest you have."

"Uh . . ."

"Have you heard of cocktails?"

He relaxes again. "Aye, ma'am. They're from America."

"I am making a special kind." She sneaks a look at me, her lips twitching. "Molotov cocktails."

"Molo . . . ?"

"They're Russian," I say.

The man glances at me and then back at Isla, who gives him an impatient look.

"I'll . . . see what I can find," he says.

"Bring out all the bottles. I will choose which I want."

---

We're back at 12 Robert Street, the New Town town house where Dr. Duncan Gray lives with Isla and their small staff. This is the house where Isla and Gray grew up, which Gray inherited along with the family business on his father's death . . . despite the fact that he's the youngest of four . . . and illegitimate. Also despite the fact that Mrs. Gray—his adoptive mother—is still alive.

Unlike English law of the time, Scottish law would have allowed Mrs. Gray to inherit the house. Yet it passed to the oldest son, and when he didn't want it, it came all the way down to Gray, leaving Isla in the awkward position of being under her little brother's protection.

While Gray and Isla have an enviable sibling relationship, it doesn't mean there aren't awkward wrinkles on either side. Which is why I am apparently tasked with telling Gray what we got up to today before he hears scuttlebutt on the street.

Fortunately, I won't have to tell him just yet because he's attending a medical lecture at the Royal College. He'd invited me along, and I honestly hated saying no, but I'd already agreed to the secret adventure with Isla. That adventure will culminate in a chemistry lesson tomorrow night when we set off our various incendiary devices and record the results. Why tomorrow night and not today? Because Gray isn't here today.

While I would never presume to fully understand Duncan Gray, I know enough to understand how this will go. I'll tell him what we did and what we're planning to do and, while he's deciding how best to handle it, I'll suggest he should oversee the actual lighting of the Molotov cocktails, which will solve everything.

After the pub stop, we spend an hour setting up the experimental parameters. Then Isla has a dinner engagement, and Alice and I return to work.

Catriona was Gray and Isla's housemaid. I've been working as Gray's assistant, but it's not a full-time job, so I'm keeping up with Catriona's tasks until Isla finds a replacement maid.

Finding a replacement should be easy enough—plenty of young women are eager to work for a decent New Town family. But Isla has a . . . unique hiring practice. She offers employment to candidates Gray's friend—Detective Hugh McCreadie—finds through his work. In other words, 12 Robert Street is also Isla Ballantyne's Home for Wayward Victorians. That explains how Catriona and Alice wound up here, though one was far more worthy of the opportunity than the other.

McCreadie did find a suitable housemaid candidate a few weeks ago: an eighteen-year-old girl who'd spent two years in prison for stabbing her abusive father. It quickly became apparent, though, that she'd set her hat on Simon, the groom, and she wasn't taking "I'm sorry, but I don't fancy you" for an answer. Simon doesn't fancy girls at all, which added another layer of discomfort, and I convinced Isla that I was fine returning to my old job until she found another maid.

I *am* fine with it. Oh, I could grumble that scrubbing chamber pots is beneath me, but that's bullshit. I cleaned houses for seniors as a teenager. There's a job to be done, and I'm not going to freeload, so if chamber pots need scrubbing, I'll do it . . . even if I am secretly dreaming of the day McCreadie finds a suitable replacement.

By now, I'm deep into the rhythm of a Victorian upper-middle-class household and all that is required to keep it running smoothly. Today is what the indoor staff consider a "light" day, with Gray gone and Isla away for dinner. Mrs. Wallace—the housekeeper and cook—gets a break from preparing the main meal, which means she can kick up her boots and relax. Yeah, not quite. While Mrs. Wallace *could* take a break, she'll use the extra time to get ahead for the next week.

We have a cold supper—Alice, Mrs. Wallace, Simon, and I—and while I personally don't see why we can't eat in the empty dining room, that's "not done." That is, it's not done by Mrs. Wallace. Isla and Gray wouldn't care, but Mrs. Wallace views their peccadilloes with the indulgence of a doting parent firmly steering errant children back in line. She treats Alice and Simon the same way. I am another matter.

"And where do you think you're going?" Mrs. Wallace calls from below as I head for the stairs at just past eight.

I turn, slowly. Mrs. Wallace stands behind me, tall and imposing. Her gray hair suggests age, but her unlined face whispers not to fall for that. She isn't old and cranky. She's just cranky. At least she is when it comes to Catriona, who is clearly setting her beloved employers up with a long-con game of playing "Mallory," some alternate personality caused by a blow to the head.

I also don't fall for Mrs. Wallace's question. I don't point out that my shift ended an hour ago, and I sure as hell never call on Isla or Gray to back me up, even when they *are* home. That's like appealing to the chief when my sergeant is being unreasonable. Handle this on my own, or face the consequences.

Step one: try to determine which chore I missed. This was easier early in my tenure when I was still figuring out the routine. By this point, I know I have completed everything on the day's list.

Step two: think harder. Could I be missing a weekly chore? A monthly one? I keep notes, and Alice helps me with that, so I don't think I've missed anything.

Step three: fall on my sword . . . as much as it stings. Don't ask *if* I've forgotten anything, and never suggest that I don't think I *have* forgotten anything.

"I'm sorry, ma'am. What have I forgotten?"

"Did you not notice the back walk when you came in after gallivanting around with the mistress?"

"I . . ." Nope, didn't notice anything. "I fear I was preoccupied in conversation with Alice. Let me go outside to see what I missed."

"Dirt. There is a great deal of dirt."

Because it's a Victorian back walkway twenty feet from the stables? Have you ever walked on the streets around here? "Dirt" is a euphemism.

This reminds me that I really need to suggest Gray invest in a back-door boot scraper. Hell, I'll buy it myself if I need to. There's a gorgeous bronze whale's tail at the front door. The problem is that the front door is rarely used by anyone except clients, who don't use the damn scraper.

I shouldn't grumble about that. The family business Gray inherited isn't a medical or surgical practice. It's undertaking, and I don't expect grieving family members to remember to clean off their boots . . . even if I really wish they would.

"Catriona?" Mrs. Wallace snaps when I'm slow in answering. In front of the bosses, she'll call me Mallory, but in private, she's not letting me forget what she thinks of this whole personality-change nonsense.

"Apologies, ma'am," I say with a slight curtsy. "I'll sweep the back path before Dr. Gray and Mrs. Ballantyne return."

She eyes me, and I resist the urge to ask if there's anything else. Catriona and Mrs. Wallace might have clashed, but I'm pretty sure Mrs. Wallace and I wouldn't do much better. I respect the hell out of her. I honestly do, and that's not just because I really want to know if she was joking about being a former circus performer. But as the housemaid, I can't ask whether there's anything else or it would seem sarcastic, especially when sarcasm is a rare trait Catriona and I seem to share.

So I wait, my gaze fixed just below Mrs. Wallace's, my expression quietly blank.

"Make sure it's well swept," she says. "Mr. Tull was gardening this afternoon, and the edges are covered in soil."

"Yes, ma'am."

The back door of the town house leads to the courtyard—including Isla's wonderful poison garden—and the stables. As Mrs. Wallace said, the part-time gardener, Mr. Tull, had been there today, and while the "edges" look fine to me, I still even them out as I sweep. I'm finishing up when a voice says, "I'm behind you and unarmed. Please do not stab me."

I shake my head and turn to see Simon walking over with his hands behind his back.

"Can't be too careful," he says. "I have something for you."

"If it's opium, the answer is still no."

He takes one hand from behind his back and waggles a finger at me. "Do not judge, dear girl. One of these days, you will have had enough of Mrs. Wallace and come banging on my door, begging for a taste of the sweet poppy."

"I don't break that easily."

"A thing you and Catriona have in common. Now, let us see what I have for Miss Mallory." He withdraws his other hand. It has an envelope and some white cards, like calling cards. "First, a favor to ask." He presents me with the envelope. "This came for Alice, and I have to go fetch Mrs. Ballantyne."

"Deliver the letter to Alice. Got it." I try to sneak a look at the cards, but he waves them about so I can't see them. "Now, Miss Mallory, in your former incarnation, you had no time for games and entertainments, yet you seem quite changed in that regard, and so I am wondering what you would say to joining me at an electro-biology presentation next week."

"An . . . ?"

He holds out the cards. "It's a show that conducts scientific experiments on audience members."

"I'm all for scientific progress but . . ."

"Not that sort of experimentation. Audience members are put into a state where they do and say whatever the scientist suggests."

"Ooh, mesmerism."

His brows rise. "I don't know that word, but I presume it is the same. Is the answer yes, then?"

I grin. "Yes, please."

"Good. We will speak later. For now, take that letter to Alice while I fetch the lady of the house. I am to be there at eight thirty sharp, and she hates it when I am late collecting her from society dinners."

"Collecting her? Or rescuing her?"

"They are the same, are they not?"

"They are." I wave the letter. "Have a good trip, and consider this delivered."

# CHAPTER TWO

I stand just inside the back door and finger the envelope. On the front, it says, in an uncertain hand, "Alice MacGillivray, 12 Robert Street." There's no postal mark, meaning it was hand delivered. The envelope has been reused a few times, with previous addresses crossed out. It's sealed with a blob of plain candle wax. I sniff it. Tallow.

If the sender was in service, they might reuse a discarded envelope, but they'd be able to take a spot of wax from a proper candle. Tallow—made from animal fat—means the sender is not only still using candles but can't afford wax ones.

I resist the urge to hold the letter to the light. I won't pry into Alice's private messages by doing more than gathering a few clues about the sender, even if I *am* very curious.

I don't know much about Alice beyond the fact she was a pickpocket. I know she still has family, but I also know that's not where she goes on her half days, so I presume there's a story there. I also suspect—though I bite my tongue against asking Isla —that Alice has part of her wages sent to someone.

Curiosity is an occupational hazard. Or it should be—an incurious cop should never become a detective. I like Alice, and I know that as good as Isla is to her, in Alice's mind there will always be a gulf Isla can't cross—employer and employee, well-to-do woman and working-class child. I can cross it, though. If Alice ever needs to confide in someone, it can be me. Yes, that's very presumptuous. I don't care. If I discover that there's someone else in her life to play that role, I'll stop trying so damn hard. Until then, I want to make up for whatever shit Catriona put her through.

I won't open the letter, but I can at least be there when she opens it, which means finding a way to do more than hand it to her and leave. That requires a trip down to the kitchen. Mrs. Wallace is in her room for the night. I still leave a note detailing what I took—that's a necessity when you occupy the body of a thief. Then I carry the tea tray up to Alice's room, on the top floor, beside mine, and I knock.

"It's me," I say. "I brought biscuits and a letter that came for you."

"Come in."

I find Alice at her desk. Our rooms are college dorm sized. Tiny compared to what I'm used to, but opulent quarters for those in service. I've been in homes where the maids all sleep in a room this size, with the poor parlormaids taking mats under the older girls' beds.

Like me, Alice has a bed, a dresser, and a washbasin. She also has a desk for her lessons, and that's where she is.

I set down the tray, hold out the letter and fix my expression to one as neutral as possible while I watch her take it. At first, she reaches out. Then she sees the writing and hesitates. Her narrow jaw sets in annoyance, and she all but snatches the letter from my hand. She rips it open, yanks out the page and reads a line or two. Then she goes still, her shoulders tensing as she pivots in her chair, putting her back to me.

From this vantage point, I can see enough to register three

things. One, the writing is in that same hesitant hand as the address. Two, while the writer is literate—over half of Scots are —there are enough spelling errors and crossed-out words to suggest low literacy. Three, I can make out one complete line of text—*He's taking me to Abernathy Hall tonight*—before Alice realizes that "turning around" gave her the opposite of privacy, and she pivots in her chair and lowers the letter.

"Is everything all right?" I try for a wry smile. "Late-night missives do not always bring the best of news."

Her gaze goes pointedly to the window, where it's barely dusk outside.

"Is everything all right?" I say, more seriously now.

"Of course," she lies.

I step back, knowing she's waiting for that . . . and also knowing that if Catriona took too much interest in the letter, it wouldn't be for altruistic reasons. The girl had a fondness for blackmail, and Alice is right to be wary.

"Tea?" I say, motioning at the tray.

"Not tonight."

"I was going to suggest cards." I waggle my brows. "With a friendly wager or two."

I've learned Alice is overly fond of cards. I say "overly" as a Victorian lady concerned for the poor child's reputation. Personally, I have no problem with it. In this world, Alice needs to develop all the income-generating skills she can.

Normally, she'd perk up at my suggestion. I'm the only person in the house who doesn't let her win, and the chance to truly hone her skills is a temptation she can't deny herself. Tonight, though, she only shakes her head.

"I'm very tired," she says. "Perhaps another time. Thank you for offering."

If Alice is using her Isla-trained manners on me, she's definitely distracted. Which means something's definitely wrong.

When I hesitate, she lifts a blank gaze to mine and fixes it there.

*Go away, Mallory.*

*Go away now.*

"All right," I say, forcing a smile. "If you change your mind—"

"I won't."

I'm in my room, considering my options as I try not to worry about Alice. In the twenty-first century, she'd be a child in middle school. Here, not having been born to a family of privilege, she's a young woman, more than old enough to be making her own way, and as horrifying as that is to me, I have to understand that she doesn't consider herself a child, either.

When Alice first came to work here, Isla had wanted to adopt her. McCreadie convinced her to hold off and Gray agreed, and she'd been furious with both. But she'd come to see they were right. In Alice's world, it would be like adopting an emancipated seventeen-year-old. Uncomfortable and even patronizing. The best Isla can do is give Alice fair employment and emotional support, along with school lessons that will help her rise out of service. And the best I can do is treat her the way I would a seventeen-year-old—offer help and stop when it's refused.

Isla will be back soon. I can see whether she's in want of company. She usually is, whether it's doing something together or hanging out doing our own thing in the same space. Until then, if Mrs. Wallace has gone to bed, I can read in the library. My room is perfectly fine, but the library is far more—

Something creaks overhead.

I go still, and my gaze rises to the ceiling. There's no attic— our rooms are in that space.

Another creak.

Someone's on the roof.

I stride to my window. It's open—even in August, it's not exactly hot in Scotland, and in the New Town, the air this high is marginally fresh. When I poke my head out, I catch the scrabble of a boot on slate. I tense, but the steps are heading in the other direction.

That's when I see Alice's window is wide open. When I was in there, it was barely ajar.

I climb up and slide partway out my window. In my head, it's an easy and graceful move, my former body having been suited for such maneuvers. No longer being in that body—and being in a corset and heavy dress—the reality involves a lot of heaving and straining as I awkwardly push my head and torso out while sitting on the sill and holding the edge for dear life, lest I topple backward.

I get out just far enough to catch a glimpse of Alice running—running!—over the rooftops. I resist the urge to glare. Not because she escaped her room, but because she can trot along the slanted roof with the ease and sure-footedness of a young goat.

It takes me two seconds to realize there is no way in hell I can follow. Even in my more athletic former body, I doubt I'd have given chase over the rooftops unless absolutely necessary. I lack the youthful confidence to think I could do that without falling four stories to my doom.

I wriggle back inside and run for my bedroom door. I make it two steps before catching a glimpse of myself in the mirror. I'm still wearing my maid's dress. If I thought Alice was staying in the New Town, I could leave it on. But that letter's tallow seal and multiple reuses tell me she's headed for the Old Town.

I yank open my wardrobe and pull out a thirdhand gown. I don't need to wear thirdhand gowns. Gray and Isla pay well enough that Catriona has two quite fashionable secondhand ones. This particular dress is my own purchase for one very specific purpose: sneaking about the Old Town without being mistaken for a sex worker.

The dress would have been mass-produced even when new, and its next life stage will be rags. It's clean, though, and well mended. The dress of a young woman with more pride than money.

I put it on as quickly as I can, which is not nearly fast enough to suit me. In the modern world, I'm quite fond of sundresses for their pull-on-and-go simplicity. There is no such thing in Victorian Scotland, and even if I can put this one over my current under-layers, there are still a dozen tiny buttons and another dozen tiny hooks and eyes.

I pause to tuck Catriona's switchblade into my pocket. Yes, my dress has a pocket—it's just a lot bigger than I'd like, meaning my switchblade sometimes gets lost in it. I'm still fastening the dress as I zoom down the stairs. If I'm sure Alice's destination is the Old Town, the back door would add a few extra seconds to my walk, so I slip out the front.

Sure enough, I'm barely at the sidewalk before Alice appears at the end of the street. I jerk back into the shadows to watch as she crosses Robert Street. She's still wearing her work dress, which gives me pause until I see she's also carrying a basket with clothing stuffed in it.

Okay, that's smart, and I wish I'd thought of it. In the New Town, the basket of clothing will make it seem as if she's a young maid running an errand. Then she can change before crossing the Mound.

There's a very clear and unmistakable boundary between the Old and New Towns, whether in this time or the modern day, with only a few spots to cross. I know where Alice is heading, and I can hang behind enough to ensure she won't glance back and see me. She doesn't glance back.

Alice hikes the uphill route past Queen Street Gardens until she reaches Princes Street. As in the modern day, Princes is a wide and busy thoroughfare, and at this time of the evening, it's the one busy section of the New Town, the rest more quietly residential.

Carriages and carts roll along several deep as the shops receive after-hours deliveries and locals partake of evening entertainment. The street is loud and fogged with smoke and stinks of horseshit and coal, and I use all that to get a little closer to Alice.

As expected, she turns to head up the hill over the Mound that separates the New Town from the Old.

I've barely turned onto that uphill climb when I lose her. I pick up speed, looking left and right. There's no other nearby route to the Old Town, so she must have—

Alice darts from behind a wall. I fall back fast and wheel to look down the hill, as if admiring the view. I count to five. Then I carefully turn back around to see her heading up again, the basket gone, her work dress replaced by a shabby brown dress I've never seen before.

Seems I'm not the only one with a special outfit for crossing the Mound incognito.

I don't fail to notice just how shapeless Alice's dress is. It's practically a potato sack. While I could pretend it's just too big for her, I know it's more than that. She's making it very clear that she's still a child, hiding any signs of blossoming womanhood, in case anyone gets any ideas. By twelve, Alice has reached the age where she needs to be careful about that, and I could say it's different in the modern world, but I'm a cop—I know better.

Alice is crossing to a part of town where I *can* find sex workers her age, and the danger she faces isn't from "base" men of the "lower orders." The ones she needs to worry about are the predators crossing from the New Town—the sex tourists who think their money can buy them whatever they want . . . and sadly, they're right. Also no different from my world.

Until a hundred years ago, Edinburgh was all Old Town. It'd been a walled medieval city, those walls meaning that the only place to build was up. Overcrowding and increasingly squalid living conditions had the effect they always have—those who can move out, do so. Thus the New Town was built, and the exodus began.

In this period, while there are working-class neighborhoods in the Old Town, there are also a lot of slums, and I've landed right in the midst of a time when people are recognizing that and organizing a concerted effort to improve the conditions. Great, right? Yeah. . . . By "improve the conditions," they mean tear down the tenements and drive the poor elsewhere by constructing new buildings with unaffordable rents. Once again, so little has changed.

When I cross into the Old Town, there's the option to just *keep* crossing—via the North Bridge—straight over the slums and into another newer part of Edinburgh. Handy for those who want to pretend the Old Town doesn't exist by literally zipping over it.

The North Bridge isn't where Alice is going. She's crossed the Royal Mile and is heading down one of those streets of newly constructed buildings: Upper Bow.

Now I need to hang back more, mostly to keep an eye on my surroundings. My dowdy dress might say I'm not for sale, but its condition suggests that could be negotiable. If I were actually a young woman in this neighborhood, looking as I do, that could be a fair assumption. It's not a matter of morality—it's a question of survival, and I'm surprised Catriona didn't go that route, given her looks.

I hang back so I don't need to duck into a doorway or a close to avoid Alice spotting me. Do that, and I'd encourage someone to follow.

I'm making my way toward the Grassmarket when a voice says, almost at my ear, "I trust you are aware you're being followed, lass?"

I spin so fast that I stumble face-first into a man's chest. When I stagger back, his hands grip my upper arms. I wrench free as I look up—

"God*damn* you," I say as I stop fighting and glare at him.

"Language, Mallory. Really, perhaps we ought to limit your visits to the Old Town if such talk is the result."

The man has the audacity to smirk. Okay, it's more of a genuine smile, but I'm not in the mood to recognize the difference.

I scowl up at him. Way up. Like his sister, Duncan Gray is tall, coming in at about six feet, which means he towers over everyone in this neighborhood who didn't enjoy his plentiful childhood diet.

Other than his size, Gray doesn't much resemble his sister. Half sister, I should clarify, though neither of them makes such a distinction. Gray is the product of an extramarital affair, his father bringing him home and dumping the toddler on his wife to raise after the boy's mother died. I say "dump." Mrs. Gray would never use such language. She recognized that any fault lay with her husband and raised Gray as her own.

That's part of the scandal that will forever stain Duncan Gray. The other part . . . Well, his mother clearly wasn't white. Gray is brown skinned, enough so that no one would mistake it for a tan even if Scotland got enough sun for that. His features suggest his mother came from India, but his father refused to say a word about the woman. He took that information to his grave and robbed his son of half his birthright.

Besides being tall, Gray is also broad shouldered and sturdy, like his half siblings. That makes him an imposing figure, with unruly dark hair and a severe face that almost always has a severe expression to match. Or it does around those he doesn't know well enough for him to relax his guard. Tonight, his brown eyes fairly dance with good humor, and any other time, I'd seize on that—it's like a blast of sunshine piercing the city's smog and coastal fog—but right now, I'm very aware of Alice slipping away.

"I presume *you're* the one following me," I say.

"Mmm, no. It was a most unsavory fellow." Gray glances over his shoulder. "Who seems to have vanished when I approached you. How odd."

I roll my eyes. Not odd at all, and he knows it, so I suppose I have to admit that he did the right thing, accosting me like that. Still . . .

"At least Simon knows not to sneak up on me like that," I mutter. "I do carry a knife, remember?"

"But do you know how to use it?" He lowers his voice to a whisper. "I have heard rumors that you do not."

I glare at him.

*Alice. Remember Alice.*

I start walking. Gray falls in step beside me.

"You're in far too good a mood tonight," I grumble.

"Because I successfully snuck up on a professional detective."

I roll my eyes. "You can sneak up on Hugh, too. You're a damned cat. It's more than that. You showed someone up today, didn't you?"

I don't look over, but I swear I hear his brows arch.

"Showed someone up?" he says.

"At your lecture. Or afterward. Someone made a mistake, possibly about a cause of death, and you proved them wrong."

"And that would put me in a good mood? How very unseemly."

"Yet you don't deny it." I shake my head. "What are you doing here anyway?"

"I was walking home from the college when I spotted you. The question, dear Mallory, is what are *you* doing here?"

In the far distance, I can just make out Alice's figure darting through a throng. I should be picking up speed before I lose her. Instead, at Gray's words, I slow. Because it is at those words that I pause long enough to fully comprehend what I'm doing.

"Mallory?"

I turn to him. "Alice got a letter. It upset her. She snuck out, and I'm following. Which I shouldn't be doing."

"If you're concerned . . ."

"How much of it is actual concern, and how much is an excuse because I'm curious? Or because I'm hoping to swoop in to the rescue and prove I'm not the Catriona she remembers."

His voice softens. "You could just tell her the truth."

I shake my head. "I'm not forcing a twelve-year-old to keep that kind of secret."

When I strain to look down the hill, Gray says, "She should not be in this neighborhood at such an hour. Yes, I understand she is probably more at home here than either of us, but I still believe it would be reasonable to follow her until we are certain she is safe."

"We . . ." I murmur.

"As your employer, I cannot let you do this alone, Mallory."

I glance over to see the twinkle in his eye that says he is, thankfully, not serious about pulling rank. I've landed in a fortunate place, and I'm very aware of that. While in the modern day we might presume Victorian men never recognized women as their equals, that's as ridiculous as saying all men in our time *do* recognize us as such.

"I'm fine with having you along," I say, "but you aren't exactly dressed for stealth."

"Continue after Alice, and I shall rectify that."

# CHAPTER THREE

I'm back on Alice's trail. She went through the Grassmarket and into Greyfriars Kirkyard. I'm hiding behind a crypt when Gray slips up beside me. I take one look at him and shake my head.

"Mrs. Wallace is going to *kill* you," I say.

"That would be most unfortunate. How would you all survive without a man in the house?"

"Promote Simon to butler."

"You've thought of this, I see."

"A woman must prepare for such things."

Mrs. Wallace won't actually kill Gray, despite the soot he's ground into his shirt. If she were going to murder her boss for stains, he'd have perished long ago.

There's always soot and ink and, often, blood on his clothing. Tonight, he's only added more soot to both his shirt and face. He's also wearing someone else's coat over his waistcoat, and I can only imagine he traded with a local who is now in possession of a frock coat worth a half-year's salary.

The coat Gray has taken is several inches too short, and he can't button it over his chest, but it's appropriately frayed and filthy. He's also discarded his top hat and run his hands through his hair to release whatever hold was left from his pomade. Add in cheeks that are already dark with stubble, and he looks downright disreputable. He's still not going to blend in, but that won't happen without a body swap of his own. Looking like this, he seems to belong, and that is enough.

I peer out to where Alice is making her way slowly through the cemetery. I tap my toe, wishing she'd move faster. This isn't Greyfriars in the twenty-first century, Edinburgh's most famous kirkyard, busy with tourists at all hours. In this period, it's bordered by some of the city's worst neighborhoods, and it's not a shortcut I'd be taking. Alice seems fine, though. There are clusters of people, either prowling or finding a place to settle for the night, in hopes they aren't rousted by the guards. None of them does more than glance Alice's way. She's too young to be a threat and too poor to be a target.

When Alice disappears from sight, Gray and I slip from our hiding place. I hook my arm through his. We've played this routine before, and it's the most obvious one—a fellow and his lady, out for the evening. We get a few glances, but they don't linger any longer on us than they did on Alice.

She seemed to be heading for the back gate, so I steer us that way. When I round the corner, I expect she'll be long gone. Instead, I catch sight of her just ahead, and we duck behind another vault.

When I peek out, she's on one knee with her fingers pressed to the ground. My heart squeezes as I watch her quietly pausing there before she rises, inhaling deeply enough for me to see her chest move. Then she lifts her chin and marches onward.

Once Alice is out the gate, Gray and I go after her. When I head for the spot where she'd knelt, Gray makes a noise in his throat. I know what that noise means. It's saying that if I'm hoping to see who she paused to pay her respects to, I'm going to be disappointed. I know that. I still have to check.

It's an empty spot of ground. No stone. Not even a tiny marker.

I remember going on a modern-day tour through Greyfriars with my nan. The guide said there were about five hundred names on kirkyard stones. So how many people are buried there? Hundreds of thousands. The only names we see are those who could afford a marker. People in modern times walk through cemeteries like this and think they're getting a snapshot of people from that time period. No, they're seeing the well-to-do, just as they would in a history book. The rest are nameless ghosts, haunting history.

Who had brought Alice through this cemetery? Who had she felt compelled to detour this way for? I'm not getting any answers here.

"Mallory?" Gray murmurs.

I nod, and we leave the cemetery.

---

"Abernathy Hall," I murmur.

"Hmm?" Gray says.

We're tucked into the mouth of a quiet close, watching Alice, who is watching a building. It looks like a former school, long since shuttered, but when a man and woman rap at a side door, it's opened, and they disappear into the darkness.

"I only saw a few words on her letter," I whisper. "Something about a place called Abernathy Hall. It said "he" was taking the writer there. I expected a dance hall or something. I'm guessing this was an old school? Abernathy Hall?"

"I'm not overly familiar with this particular street," Gray says. "I believe Hugh did bring me to a murder scene in this close here." He peers down the alley. "Yes, I'm quite certain it was this one. It was before Hugh and I had the arrangement with Addington. Hugh snuck me in for a look at the body before the police surgeon arrived."

Dr. Addington is the current police surgeon—Edinburgh's version of a city coroner. He's young and recently elected to the position. A forward-thinking fellow, he recognizes Gray's expertise and allows him to examine the bodies in Gray's laboratory. Yeah . . . not quite. Addington *is* young. He *is* newly elected. And he's the worst type of elected official, one who got the job through pure nepotism and considers the post merely honorary, an extra source of income, for which he must unreasonably be expected to work.

Being both lazy and entitled, Addington refuses to use the "dead rooms" of the police offices, which is where Gray came to the rescue by offering his laboratory. He even includes snacks, delivered by a "fetching" young maid. In Gray's defense, he hasn't quite realized why Addington likes me delivering his tea and biscuits, but that's fine—I've learned I have more of a knack for manipulative flirtation than one would ever have imagined. All this means that while Addington is an inept ass, his ineptitude and ass-itude allow Gray and McCreadie full access to bodies, and the city is better for it.

"Yes, it was definitely this close," Gray says. "It was a most interesting case. Strangulation. The killer . . ." He shakes his head. "This isn't the time. Apologies."

I glare at him. Not for the diversion but for teasing me with it. The corners of his lips twitch, proving he knew exactly what he was doing.

"Later," he says. "Get your answers on Alice, and I shall reward you with a story. Manage to do it without Alice spotting you, and I'll toss in a glass of whisky."

"Woof."

He motions as if patting my head. "Now stop playing about. The game is afoot."

I sigh. I should never have told him about Sherlock Holmes. It's bad enough Gray has decided to call himself a consulting detective. I feel I owe Conan Doyle an apology, for the day when someone might dig into the records and realize he seemed to "steal" that moniker from an Edinburgh forensic scientist. Ironically, one of the actual inspirations for Holmes was an Edinburgh doctor, Joseph Bell, under whom Conan Doyle will come to study.

I peek out. Alice is still in her spot. She's watching the building from the shadows, where she seems to be considering her options. After a moment, she checks to be sure no one is watching, and then she takes off . . . heading straight for us.

Gray and I scramble down the alley only to find it ends in a courtyard. Damn it! That's the problem with Edinburgh "closes." The word can refer to an alley linking two streets or to a passage into a courtyard. This is the latter, and that's a problem.

Gray plucks my sleeve and runs for what looks like . . .

Oh God, not a rubbish heap. Please, not—

He ducks behind the heap. I send up a silent prayer to whatever feckless god rules my fate, and I dive in with him.

People talk about the state of Victorian city streets. The horseshit and the chamber pot contents that turn already muddy roads into a cesspool of filth. By this period, it's not as bad as I feared. By that, I mean I can usually avoid stepping in piles or puddles deep enough to soak through my boots. But then there's the trash.

We're in a time when very little goes to waste. There's always someone worse off who can make use of your raggedy clothing or broken dishes or rusting tins. But there are still piles and bins of rubbish waiting to be picked through or carted away or just left to rot. The smell of this particular heap is like

New York on a hot summer day after a month-long garbage strike.

My gorge spasms, and I'm struggling to remind myself that the town house has running water and I can wash up after this. I'm so focused on that reassurance that I forget why we're here until Gray whispers, "She's gone."

I look over at him. He's stepping out from the heap and pointing. "She only came that far. Then she went up."

Up a staircase, he means. There's a set of stairs leading up to higher floors. We're in one of the areas that hasn't yet been condemned. That means the tenements soar into the sky. When the law forbade buildings over a certain height, people soon realized that referred only to stone, so they added extra stories in wood. Buildings are as high as they can safely go . . . and then another story or two after that.

Gray strides to the stairs. Then he glances back, frowning. "Mallory?"

*Mallory? Why aren't you right behind me . . . if not racing past me, eager to continue the chase? What ever could be wrong?*

The stairs are wood. Rotted wood. With no handrails. And there's a dark spot on the cobblestones below.

"Is that blood?" I ask.

Gray peers at it. "Seems to be. Someone really should clean that. Perhaps they lack the proper chemicals."

"Or it's been left as a warning."

He frowns. I motion at the stairs. He keeps frowning. Then, giving up on figuring out what I mean, he trots up the rickety steps as if they're concrete.

I no longer wonder at Victorian mortality rates. Now I just marvel that anyone survived at all.

I take a deep breath—regret it immediately—and begin to climb. After a couple of flights, I get the hang of it. Look where I'm going, trust my feet, and don't try to keep up with Gray.

When he pauses five stories up, I wave for him to keep climbing and motion as if I'm winded—blame Catriona's body—but he shakes his head and points.

I keep climbing until I'm on a landing with him. Then I see what he was indicating. The stairs keep going, but we're on level with the roof of the adjoining building. That's where Alice must have gone—using the stairs to hop onto that roof, which is next to Abernathy Hall.

At least the roof here is flatter than the town house one, and I can follow Gray as he moves across it, the damn man as sure-footed as Alice.

When we near the other side, he motions for me to pass him. I do, and I continue to the edge, where a narrow alley separates the building from Abernathy Hall. One floor down is an open window. From Alice's vantage point earlier, she would have spotted that and climbed to it this way.

Thankfully, the alley really *is* narrow, barely a crack between the buildings. I don't need to hesitate or look for another route. I can be myself, size it up and say, "Ninety-three percent chance of survival—good enough."

Gray could lean in and point out possible routes. He's not that guy. He knows I have this under control, and we've reached the stage where, if I don't, I'll admit it and ask for advice. Taking that into consideration, I resist the urge to prove I can handle it and instead point out my proposed route. He nods, and I strike out.

I make it across. Getting into the open window is the tougher part. My corset might slim my waist, but it does nothing for my hips and it does the opposite for my bosom. Focusing on those two sticking points, I maneuver inside, which is tough when my corset doesn't let my torso bend. Then I check my surroundings.

It's dark.

Yep, really dark.

We've entered the age of gas lighting, and while the better homes in the Old Town have it, ones like this do not. That's a boon here, because I can make out the pale shape of a candle with a matchbox nailed to the wall.

I light the candle. I'm in a tiny room with a bed. It's maybe the size of my walk-in closet at home, but the fact it has only one bed means it's downright penthouse quality for this building. The only furniture is that lumpy mattress on the floor. Oh, wait. There's also a safe. An open and empty safe with a wooden toolbox beside it. Odd . . .

I shake off my curiosity. What matters right now is that the room is empty and the door is shut. I push the window open wider just as Gray makes the jump to this side. One boot slides, and my heart stops, but he gets his balance and barely seems to blink at the slip.

Even with the wider window opening, he struggles more than I did getting inside. I resist the urge to help. That's not about trusting him to do it. It's about him being a Victorian man, and whatever untruths and exaggerations abound regarding the Victorians, this one is true: there are very strict limits of propriety, which include physical contact.

It's not as if Gray would object to me grabbing him to save his life. He's obviously fine with putting his arm around my waist when we're playing a role. He's even held my hand in comfort. But if I were to take hold of his leg to tug him in, I'd startle him enough that he might fall. Basically, when it comes to my new Victorian friends, I think of them the way I'd think of modern friends with strong personal boundaries. Don't touch unless I'm absolutely sure it's okay.

Gray gets through just fine, although I'm not the only one annoyed by the effort our entry took, given the way he rolls his shoulders and straightens his tie.

"Tight squeeze," I say.

"Hmm."

He takes one look around the room and goes straight for the safe. He crouches before it and fingers the tools in the box below.

"Safe cracking," I say.

"Really?" His voice rises with interest that makes me smile.

*Ah, Dr. Gray, if only I planned to stay in this world a little longer . . .*

Nope, none of that.

"Someone was practicing opening a safe." I notice something behind the safe and walk over to lift a board covered in padlocks.

"Seems Abernathy Hall is still a school," I say. "A school for thieves." I look around the room. "Do you think Alice trained here?"

"Possibly. It would make sense."

"And now an old friend sent a message, urgently summoning her back."

I walk to the door and ease it open a crack. Voices tumble up from below. Someone laughs. Someone shouts. Then . . .

"Music?" I say, frowning.

My first thought is that it's just someone playing music as background noise for a party. Except this isn't a world where you can hit Play on your music app. I'm hearing live music.

Curiouser and curiouser . . .

"Shall we take a look?" Gray says.

Absolutely.

# CHAPTER FOUR

I might be wrong about this being a former schoolhouse. Or, more likely, it was at one time, maybe back when this was a neighborhood populated by the well-to-do, the tenements still private homes. It seems as if the last incarnation was more of an entertainment venue. Up here on the top floor, it's a warren of tiny rooms. Same as the next level down. Lodgings for the entertainers or rooms to let.

The second-story rooms are all along the perimeter, with the doors closed, muffled voices wafting from within. The center is open to the floor below, and there's a wide balcony around the edge.

On the far side of the balcony, men lounge around what looks like the box at a sporting event. They're drinking, talking, and occasionally glancing down at the festivities below. Those "festivities" are a dance, and when I see that, I have to smile.

This isn't the sort of grand Victorian ball I've read about in novels. I am rather fond of those—all the bright gowns and courtly manners—but this is far more interesting. It's the working-class equivalent. A dance hall, where average young men and women put on their best outfits and come for an evening of music and dancing and maybe a little romance.

I presume the men in the box are chaperones. Fathers and uncles, come to watch the young women while giving them some space. Gray and I give those chaperones space, too. From the way the windows are blackened, we presume this is a private event, and we can't let anyone see strangers wandering about.

Fortunately, it's not hard to find a vantage point out of sight of that chaperone box. Most of the remaining balcony space is in disrepair, as if the owners only restored that one area. There's no one else on our side, and we creep through the shadows until we find a place where the chaperones can't see us. Then we step out and gaze down below.

It looks more like a country dance than a ball. I don't know my minuets from my waltzes, but I'm going to guess most of these attendees don't, either. They're following a dance far more lively than those in my Victorian-ball scenes.

I lean on the balcony railing, smiling, as I watch the teenagers spinning and whirling. Their gowns might be shabby, but I can't tell that from here. They might be outdated, but I wouldn't know the difference. All I see is happy young people, dressed to the nines for an evening at the club, laughing and dancing and flirting.

"Do you dance?" Gray asks.

I look over to see him leaning beside me, his long legs braced behind him, arms folded on the railing, hair hanging around his face as he looks down to watch the dancers. When I first arrived in this world, it was hard to see people as people. To me, they were characters in a period drama. Even when I got past that, there was still a divide. They were from another world. Alien. But then I began to catch glimpses of them like this. Relaxed. Casual, even. That's uncommon in this world, where the only people who sprawl on sofas are young men in the company of other young men. Gray in particular keeps his walls up, from a lifetime of experience. But when he does relax, I look over and I don't see a Victorian doctor. I see a regular guy, as if we've dressed up for a costume ball.

Gray raises one brow. "Tell me there isn't blood on my cheek."

I smile. "No. Just dirt."

"Excellent. That is intended. You were looking at me as if I'd forgotten to wash off the blood after today's lecture, and I was quite careful about that."

"Blood? In a *lecture*?"

"It was a surgical procedure. An amputation using a new technique. There was still some fluid spray, but such demonstrations are no longer as bloody as they were before the development of anesthetic."

"I . . ." I stop. Then I shake my head. "I was going to say, 'I can imagine,' but then realized I'd rather *not* imagine it."

He smiles. "That was before my time. At least, before my time in a surgical theater. I have heard stories though, many of Robert Liston, from the Royal Infirmary, known as the fastest man for the job. Also known to have had the highest mortality rate for a single surgery."

"Highest mortality rate?"

"Three hundred percent."

"Three people died in *one* surgery?"

"It was quite a feat. Remind me to tell you about it sometime. For now . . ." He waves at the sight below. "We are looking for our dear Alice."

"She's over there," I say, pointing to where Alice is almost hidden behind a post.

"You have excellent eyes," he says.

"Catriona does. My own needed contact lenses."

When I don't go on, he glances over. "Are you going to explain what that is?"

"Remind me to tell you about it sometime. For now . . ." I gesture below.

His lips twitch. "Touché." He peers down. "So we have found Alice. Is it possible this is what she came for? She is slightly younger than the dancers, but there are a few close to her age. The message was that 'he' was bringing the letter writer here. Perhaps it was a friend telling Alice that she was being escorted to the dance by her beau, and Alice hurried out to sneak in and see them?"

"That'd make sense."

I'd like to think that's the answer. It would show a side to Alice I haven't seen, a flicker of frivolity in a girl who is otherwise a little too serious for her age. A girl who had to grow up too fast.

I try to see whether Alice is watching anyone in particular, but her gaze seems to move from dancer to dancer. At first, I see only a pirouetting mass of young people packed into a small dance floor—not unlike a modern club. Slowly, I begin to distinguish faces and mini dramas.

A couple of dark-haired young men battle for the attention of one pretty redhead, who pretends not to see their rivalry. A girl with skin only a shade lighter than Gray's hovers closer to the edge, her gaze sliding toward the door as if hoping for escape. It's only once I notice her that I begin to realize it's not a dance floor of *entirely* happy young people. The boys all seem happy enough, and most of the girls do, but several keep looking toward the exit and several more cast furtive looks at the chaperone box above.

I zero in on those girls. I remember dances from when I was young. Awkward as hell for a girl who'd rather be kicking back in a corner with friends. While I liked clubs just fine, I had friends who'd been just as uncomfortable there. Is that what I'm seeing? Girls who've been dragged out by friends crowing, "It'll be fun!"

With that in mind, I study the girls who seem uncomfortable, and I don't see boredom or social anxiety. I see fear.

That's when I notice that some of the girls who *do* seem to be enjoying themselves are smiling a little too widely, their faces slick with sweat that I suspect comes more from nerves than exertion.

I'm about to speak to Gray when he says, "There."

I follow his gaze to one of the girls who'd been looking up at that chaperone box. She has been angling her dance partner toward the edge, and now that she's near it, a young man strides across the room, his face tight with anger. He shoves the girl's partner away and takes his place. When his grip makes the young woman flinch, I tense.

Gray makes a warning noise, but he doesn't say anything. I'm not about to run down there and interfere. I'm just noting the situation and noting that the situation is not good.

"That's who Alice is here for," Gray murmurs. "I noticed her looking at those two more than others. I'm guessing they're related to her. Siblings or cousins."

I glance over.

"Note the shape of their faces," he says, his gaze still on them. "The chin. The nose."

He's right. I can kick myself for *not* noticing it, but he's a whole lot better at those subtle observations.

I also see that he's right about Alice's gaze fixing to these two more often. Now that there's some tension, she's on high alert, slipping behind posts for a better view of the two, who begin dancing together. Or they appear to be just dancing, until I realize the young man is whispering into the young woman's ear. Whispering angrily, from the expression on his face.

The girl is tense but making no move to escape. The boy appears to be in his late teens, the girl a few years younger. I can see the resemblance to Alice now. Neither shares her coloring, but the similarity goes deeper, in their features and their builds, both slight and short for their ages. The boy is average looking, like Alice. The girl, though, is very pretty, in a doll-like way. That has my stomach twisting as I begin to comprehend what might be going on here.

Not a simple dance. Not at all.

*He is taking me to Abernathy Hall tonight.*

"Whatever is happening," I begin, "Alice is concerned for the young woman, who is her sister or cousin. I suggest—"

A flurry of activity below catches my attention. A man somewhat older than the dancers—maybe late twenties—cuts through the group, jostling and bumping. No one glares at him. Instead, they get out of his way. Fast.

The young women notice him the most. Some primp and posture, deflating when he strides past. Some shrink away, as if they can hide behind their partners.

The man wears clothing closer to what Gray had been in before he changed. A frock coat, a waistcoat, white shirt, trousers, and a top hat. It's not the same quality as Gray's—I'm learning to recognize the differences, which aren't as obvious in a world where so much is still tailor made that it all looks fancy to me. The difference is partly in the fabric and the cut, but mostly the way none of it fits quite right, suggesting a second-rate tailor.

A man who isn't in Gray's socioeconomic class but is trying to look as if he is, and partly succeeding, meaning he has more money than anyone here. Is that why they make way for him? I don't think so. I'm beginning to fear I have the answer to this particular puzzle, and I don't like it. I don't like it at all.

The man stops in front of one of the primping girls. He

doesn't seem to say a word. He only crooks a finger, and she gives a grin of delight and hurries along after him. As he heads out of the crowd, he stops again, indicating another young woman, this one with that sheen of nervous sweat. She glances at her dance partner, who is taking great interest in something across the room. Her shoulders slump, and she dutifully follows the man.

I move along the balcony to keep track of the trio. I'm almost certain where they're heading, and soon they appear along the balcony, the man leading the girls to that "chaperone" box, where a man in his forties steps forward. He wears an outfit similar to the other man's attire, but his is the real deal.

I hadn't paid enough attention to the men in the box. I realize that now. I'd made the unforgivable mistake of presuming I knew what they were there for and dismissing them.

They aren't fathers and uncles and other chaperones. They're gentlemen, at least in the sense this world uses it: to describe men of means, like Gray.

If I'm assessing correctly, the man stepping away from the others is another rung or two up the social ladder from Gray and Isla. Upper class, probably with an estate outside the city and a title tacked onto his name.

When he moves forward, the man escorting the girls steps back. The older man takes each girl's gloved hand in turn and pats it like a kindly uncle. Then he produces two necklaces from a pocket. I can't see them well from here, but I'm sure they're cheap trinkets. To the girls, though, they might as well be gold and diamonds. Even the nervous one's face lights up, her mouth forming a little "O" that has the man chuckling.

The young women take the necklaces, and the nervous one hesitates, and I swear I can hear her thoughts from here.

*Maybe this is why we were summoned. Maybe he only wanted to give us a prize for our dancing.*

No, honey, I'm sorry. That's not it.

The man turns the bolder girl around, and she pivots, her giggle reaching us. It looks like a dance move, but he's only getting her turned around. He does the same to the other girl. Then he puts his arms around both their waists and leads them away from the other men. The nervous girl's knees must lock, at the moment when she realizes that what she fears is happening, because she does a little stutter step before he sweeps her along.

I rock on my toes, feeling the urge to go to her rescue. I know I can't. I still want to. I'm furious for what has happened to her. No, I'm furious for what is about to happen, knowing there's nothing I can do to stop it.

If she'd done more than hesitate, I'd have known it was more than a business transaction, and I wouldn't have been able to stop myself from running to her rescue. Does that lack of screaming or fighting mean she's okay with what's happening? It does not, but it does mean interfering will only cause trouble for her.

"Oh," Gray says.

I turn to see him by my shoulder. I prod him back into the shadows, and as his gaze swings in the direction of the box, his lip curling in disgust, I realize he has just figured out what's going on. He's faster at deciphering some clues, and I'm faster at others. It's why we make a good team.

"I thought it was a dance," I mutter. "Young men and women having a good time, with their chaperones overhead watching. Chaperones." I snort. Then I glance at him. "What did you think they were?"

"Not chaperones," he says. "I could tell they were men of means. I was still working out the purpose of their gathering. I thought it might be unconnected to the dance below—men making unsavory deals in an unsavory place. Or they might be considering purchase of the venue, if it seemed profitable. Or perhaps they were simply enjoying an evening gaping at residents of the Old Town, as they are wont to do, possibly amusing themselves by betting on the dancers. Such men will wager on anything." He looks back toward the box. "Now that I understand their purpose, I feel rather foolish for not seeing it."

"You and me both," I mutter. "On the other hand, I'm not sure I want to be someone who sees older men watching girls dance and presumes they're looking to buy one for the evening."

"Hmph."

I glance over the railing again. The music continues to play, and the dancers have resumed. When a motion near the center catches my eye, I zero in to see the couple Alice was watching. The young man grips the young woman's forearm. She gives a tentative tug and then winces as his grip tightens.

"Shit," I whisper.

Gray doesn't bat an eye at the profanity. He only follows my gaze and then murmurs a more period-correct curse of his own.

"Alice is here because of that," I say. "Her cousin or sister is being prostituted by another family member."

I could express shock at that . . . but then I'd have to admit I've seen the same thing in my world.

"We need to break this up somehow," I say. "Stop it from happening tonight, and then I'll find a way to broach it with Alice and see what can be done longer term. You do have an opening for a housemaid . . ."

"We do."

"The question is how to stop it tonight . . . without exposing Alice. There's a reason she's not marching onto the dance floor to help."

"It would not go well for her," he says.

"She's trying to figure out another solution. Do you see one?"

"Only what you mentioned. Interfere in some manner that

doesn't involve Alice and preferably doesn't let her know we're the ones interfering. I have a thought."

"Good."

"As you pointed out, I am not inconspicuous, whatever my attire. People notice me and they know whether or not I belong, particularly in what seems to be a private event. I believe I can use that to my advantage."

"Infiltrate the crowd and cause a commotion?" I say.

"Yes, and while it will not be enough to 'break it up' as you say, it would seem that the young woman is quite prepared to take advantage of any distraction."

I nod. "Cause a commotion and give her time to flee."

"Yes, now . . ."

He trails off with another curse, and now I'm the one following *his* gaze. Two men have just entered. One is about forty, dressed similarly to the fellow who went downstairs to collect the young ladies—in a good but ill-fitting suit. The other is younger and makes no such effort with his attire, wearing clothing not unlike that of the other young men below.

The older man leads the way with his chin raised. The younger one looks about anxiously, and when someone glances in their direction, he turns away and raises the collar on his jacket, as if to hide his face. That makes the older man laugh and chide him.

"You know them?" I whisper to Gray.

"The older gentleman is Detective Harry Broun."

I could say this is an excellent development. The police have arrived to break up this event, and everything is fine. Yeah. . . . Policing might be relatively new in this era—about fifty years old, with detective work being even newer—but officers already know better than to march into a place like this without subterfuge and backup.

There's a reason Broun's young constable tried to hide his

face and a reason Broun laughed at him. Broun is on the take. His constable knows it and didn't want to be recognized, and Broun is amused by the idea that it would matter. They are police officers, after all, and this is a hall full of would-be sex workers and gentleman johns and young men that I presume are either hired to dance or pimping out the girls. No one here is going to run to a police office and snitch on Broun.

Sure enough, the man who'd escorted the two girls upstairs hurries down now, all smiles and diffident nods as he leads the officers toward the balcony stairs.

I glance at Gray, who has backed away from the railing.

"I take it he'll recognize you if you cause a disturbance," I say.

Gray presses his lips into a grim line. Then he rolls his shoulders, throwing it off, and I understand the full problem. Broun won't just recognize Gray—he'll cause trouble for him, which means causing trouble for McCreadie.

Gray is a doctor devoted to the study of forensic science and criminal investigation. His life's work is helping police, without any financial reward or recognition. Clearly, the police recognize his efforts and appreciate them, right? Hardly. I've seen firsthand the way they treat him, as if he's a ghoul who takes far too much interest in dead bodies. The only reason they tolerate him is out of respect for McCreadie.

I won't say McCreadie is universally liked by his colleagues —he's too good at his job for that—but he is popular, and those who dislike him wisely know to keep it to themselves. They do not, however, need to do the same with their distaste for Gray.

"If you cause a commotion," I say, "Broun will recognize you, and because he's here taking bribes, he'll do backflips to turn this story around. He'll say he was conducting an investigation and you ruined it."

"Yes, and he'll claim I was acting at Hugh's behest. He's had run-ins with Hugh before, and if he has the chance to professionally embarrass him, he'll seize it."

"Then we're not taking that chance."

"No, I can find a way—"

I shake my head. "Let's not. Please. We'll tell Hugh about this later. There are ways for him to shut this place down without Broun knowing he had anything to do with it. For now, I have another idea." I peer down to where Alice still hides behind a post. "Which starts with me coming clean with Alice."

# CHAPTER FIVE

Gray suggests other solutions, but this is the right one. Fall on my sword and admit I followed Alice. I don't want Gray or McCreadie taking the blame for something I started, which means the person who needs to take the blame is me.

This isn't going to help my relationship with Alice. I know that. I can only hope that any help I can provide with the situation will balance out the fact that I followed her here.

I should have come clean from the start. The old Mallory would have, without hesitation. Take my lumps and do the right thing, which is obviously to speak to Alice, find out what's happening and help stop it. So why hesitate? Because even after three months, I haven't quite found my footing here, and I'm uncomfortably reliant on the support of others.

Don't get me wrong—I'm no lone wolf. I work best with others, which is why I chose policing instead of private investigating. I'm just not quite so accustomed to being at the mercy of others, even when those "others" are good and decent people like Gray, Isla, and McCreadie. Without them . . . ? Well, I might be able to muddle through, but I wouldn't be in the place I am now, enjoying this time-travel adventure, however much I long for home.

My world, though, goes beyond the three who know my real story. It includes my fellow household employees. I have Simon on my side, but he's outdoor staff, not a fully integrated part of the household. I'm beginning to despair of ever winning over Mrs. Wallace. Alice, though? I want her to be comfortable in her home, which means accepting that I'm not Catriona and I can be trusted.

Am I going to ruin what progress I've made? Possibly, but this isn't about me. It's about someone Alice cares about, which means it's also about Alice.

While Gray stands watch, I slip over toward the stairs. That's the only route down that I can see. Well, I could go over the railing, but some things are really best not done in five layers of dress, especially when my underwear is crotchless. The crotchless part is *not* a personal choice, believe me. It's a practicality with the aforementioned five layers and the occasional need to use a water closet.

I make sure no one is around, and then I trot down the stairs, which thankfully lead into a side hall rather than straight onto the dance floor. It takes me a moment to find a back passage to that dance floor, but eventually I do, allowing me to sneak out into the crowd.

Before I left the upper floor, I checked my outfit. Primped as best I could, while knowing I'm going to be a wren among peacocks in this drab dress. At least I'm roughly the right age. A straightening of my dress, a pinching of my cheeks and I head into the main room.

I make a beeline for the post Alice has been hiding behind. I'll come at it from the back and hope that, between the candlelight and the thin layer of woodsmoke, no one will get too good a look at me.

I reach my target and . . .

Alice is gone.

I glance about. There's no sign of her. The dancers are in full swing, with no disturbance to indicate a twelve-year-old storming onto the floor.

A few of the dancers have paused at the side where they're enjoying glasses of what looks like lemonade. Behind them, I catch a glimpse of a figure Alice's size.

I make it three steps in that direction before a voice sounds behind me.

"Mrs. Wallace was right."

I spin to see Alice with her arms crossed.

"You haven't given up your old ways at all," she says. "You're still the same old Catriona, come skulking about to conduct your business."

"My business?" I say. "I never traded my favors."

She rolls her eyes. "I mean thieving, obviously."

I remember what we found in that upstairs room. The safe and padlocks. I'd thought they looked like a practice room for a thief.

I shake my head. "Whatever this place is, I've never been—"

"You know exactly what it is. Abernathy Hall. Where your sort come to buy lessons and find work."

I look out at the male dancers. So that's where they come from. "This is a thieves' guild?"

"A what?"

I shake my head. "If I spent time here, Alice, I truly do not remember it. I followed you here. You came down Upper Bow and into the close and then climbed the stairs to hop over and cross through an open window on the top floor."

I'm expecting the details will prove my story, but her eyes only narrow. "You followed me to see what I was doing. In hopes you could use it against me like you did before."

*Damn it, Catriona.*

"No," I say firmly. "If I did that before, I apologize. I was concerned, Alice. You were obviously upset by that letter, and you didn't want to discuss it. That was fine. It's your private business. But then I heard you on the roof, and I thought about the letter, and I was worried."

Her gaze bores into mine, and sweat beads on my forehead. She eases back, shaking her head. She doesn't say she believes me, but I can tell I've convinced her enough that she'll give me the benefit of the doubt.

It's the sweat that did it. Something tells me Catriona never sweated, no matter who doubted her story. That requires a conscience and the ability to give a shit.

"I think I understand what's happening," I say. "I was watching from upstairs. The person who sent that letter . . ." My gaze tracks to the young woman. "That's her. She's related to you."

"My sister," she mutters after a moment. "Mae."

I nod. "And the boy with her is also a relative."

"Boy? Felix is *your* age, Mallory. He's my brother."

"Felix brought Mae here," I say, "and she's concerned. She fears . . . something untoward."

She snorts. "I'm not a child. I know what goes on here. I tried to warn Mae. For years, I tried to warn her. There was a reason Felix didn't make her work for her keep, like he did with me. She thought it meant she was special." Alice's lip curls. "She is, but not that way. She's pretty, and she does as she's told. He brought her here to find a man."

"A . . ." I search for the period-appropriate word, but I'm not sure of it. "A man who will look after her in return for her favors."

"Favors." She rolls her eyes. "You've been in the New Town too long. But yes, the man will pay Mae's keep, and Felix will get his cut. Then, when he tires of her, Felix will find her another man and another and another until she's old and useless, and then he'll abandon her." Her thin jaw sets. "I told her. I warned her. But she said I was just jealous because Felix liked her best."

"And your parents?" I say softly, though I think I know the answer.

"Dead," she says, the word almost a snap. "Mama with a babe when I was five, and Papa was carried off by the fever when I was eight, along with the two little ones."

"I'm sorry."

Her chin lifts. "Don't be. It happens all the time. Good people die and the wrong ones live. Felix got sick, and I hoped the fever would take him, too. Mae hit me when I said that. Slapped me so hard my nose bled." She raises her voice to a falsetto. "Whatever will we do if Felix dies, too? Well, we will not be sold to a man, that is for certain."

When I don't answer, her gaze rises to mine, defiant. "You think I was a monster for wishing him dead."

"No, I think the monster is the brother who'd prostitute his sister. I'm presuming you want to help her?"

Alice shrugs, struggling to keep her face impassive. "Maybe. She asked for my help. I don't know why. She never helped me when I asked. First, he made me play the bait for his own thieving. When I got hurt, I begged Mae to speak to him. She said I needed to be more careful. So I found a job in service. It wasn't like with Mrs. Ballantyne. The housekeeper hit me if I didn't work fast enough, but so did Felix, and at least it was regular work. He ruined it. Stole from them and made it look like I did it. Then he 'saved' me from being arrested and made me steal for him and his friends. Again, I begged Mae for help. She believed him—that I'd stolen from my mistress and that he rescued me."

Alice takes a deep breath and looks off to one side, her cheeks reddening. "I did not mean to say all that."

"You're angry with her, understandably. She doesn't deserve your help." I pause. "But you still want to give it."

"If I can," she mumbles as if embarrassed by the admission.

I look out at the dance floor. "I think I can get to her. I'm the right age. I'll get close enough to distract your brother. Then you let her see you and get her out of here. I'll look after Felix."

"What? You can't go out there, Mallory."

"It's fine. I'm not quite dressed for the part, but I'll pass." I head for the dance floor. "Just wait here and be ready."

She lunges. "You can't—"

"I've got this," I say, and then I'm gone.

There are times when I like being in Catriona's body. Not the younger-and-prettier part so much as what the younger-and-prettier part can buy me, in terms of an investigation. Does it help that it's not *my* body? Do I feel more confident in her attractions because I didn't grow up looking like this, and I can assess her as an outsider?

Oh, I'm sure Catriona knew just how pretty she was—and used it to full advantage—but for me, it does help to have that distance. In my own body, when guys called me beautiful, I knew they wanted something. In this one, I can—without pride —accept that it's true and channel Catriona in using it.

I stride across the dance floor, not as a wren among peacocks but as the cocky pigeon who knows she doesn't need a fancy dress to shine. Chin up, gaze twenty-first-century bold as I sweep through like I'm Queen Vic herself.

Does anyone notice? Hell, yeah. I don't even make it across the floor before some young buck abandons his partner—who huffs in outrage—and offers his hand. I look him up and down, as if considering. Then I nod and allow him to lead me into the fray.

Earlier Gray asked whether I could dance. I hadn't answered. The truth is that I love to dance . . . and I can only vaguely recall the last time I did it. A cousin's wedding, I think? I won't say I'm good at it. Won't even say I'm decent at it. But I do love it, and the fact that I haven't done more than dance at weddings in nearly a decade is proof of how lost I'd gotten chasing my career goals.

I let the young man whirl me into the dance, and it's nothing like a dance at home, but I'd been watching from upstairs, and now that I'm out here, it's just a matter of following his lead. In this era, a woman always follows a man's lead.

It helps that I don't think the poor boy would notice if I flopped around the dance floor like a beached fish. He's too busy staring at my breasts bouncing along over my neckline. For once, I'm glad a guy isn't looking me in the eye. It makes it easy for me to look elsewhere, too, as I scan for Alice's siblings. I spot them only a few couples over. Mae has given up her token protests and is quietly dancing with Felix, her gaze fixed on his collarbone.

Distraction. I need to create—

"There you are," a voice says. "You're late, pet. As always."

I pay no attention until my dance partner stops and glares, and I follow that glare to a young man just behind my shoulder.

He puts out his hand. "Did you forget what I look like? Or did you see something you liked better?"

He's smiling, calm and affable. I glance at my partner, who simmers in silence. The newcomer is a few years older. Higher in the pecking order. Too bad. A fight would have been the distraction I need.

Hmm. Maybe if I refuse—

"Cat?" the newcomer says, still smiling. "Come on now."

The hairs rise on the back of my neck. He recognizes me. Recognizes Catriona.

I return the smile with a toss of my hair. "I'm not the one who is late. If you make yourself so difficult to find, I must locate another partner." I nod and smile at the younger man. "Thank you for being so kind, but I fear I must cut our dance short."

He nods stiffly and backs away. I turn to the newcomer, smile and extend my hand. As he sweeps me into the dance, I channel Catriona and stay calm, despite my tripping heart.

"Dare I ask what you are up to?" I murmur, as unruffled as can be.

"Me? You're the one waltzing in here, brazen as can be. Has your fancy New Town life become so unbearable that you wish to end it in the most spectacular fashion?"

End it . . . ?

Catriona, what the hell did you do?

I keep my sphinx smile in place. "Whatever do you mean, dearest?"

He rolls his eyes. Then, as he sweeps past, he lowers his voice when it's near my ear. "Whatever it is, I want in."

I arch my brows.

He waits until he passes again. "I bear you no ill will. You did as a young woman must, if she seeks to avoid the fate of these chits. Of course, I also made myself useful enough to give you no reason to double-cross me."

"True . . ." While I may not know exactly what he's talking about, I know Catriona's track record, and I can fill in the blanks well enough.

"I believe you could use my assistance," he says. "If not with whatever scheme you have, at least in ensuring you are not killed in the execution of it."

"A reasonable precaution, as you are correct that it is somewhat unwise for me to be here, in a place where I . . ."

I trail off, and he says, "Made so many enemies?"

"It was not my fault."

He grins. "I would halfway agree, Cat. If men are willing to teach a girl their trade, in return for favors she never promised, that is not her fault. Were a woman to offer to teach *them* because she hopes to gain *their* favor . . . ?" He shrugs. "I would expect most would seize the opportunity."

"They would, and yet it is different for me, because a woman should not best a man. A *girl* should especially not best a man. It is unseemly."

He laughs at that, and I process what he's said. Catriona learned her trade here, from men who thought they'd get something in return.

No wonder Alice tried to stop me from coming onto the dance floor.

I should have paused a second to listen to her. Or, better yet, worked through the implications. That's a mental leap I'm struggling with. I don't need to just remember that I look like Catriona. I must remember that I *am* Catriona . . . and her history is mine.

Which means don't be swanning into a damn den of thieves while pretending to be an ordinary girl.

Still, that suggests there's an easy way to cause a distraction.

Yeah, if I want to get hauled into a back room and beaten within an inch of my life. Catriona wasn't nearly strangled by a stranger. It was someone she'd double-crossed.

I'm a young Victorian woman in a room with men she offended, who feel betrayed and humiliated. I'm in danger of more than a beating.

I glance up at the balcony, trying to spot Gray, but there's no sign of him.

*Okay, just play this cool. Get closer to the door before causing a distraction. Alert Alice and get her out—*

"You!" someone says, and my dance partner deftly catches my wrist and tugs me behind him.

"Now, now, Felix . . ."

Felix? I glance around my defender to see Alice's brother bearing down on me.

Bearing down on me . . . while leaving Mae unattended.

Okay, distraction provided. Alice? I hope you're seeing this and acting fast.

"Felix," I say. "Good to see you."

He lunges at me, but I dart out of the way. Felix stumbles, and I think he just tripped, but then I see my dance partner pulling in the foot that tripped him. My partner grasps Felix's shoulder.

"Come now, lad," the older man murmurs. "None of that tonight."

"Is that Catriona Mitchell?" someone else says.

Out of the corner of my eye, I see Alice darting for her sister, who is looking around as if only now realizing she can run.

*Go! Get out—*

Then everyone stops, including Felix and my defender. I glance toward Alice. She freezes for a heartbeat before scrambling backward as the crowd parts.

It's the guy from upstairs. The one who came down to escort the chosen girls upstairs. I go as still as everyone else. Then I think better of that and ease behind the girl closest to me, getting out of sight.

The man doesn't look my way. He has his goal in sight.

And his goal is Mae.

Before I can react, he has his arm on her shoulder, and he's propelling her through the crowd. Felix hurries to catch up with him. The man pauses only long enough to nod Felix's way. Then he continues on.

Felix hesitates a second before remembering me. As he bears

down, I backpedal, only to have another young man stop me with, "And where are you going?"

I look at Mae and her escort. Then I take a deep breath and swan toward them, elbowing aside anyone who gets in my way.

"Sir?" I say. "I believe you forgot *me*."

Mae's escort only half turns, barely enough to give a glance and a dismissive wave. His hand is already lifted for that wave. Then he sees me, sashaying forward, bodice discreetly adjusted to display my assets, blond hair tugged coyly over my shoulder. I lift big blue eyes to his.

"You did miss me, did you not, sir?"

He looks me up and down like a heifer at market. "I believe I did. Wherever did *you* come from?"

"My cousin"—I cast a withering look into the crowd—"stole my gown, and I could not find another in time. I almost did not come, but I decided I would take a chance on some kind gentleman seeing past my unsuitable attire."

"Indeed. I do believe you are quite exactly what they're looking for. Do you have a patron among these young gentlemen?"

I look back at my defender, who looks worried. I shake my head and mouth, "I am fine," and then I nod toward him.

"That young man was most kind to me tonight. He should receive a patron's share of my earnings."

"I'll be sure he does. Come along then."

# CHAPTER SIX

Stroke of genius? Or reckless idiocy? As I climb the stairs, I don't dare guess which end of the spectrum this move will land on. The jury lies above, ready to rule.

It was impulsive. I'll accept that. It also seemed to be the only way to help Mae once she was taken from the dance hall floor. And by helping Mae, I really mean helping Alice. Yes, I'm sure Mae doesn't deserve her fate, and I'd certainly help her if I could do so easily enough, but offering myself up for a Victorian three-some wouldn't have been my personal choice of "easily enough."

I can be impulsive. I can be reckless. I can even be a wee bit too cocky for my own good. But I'm also a woman and a cop, and I do not go up those stairs confident that I can just say no, or if "no" isn't accepted, fight my way out. I have interviewed survivors much smarter and much more physically adept than me.

I'm in danger. I think I can handle it, but I fully acknowledge that I may have bitten off more than I can chew. I just need to set that aside and convince myself otherwise.

Like I told Alice, I've got this.

Or at least I can pretend I do.

When we reach the top of the steps, I don't look for Gray. There's no way he could have missed the upheaval downstairs, and while he'll be shaking his head, he'll be watching, too.

My resolve not to look for him lasts for three steps. Then I start to worry that he might think I'm in grave danger and come to my rescue. I'd never say I *don't* want him coming to my rescue if I need it. I'm a feminist, not an idiot. I'm more than happy to accept help from any quarter, and I trust his help above most others. I just don't want him thinking I'm in serious and imme-diate danger and swooping in before I have a chance to escape with Mae.

So I look. I pretend that my boot has twisted, and I pause to give it a shake while I glance over to where I last saw Gray.

He isn't there.

From this vantage point, I can see right into our hiding spot, and there's no sign of him.

He must have moved then. He needed a better line of sight, so he changed position.

Except I see no sign of him anywhere around the balcony.

Because he's hiding.

But if he saw me looking for him, he'd peek out to reassure me.

I go to scan again, but my escort has a hand on my elbow and he's steering me toward the box. When we reach it, he pauses as a man in his forties comes out. He's as tall as Gray, with silvering hair and a squint that suggests he should be wearing glasses. While I might be able to use that to my advantage in a fight, when his gaze lights on me, his expression suggests his eyesight isn't *that* bad.

"Yes," our escort says. "You only chose the one girl, but I thought someone might like this one. She was newly arrived."

Another man steps forward, mouth opening.

"No, I'll take both," the older man says.

Good. I hadn't considered the possibility that I might be separated from Mae once I got here. I sneak a look at the girl. Gray is right that she physically resembles Alice, but I understand now why I didn't see it myself—she otherwise doesn't remind me of the little parlormaid at all. She stands there, doe eyed, the proverbial deer in the headlights.

I could grumble about that. I could even dismiss her for it. But I also recognize that at Robert Street, I'm surrounded by women who don't fit the mold of the classic Victorian female. Not Isla, not Mrs. Wallace, not even Alice. Mae is a more common example of the breed, though I *still* fault her for not helping her little sister. That's unforgivable in any era.

I turn from Mae. As a cop, I didn't pick and choose who was worthy of my protection. Sure, I'm no longer a public servant, but I didn't get into police work for the pay. Mae doesn't deserve her fate, and Alice *does* deserve my help. Good enough.

I realize I haven't reacted to being introduced to my "gentleman for the evening." Then I realize no one expects me to. He takes me from the escort and, together with Mae, steers us along the corridor.

There's no small talk. Not even an awkward "So, how are you young ladies this evening?" We don't warrant the effort, having been bought and paid for, like those market heifers.

In this case, I appreciate the lack of attention. It lets me assess my surroundings and our captor. While the man is tall, he doesn't seem particularly sturdy.

The biggest difference between the physicality of Victorian men and those from my era is the spectrum, which is narrower here. There aren't a lot of gym rats, and when I saw a poster for a circus strongman, I almost laughed—I knew a dozen guys on the force with more muscles. Most men tend toward the average, either lean muscled from athletic endeavors or softer from the lack of them. Gray is among the former, and this guy is among the latter. As a gentleman, he'd have the opportunity to wrestle or box for sport, but he doesn't seem the type who has done it since his school days. That will be helpful. He's significantly bigger than me, but that will likely be his only advantage.

I pay attention to my surroundings as he leads us up to the third level taking a different set of stairs than Gray and I came down. There are at least two staircases then. Good. I also know where to find an open door and window on the next floor, though something tells me I won't easily get Mae out through it. No matter. There were also open rooms on the second level, and I can find one with a window.

The man leads us all the way across the third level . . . to the set of stairs Gray and I used.

Hmm, not what I expected, but okay.

Instead of going up, though, he heads *down*. Back to the level we just left.

When I hesitate, he pokes me in the back. No words. Just that poke.

I keep descending. Maybe we're heading to a room that's inaccessible from the box where the men were hanging out.

But that makes no sense. That floor is one big square around the open center overlooking the dance floor.

Gray and I came down these stairs. I know where they lead and—

And we don't stop at the second level.

We're going back down to the dance floor?

My brain struggles to parse out the reasoning. Why take us up and then bring us back down? I can only come up with one answer—the guy doesn't really want us and only took us to show his friends he was game. Catch and release.

Then why bring us back this way? We'll be recognized if he

takes us near the dance floor. Better to just escort us to a room for twenty minutes and pay a half crown for our silence.

We reach the bottom. I'd come this way earlier, when I descended to speak to Alice. Unlike the main stairs, these ones don't open onto the dance floor but into a hallway. When I turn the way I'd gone before, the man gives me a push in the opposite direction. I slow my steps, taking in my surroundings.

We're in a hall with the dance floor to our left and a few closed doors to our right. Does he plan to use one of those? My spatial sense tells me those are tiny rooms, more like closets, and I don't understand . . .

We reach another hallway, this one short and ending in a door. When he opens the door, a cart rumbles past along the street beyond. I balk, digging in my heels.

"Sir?" I say.

He only prods me onto the narrow street.

I turn and repeat, "Sir?"

"What?" he says with some exasperation.

"I was not told I would be leaving the building. I wish to know where we are being taken."

"What business is that of yours?"

The question is so ridiculous that it takes me a moment to formulate an answer. Before I can speak, Mae says, in her soft voice, "I was not told of this, either, sir. My brother expects me here and will be most concerned for me."

His lips twitch in a humorless smile. "Your brother is well aware of the arrangement. He simply did not see fit to share it with you. Did you think I was going to enjoy myself in some stinking room in that place? In a bed crawling with lice? Sheets that haven't been washed since the queen took the throne?" He nods toward a shiny black coach. "See that? It's waiting to take you to a place I am certain you will also find far more to your liking."

When I glance about the street, still not moving, he sighs. "Stop being such a child. I am a gentleman. I aim to treat you as a gentleman would. We shall have a bit of sport, and then you will enjoy a night in a grand room, with a grand breakfast, before I put you in a grand coach and send you home with a guinea in your pocket. Now come along, before I lose patience."

*And if you do?*

That's what I want to ask. What happens if you lose patience, sir? Do you abandon us by the roadside? If so, that is the answer to my problem. If not . . .

I'm considering, but Mae is already moving toward the coach. I follow, slowly, still thinking. Then I hurry to catch up and whisper to her, but she's climbing into the coach without even a glance around.

*Damn it, girl, do you have any sense of self-preservation?*

When I turned eleven, my mom took me to a self-defense course. One thing they said that has stuck with me—and I have passed down to girls, boys, and women alike—is that if you're ambushed in public, do not let your attacker take you to a second location. Don't get in the car. Fight, scream, do whatever you can, even at risk to yourself, because you have a chance of bringing help or spooking your assailant, which you lose as soon as they get you someplace where they feel safe.

I am being taken to a second location.

Logically, I can say this isn't the same thing. It's Lord Horny who just wants a little "sport" with two barely adult girls, bought and paid for in what he considers a legitimate transaction. But that doesn't mean it's safe. Every time a sex worker goes to a new client, they take a risk. Hell, every time a person hooks up with a new lover, they take a risk.

I don't have a cell phone. I don't have a gun. I have a switch-blade that—yes, Gray was right—I'm not exactly adept at using yet. I also have a corset and layers of skirts and heeled boots, none of which are made for fighting or fleeing. I've been teaching myself how to adapt my skills to these outfits, but it's a slow process.

Still, Mae is in that coach, and until I see obvious danger, I'm committed to helping her. The man's rationale for leaving makes sense, and this is a horse-drawn coach, not a car capable of high speeds. If I see a clear threat and I need to save myself, I can throw open the door and jump out.

I glance around, hoping to catch some glimpse of Gray. I don't.

I should have told Alice he was with me. Should have told her where to find him if things went wrong.

Gray must be here somewhere. He's brilliant and resourceful. He'd have figured out that I was in trouble on the dance floor and found a way to observe me. He only needs to hail a hansom cab and give chase at a discreet distance.

The man gestures for me to get into the coach. I pause to get a better look. It reminds me of Annis's—that's Gray and Isla's older sister, Lady Annis Leslie. A cloth covers the crest on the side. Definitely nobility then. I resist the urge to peek under the cloth—not as if I'd know one family crest from another. Otherwise, it's a high-class coach, new enough that I still smell the leather.

The man prods me impatiently, and I climb in. He makes no move to help me. Gray would. McCreadie would. If neither of them was there, Simon would hop down to do it. That's not like opening a car door—it's actually difficult to climb up into a coach in a Victorian dress. At least, it's difficult to do it gracefully. This guy doesn't care. He just keeps nudging me until I scrabble in.

I take the spot beside Mae, who gawks around like she's in her first limo, which I guess is an apt analogy. The man climbs in and knocks on the roof, and the driver sets out.

It's a slow ride out of the Old Town. Most of the streets are too narrow for a coach this wide. That's one reason Gray prefers to walk, the other being that he simply prefers to walk.

The coach moves in stops and starts as the man across from us grumbles and sighs with impatience.

I turn to Mae. "I'm Cat. I know your little sister, Alice."

Mae stares at me blankly. Not as if she doesn't know who I mean, but as if she doesn't know why I'm speaking to her.

"Enough of that," the man says.

"Enough of what? Talking?"

His eyes narrow, as if sensing sarcasm but unsure of it, meaning he obviously doesn't have much familiarity with the concept.

"There's no need to introduce yourself," he says. "You aren't here to make friends."

"I only thought to be polite," I say, "as we are about to experience a rather intimate situation together."

Mae's face turns bright red, and spots of color even tinge the man's cheeks. Victorians. It doesn't matter how prettily I word it. Don't discuss sex. Even with someone who's paying you for it.

"My apologies," I murmur. "I am quite nervous, and I only wished to ease any discomfort."

He grunts. "Well, there is no need. She does not care who you are or what your name is. What matters here is me."

"All right then. What is your name?"

"Sir."

"Apologies. What is your name, sir?"

"I meant that *is* my name, as far as you two are concerned. Sir. Now hush. Your prattling is giving me a headache."

---

I don't like this. Don't like it at all.

*Oh, really? Weird. You've been taken away in a coach by a stranger, for paid sex. What's not to like?*

Yes, obviously I'm anxious, as hard as I try to hide it. I'm sure Gray is nearby. I'm sure I'm safer than I feel. But we've left the Old Town behind, and we didn't head into the New Town, and I'm no longer quite sure where we are.

No, that's not entirely true. I do know one thing. We seem to be leaving Edinburgh.

"Sir?" I say.

He makes a noise in his throat, half exasperation and half warning growl, as if I am a child who has indeed been "prat-tling" for the past half an hour instead of sitting in stolid silence.

"We appear to be leaving the city," I say.

"Yes."

"Might I ask—"

"No."

I glance at the window and then sneak a peek toward the door.

The man sighs. "Curiosity is not becoming in a young lady."

"No?" I look at him, brows arching.

He catches my meaning, and instead of blushing, he gives a thin-lipped smile. "All right. Perhaps it is not *always* unbecom-ing. Likewise for boldness, both of which you seem to possess in abundance."

I've barely said anything that I'd consider either curious or bold, which is a reminder of my expected place in this world. At least, my place in this man's corner of it.

Mae is still beside me, but has been completely silent, watching out the window.

He continues, "I am taking you to my country estate. My family is not there, and my staff is very discreet. I think you will find it quite a treat." That thin-lipped smile again, his gaze locking on mine. "And if I find your company enough of a treat, you may win yourself an extended stay. A lavish country home, with a full complement of staff, all to yourself, except for my occasional visit."

I lower my lashes. "I could only dream of such delights."

He throws back his head, his laugh so sudden it startles me. "You *are* a minx. It almost makes me wish . . . Well, perhaps we can both do more than wish, can't we."

I look up at him through my lashes, channeling full-on flirty Catriona. That's the way to handle this. Play the game. Lower his defenses that way.

The coach continues until I catch the smell of . . . seawater? I glance out to see the haar rolling in as the night cools quickly. The thick fog swirls, obstructing my view.

"We are by the sea, sir?"

"We are. My house overlooks it."

That's not so strange. Edinburgh is a port city. But something doesn't seem right. While I struggle to see through the fog, I can make out a ship-like clank, as if we're nearing a dock. A distant banging. Then distant shouts of working men.

*Not right*, the voice in my head whispers. *You know this isn't right.*

I move closer to my window.

"Get back from there, child," the man says.

"I'm only trying to see."

"*Back.*"

The fog clears, and out the window, I catch a glimpse of what is definitely a port, complete with massive ships. And the coach is heading straight for it.

"Sir?" I say. "Why are we going this way?"

He waves at the ocean.

"That's the docks, sir. There are no country estates there."

His lips tighten. My curiosity and boldness are becoming far less charming with each passing second.

"Yes," he says with exaggerated slowness. "We are near the docks, as we are heading toward the sea. There is a road right there that will take us along the coast."

He points. When I shift to see better, he makes way on his side for me, and I carefully move over there and peer out. I see only fog and ships and warehouses. There is a smell, though, suddenly strong and pungent, and I turn just as the man slaps a rag to my face.

Chloroform.

Goddamn Victorians and their goddamn chloroform.

Even as I think that, I lash out, of course, backpedaling as fast as I can, but he holds me tight, shoving me down to the seat with the drug-soaked rag over my mouth and nose.

I go for my knife, only to discover that pockets in gowns aren't like pockets in jeans. I fumble to get the blade out through the folds of fabric, and I can't manage it in time. As the sedative drags me under, I cast one look at Mae—half pleading, half urging her to do something. She sits there, staring at me, eyes wide.

Goddamn it.

I slide into darkness.

# CHAPTER SEVEN

I wake in darkness, and I think I've gone home. One of these days, I will be drugged or hit on the head—both a given, considering my work with Gray and McCreadie—and I will open my eyes to the twenty-first century.

I already know there is a guaranteed route back. Die. When I first crossed, someone crossed with me, and in the moments of his stolen body's death, the former occupant returned for a few seconds before he died.

Yeah, I don't want to go back *that* badly.

Here, when I rise to that darkness, it's exactly as I came into this world. It's quiet and dark, and I'm lying on my back, disoriented, and so what pops into my mind is "I've crossed back."

*I've crossed back.*

The thought should come with sobs of relief. I am home, in a familiar time, back to my family and my friends and my job. I am me again.

When I picture that moment, I am giddy with it. Yet it comes, and all I feel is . . .

Loss.

I feel as I did when I first crossed, as if I've been wrenched from my life, and I want to scream, "Wait!"

*I'm not done yet. I'm not ready yet.*

*I don't want to go yet.*

On the heels of that comes overwhelming guilt. When I left, my beloved grandmother was dying. I need to get back in the faint hope she's still alive. I need to get back for my parents—I'm their only child. I need to get back in case Catriona is wreaking havoc in my old life.

I *should* be sobbing with relief, and instead, it's as if I am sixteen again, at a party and having the time of my life, my parents texting to remind me to call when I'm ready to go home, hinting that it's past time. I want to put the phone away and pretend I never got the message.

*I'm not ready.*

I blink, my insides twisting with fear and guilt. Then the darkness lightens as my eyes adjust, and I see Mae sitting in a corner, her knees pulled up as best she can manage.

I'm still here.

That fear and guilt turns to relief with only a flicker of disappointment.

I didn't go home.

I didn't *want* to go home yet.

I push off the confusing muddle, blink more and lift my head.

I focus on Mae, and after a moment, irritation chases away the last vestiges of that confusion.

"Why didn't you do something?" I say.

Her gaze turns to mine, eyes widening.

"You could have done something," I say. "When he was drugging me. He wasn't paying any attention to you."

She continues to stare, as if I'm speaking a foreign language.

"Hello?" I say. "You just sat there while I was being *drugged*."

"What else could I do?"

"Kick. Punch. Scream. Anything that would have startled him enough to let me go."

"But he is a man. A gentleman."

"A gentleman doesn't buy young women for sex."

Her jaw drops. Then she recovers and says, meekly, "It was my brother's will. He is my protector, now that my father is dead."

"Oh for fuck's sake."

She makes a choking noise, gaping at me. I don't normally use that particular profanity, but nothing else seemed appropriate. As she continues to stare, I realize it's not just the strong language. It's that profanity . . . coming from a woman.

"Whatever," I mutter as I pull myself up. "Just to be clear, if I can get out of here—which I fully intend to do—should I take you along? Or do you just want whatever's happening to happen, as your brother deems fit."

She continues to stare. I replay my words. Right. It's not just the profanity. I'm talking like Mallory.

Normally, if I do this, I backtrack fast with some excuse, but I can't be bothered for Mae.

"Do you hear me?" I say, my tone more era-appropriate. "If I manage to escape, do you want to come with me? It's what Alice wants, and it seemed to be what you wanted, but I am no longer certain."

"Escape?"

I give up. We're alone in . . . wherever we are, and I'm wasting precious time arguing with a girl who—giving her the benefit of the doubt—might be in shock. When I figure out an escape plan, I can give her the option again, and honestly, I'm not sure how much "option" there is. I can't go back to Alice unless I can say that I tried everything to get her sister out.

I move my switchblade to my bodice, where it'll be easier to grab. Then I turn my attention to our surroundings. There's no light, but outside something is bright enough to seep through the cracks. We're in a small room that reeks of old wood and salt and fish. When my shoulder knocks against something, I reach out to feel a damp crate, slimy on the edges and crusted with barnacles. Under me is what feels like a ripped-open canvas sack.

I tilt my head to listen. It's the same sounds I heard earlier, only louder. Dock workers talking and shouting orders and laughing. The clang of metal. The blast of a ship's horn.

We're definitely still at the dock.

Yep, I *earned* my detective shield.

The dock part is obvious, and I'm beginning to fear that the "why" part is also obvious. What are the chances that our john has a kink for sex in dock warehouses? There's no sign of him, either. It's just Mae and me in this tiny room.

As I think that, I pick up another voice. One much softer than the rough male ones outside.

"Wake up," a young female voice whispers urgently. "Come on, Nancy. Wake *up*."

The voice comes from my left. I walk over and nearly bash into a wall. I feel along it. Definitely a wall. Such a good detective.

"Hello?" I say in the loudest whisper I dare. "Is someone in there?"

A pause, and then, "Who are you?"

"Cat. I'm with Mae. Felix's sister."

I have an idea who I might be talking to, and I'm hoping something in my introduction rings a bell.

"I don't know you," the young woman says with an Irish lilt. "But I do know Mae."

"I know Mae's sister, Alice, so I came to help Mae, and I seem to have done a rather poor job of it."

The girl laughs as she obviously relaxes.

I continue, "You came from Abernathy Hall, didn't you? Two girls were chosen before us. Is that you two?"

"It is. Our gentleman said he was taking us to his country house, which I knew was not how the dances are supposed to work. We should go upstairs to a room with the gentleman. I did not like this change, and I planned to escape when we arrived. Only once we reached the docks, Nancy became quite excited, and he—" I don't know the next word, but I presume it is slang for being knocked out with chloroform. Just as I presume, by "excited" she means that Nancy panicked.

She continues, "I still thought I might escape, but once we stopped, I was quite overpowered."

"I'm guessing we are about to be taken on a ship."

"Ship?" Mae squeaks. "What ever do you mean?"

The other girl ignores her, voice calm. "I fear so. I pretended to faint so that I might hear their plans. They did not say as much as I hoped, but I was to understand that more lasses will join us, and then we will be taken somewhere." She pauses. "I also understood that our patrons realized what was happening and were handsomely paid."

I curse, and the girl gives a strained chuckle. "Indeed."

"What is she saying?" Mae squeaks. "That my brother knew of this?"

"That is precisely what I am saying, Mae," the girl says, speaking slowly. "Your brother. My man. Nancy's, too."

"Your . . . man?" I search for the right word and can only come up with, "Suitor?"

She laughs louder now. "Oh, lass, you *are* an innocent. He's my man. My fancy man."

Fancy man. I know that term. Her pimp.

"You have a fancy man?" Mae says. "That cannot be. The ball

is for girls who have not . . . That is to say, it is to find protectors for girls who have not yet known the marriage bed."

I swear I hear the other girl's eyes roll. "Did you believe that, Mae? You really are rather simple. That is what the men believe the situation to be, but what do you think happens when a lass is chosen and a gentleman chooses not to engage in a longer arrangement?"

"Recycled virgins," I murmur, too low for anyone to hear.

"You would have learned the truth soon enough," the girl says. "We all did. It is a game our men play with the gentlemen, who seem to believe there is an unending supply of untouched girls in the Old Town."

I clear my throat. "Setting that aside . . ."

"Yes," the girl says. "There are more important matters at hand."

"Such as escaping. Also, your name?"

"Bren. As for escape, I hope that if they've brought you and Mae, that means they'll be bringing more."

"Collecting us two by two for Noah's ark."

She snorts. "I do not believe we will be transported to the promised land."

"To an area in need of young women," I say. "The cities have plenty. The countryside then? Or a smaller munic—comm— town?"

"I thought London, but you are correct. There are more than enough girls in London, and my kind are no more welcome in England than Scotland."

Irish, she means. We're twenty years post-famine, but the Irish are still considered the illegal aliens of their day, snatching up jobs and land that "rightfully" belongs to Scots.

I say, "At this point, it matters little where we are going, presuming we do not *wish* to go *anywhere*. As you said, they will likely bring more girls. That's why they're holding us here. We must escape before they are finished collecting. Have you checked the whole of your room?"

"I have. There is a door, but I cannot open it. Otherwise, there is nothing."

"You keep trying to rouse Nancy, and I'll search this room."

# CHAPTER EIGHT

At first, it seems that Bren is right—there's just a door, with no other exit. No windows. Solid walls. Stone floor. Ceiling eight feet overhead, out of reach. Then I remember the crates. Even as I stack them for climbing, I know I'm getting desperate. The light infiltrating the room comes between the thick wooden planks used for constructing the walls. The ceiling is pitch dark. That means the roof is solid.

Still, I have to check, which would be much easier if the crates weren't rotted. I check each manually, running my hands over moldy wood in the dark, which is as much fun as it sounds. I end up with so many slivers that I could use my hands as spiked maces.

Eventually, I find boxes that will support me enough to get to the top, where I discover it was worth the effort. It's not a roof over our heads. It's a ceiling, with another floor overhead, and that's why I didn't see light coming through. Not that the ceiling is airtight—just that the floor above is pitch black. From atop the crates, a breeze brushes my cheek, and I adjust my stack until I find the source: a hatch in the ceiling.

I snort at that.

You threw us into a prison cell with an actual escape hatch?

*Why not? We're just silly girls who'll be too busy sniveling and shivering in the dark to think of exploring the ceiling, much less find a way to do it.*

They aren't entirely mistaken. Out of the four girls they've captured, one is still unconscious and one is indeed shivering in the corner. I'm busy trying to find a way out, and not once does Mae evince even a shred of curiosity, much less offer to help. So when I find the hatch, I don't bother to tell her. I just get it open and heave myself through.

Once I'm up there, it's too dark to see. By feeling my way, I can tell I'm moving across rafters. An attic then? Maybe. I focus on moving to the section above Bren and Nancy's room.

Turns out that Bren *was* right about her cell being solid. It doesn't have a hatch. It does, however, have a loose board that I'm able to pry up, along with an adjoining one.

"Here," I whisper as I lean into the hole.

In the near dark, I can make out a young woman standing below me, with another rousing herself from the floor. I knew which two young women I'd seen leave, and if asked to speculate which was "Bren," maybe I should have guessed the confident and bold one. But I'd have picked the quiet girl who'd seemed uncertain, which is the one standing below. Bonus points for me, which is always a relief. A detective needs to be able to read people and make judgments, and I *do* screw up, but it's reassuring when I get it right.

The quiet girl had seemed nervous, but that didn't mean she was flighty or frightened—just understandably concerned about the situation. That's Bren. The bold one is Nancy, still recovering from being drugged after she got "excited" on realizing what Bren already knew . . . that this was not a simple evening of paid companionship.

When I peek down through the hole, Bren starts to smile.

Then she stops, and her face tightens. I almost check over my shoulder, as if someone's there.

"You," she says, taking a slow step back. "You're *Cat*? You mean Catriona."

Nancy pushes to her feet. "Catriona Mitchell?" She peers up at me and then spits on the ground.

Why couldn't I be like time travelers in books, plunked into a new era in my own body?

Because then I wouldn't have met Gray and Isla, and I wouldn't be here. Which, at the moment, doesn't seem like a terrible idea, but I'm just being grumbly. I like where I landed, and I wouldn't give it up, even if it meant not having to deal with the fifty percent of Edinburgh that Catriona has pissed off.

I open my mouth to say . . .

To say what? That I've changed? A classic line that means someone absolutely has not changed one whit. Say that I hit my head, and I'm a different person? Yeah, I'm not even starting that tale when we have mere minutes to escape before being loaded onto a ship for parts unknown.

"It's a long story," I say, also cliché, but also *so* true. "Think of me as Catriona's twin sister. I look like her. I'm not like her—not anymore."

"You expect us to believe that?" Nancy says.

Bren motions for her to keep her voice down.

Nancy sniffs. "Princess Catriona, too good for the likes of us. Too good to even *talk* to the likes of us. Now you've fallen right beside us in the gutter. Serves you right."

I don't argue. If that's her take on the situation—that Catriona has tumbled off her high horse into the sex trade she scorned—then let her have that victory.

I reach down my hand. "Pull over a crate and climb up."

Bren only peers at me in the darkness. "You said you're here for Mae's sister, Alice. You work with her, don't you? For that doctor fellow who cuts up corpses?"

Great. If it's not Catriona's reputation causing trouble, it's Gray's.

"Just come on up," I say.

To my surprise, Bren pulls over a crate, tests it and then steps on top.

"I like Alice," she says. "And I don't care what they say about that doctor fellow. His sister sent Alice with a balm for my wee cousin."

Nancy sputters. "But *that* is Catriona Mitchell, not Alice or the doctor's sister."

"I know, but she is helping us escape, and I do not see any way it might be one of Catriona's tricks."

"It's not," I say. "I'm here to get Mae free, and I'm offering you the same. Just don't think of me as Catriona, all right?"

Nancy's eyes narrow. "So where is Mae?"

That's a fine question. Last time I saw her, she was still in that damn corner. Even me disappearing into the ceiling wasn't cause for surprise or even interest. I'll blame shock. It has to be shock, right?

"I will get her now," I say. "She has had quite a fright, and I wanted to give her time to rest her nerves."

Bren makes a noise that sounds like a snort. She says nothing, though, and when I reach down, she lets me start hauling her up. That's made more difficult by the fact that she's not wearing layers of skirts. She's wearing a crinoline cage, which gets stuck.

She curses under her breath and tells me to set her down. Then, in a few moves, so deft that I am in awe, she has removed the cage and tossed it aside. After that, it's much easier to pull her through that narrow gap.

"Get Mae," she says. "I'll help Nancy."

I crawl across the floor, which is no less filthy on the return trip. This dress is done for, and that's not like ripping a T-shirt in the modern world. I try not to calculate the cost of replacing it. Oh, Gray would happily buy me a new one, and Isla would be horrified to know I was even worrying about such a thing—rather like a guest worrying about replacing a ripped hand towel. But I really do want to make my own way, as much as I can.

Right now, the dress is inconsequential. I have a bigger concern. Mae. If she's in shock, how the hell am I going to get her up here? Can I sneak down and open the door instead? What if even that doesn't work? I can't *carry* her out.

And all that is unnecessary fretting, because when I lean through the hatch and say, "Come on," she only says, "Is the way clear?"

I hesitate, thinking I've misheard.

"Have you cleared the way?" she says, her voice calm as she gets to her feet.

*Have I cleared the way?* She's not in shock. She's sitting on her ass waiting for me to prep a damn escape route for her.

"Yes, your highness," I whisper down. "I even scrubbed the path."

Her lips tighten. "You sound like Alice."

"Good," I mutter.

When I look out again, she says, "I need help."

"That much is obvious," I mutter. "Climb up the crates."

She hikes her skirts and struggles to get her boot up high enough.

"Bloody hell," I say, and I lean out as far as I dare. "Take my hand. Work with me, all right? I can't pull you up on my own."

I still end up doing more pulling than necessary. It's like rescuing a terrified cat. I even end up with the scratches, and I'd be a lot more understanding if she *were* terrified. She's not. She's a pretty girl who has grown up being treated like a china doll, too delicate to do anything for herself. Learned helplessness combined with the expectation that she will be helped. She deserves it . . . for being pretty.

For all my grumbling about Catriona, I can at least give her credit for not turning out like this. Catriona could look after herself. It's what she did to others along the way that's the problem.

I finally get Mae into the attic. She says something about not being able to see and something about the floor being dirty, and I tell her—in a period-appropriate manner—to shut up. I also don't shove her back down the hatch, proving I am *not* Catriona.

Mae does quiet down . . . after Bren tells her to. Both Nancy and Mae seem to listen to Bren, which means they do have a sense of self-preservation, if somewhat undernourished compared to Bren's. I make note of this, though. Let Bren herd them while I focus on finding a way out.

I don't mention that I haven't found an escape route yet. It seemed safest to just get everyone up here first. At least now if our captors come for us, we won't be in our cells.

Also, I've been up here long enough for my eyes to adjust. There's a little bit of light peeking in. Leaving the girls behind, I make my way toward that light and find a set of doors, like those on a hayloft, as if for hauling goods into the loft.

I push on the one door, very gently, and it moves an inch and then stops. Locked? I maneuver around until I can peer through the crack when I push again. Nope, not locked. Just latched.

More maneuvering, during which I do something I probably should have done earlier. Following Bren's example, I shed some of my bulk, in my case, peeling off my underskirts.

It's not as if I didn't consider this as soon as the skirts got in my way. I am just very aware that I only have two sets of them. Also, part of me likes to do this sort of thing in full Victorian garb. There will be times when I don't have the option of stripping off layers. I need to be able to work with what I have.

For now, though, the skirts have become an encumbrance that I can't afford. Off they go, and without them, I can get into the right position to snake my arm through the gap as I push on the door.

I undo the latch while holding the door shut. Last thing I need is to throw open the escape hatch . . . and have a bunch of dock workers look up and see me. The voices seem distant, but I'm still careful.

I hold the doors shut and peer through the crack. No sign of anyone. It helps that the doors are on the opposite side from the rooms where we were kept. Those seem to open to a road, while this opens over a dock—with a boat there—it's dark and quiet.

I go back for the others. We all crawl to the doors with a minimum of fuss. Then comes the "getting down" part. I go first. No one argues with that.

As I guessed, the doors are for hauling up goods. That means there's a pulley, and a pulley means a rope. It also helps that it's no farther going down than it was climbing up on those crates. In other words, it's roughly an eight-foot drop. I use the rope to get low enough, and then I'm on the ground easily enough and ready to help the others.

Bren comes down first. Without me needing to ask, she slips off to stand watch while I help the other two. Once all of us are on the ground, I wave them farther along the building wall to a shadowed spot where we can catch our breath.

"Wait here, and let me scout," I say.

I slip off. I've mentally mapped out our surroundings. In front of us is a dock with a small boat and water beyond. To the right, a short row of more docks ending in a darkness that looks like scrubby fields. The voices and noises all come from the left, where the docks continue on. I head right.

When I try to go farther, Mae yelps, and I turn to see Bren hushing her. I point in the direction I'm heading, trying to convey that I'm checking a potential escape route, but I'm sure Mae thinks I'm fleeing and leaving them to their fates. Bren manages to shush her.

I still don't go far—at some point, even Bren would get suspicious. I confirm that there is indeed open land beyond that next dock, with enough dark shapes—trees? Buildings?—for cover that we could make our escape in that direction.

Then I return and check the other way. I know better than to just make a run for it. I need to see what we're up against. Stationary guards? Patrolling guards? No guards?

I take it slow and give thanks for my dowdy dress that blends into the shadows. That's going to be a problem for the other girls, all wearing more typically bright Victorian gowns. Mine keeps me hidden as I peek around the corner to see, as expected, more docks.

While men are clearly hard at work, they're all much farther down, allowing me to continue around the corner and to the next one. And that's where I see what we face. Two men, both of them neither stationary nor patrolling but just restlessly wandering along that side of the building. It's where the doors to our cells exit, so there's no need for the guards to go much farther. And they don't. They presume the young ladies are languishing in their cells, having thrown themselves on the altar of fate.

I hurry back to the others. "There are two guards staying on the other side of the building, by the doors. Past that dock there, it's clear. We only need to—"

Hooves clatter on stone, and I peek out to see the black coach we arrived in, crest still covered. Seeing that covered crest, I finally take a moment to fully understand what was happening back at Abernathy Hall. The building was used by thieves, including Catriona, for learning their trade and, presumably, networking—students getting jobs from experienced thieves for a cut, older ones teaming up together for more difficult jobs. The hall also held dances, during which young women would dance with the young thieves, while gentlemen above would select a companion for the evening . . . with the possibility of a longer relationship, which encouraged the girls to take part. Tonight, though? Tonight had been different.

Tonight, those gentlemen hadn't been looking for an Old Town girl to warm their bed. They'd been there to make money . . . by sex-trafficking the girls.

Rich men of the so-called nobility making a few bucks on the side selling girls who wouldn't be missed. Pass their pimps extra cash and let them tell others that the girl was one of the lucky ones.

*Remember Nancy, Bren, and Mae? They found themselves a gentleman lover, who keeps them in a fine house in the country. You could be next.*

I want to throttle the young men who did this to the girls, with Felix first in line. Yet their crime is heartlessness mingled with a desperate drive to do whatever it takes to scramble out of the cesspool life threw them into.

The gentlemen have no such excuse. They have food on their tables and roofs over their heads. They are men of wealth and privilege, and yet they're happy to make a little extra selling teenage girls into sexual slavery. Why? Because they can. Maybe they have debts—gambling, drugs, mistresses—and the world owes them a way to pay those debts, which it provides by throwing these girl-shaped bags of money at their feet.

I watch that coach, and a fire takes hold inside me. A spark that I am going to use to light Molotov cocktails under those men's asses and burn it all down.

I know it's a drop in the bucket, but as Mrs. Wallace says when Isla despairs over how little she can do, that drop is rain on parched earth, and even if it only revives a tiny patch, that patch still wasn't there before. We do what we can, and I will take pleasure in lighting this fire.

That will come later. What matters first is the girls who need to get away *now*, not after a police investigation that won't find them, much less free them.

The problem, of course, is that I've no sooner found an escape route than more potential victims arrive. I want to help them, too. Inside me, there is a pint-sized superhero, five-year-old Mallory who carried her golden lasso everywhere. I might have a bit of a savior complex. Oh, hell, I have a full-blown savior complex that got me into this damn situation, first running into an alley to save a woman in trouble and then leaping up tonight to join Mae. But now the adult in me needs to take that golden lasso away.

Get Bren, Nancy, and Mae to safety. Find Gray. Tell him what happened while we're hauling ass to McCreadie in hopes of stopping the ship before it sets sail with its human cargo.

Bren has snuck up behind me, and I turn to whisper, "I'll send help back for them."

She nods, validating my plan as the sensible one.

"We just need to wait until the coach leaves," I whisper. "I don't want to be running across that dock when it turns around."

"Agreed."

The other two have made their way over, and she explains to them as I watch the coach pass—

I blink hard. Am I seeing someone clinging to the back of that coach?

For a moment, I think of Gray. I don't know what happened to him. I can only guess that he lost track of me. I'd love to see him hitchhiking on that coach, but yeah, he wouldn't get far without being spotted. This figure is much smaller.

I squint, trying to make out . . .

It's Alice.

# CHAPTER NINE

I've seen children do this in the city. They grab onto the back of a coach and hitch a ride until the driver notices. Oh, people see them, but if they're riding on a fine coach through a less-than-fine part of town, the average passerby is too amused to tattle.

Being small and clad in a dark dress, Alice has managed to escape detection. She's clinging like a barnacle, and I would be utterly impressed if I wasn't busy madly waving for her to jump down while she can. The coach is barely moving, and if she gets off now, she can scamper to safety before it stops.

Except she doesn't know the coach has reached its destination, and she's not going to leap off at the docks otherwise. She can't see me waving, either. Her face is turned toward the coach as she holds on for dear life.

Distraction. I need to create a distraction before—

The coach stops.

"Is that Alice?" Bren whispers.

I nod, and she curses, adding a murmur of, "Seems the little one got all the bravery in that family."

True, but I'd rather she were a little less brave right now. I reach down and pick up a stone. It's a clichéd distraction technique, but I've used it before and I'll use it as long as it works. Anything else would risk calling attention to Bren and the other two.

I stand there, holding the stone as I watch. The driver hops down, and the two guards stroll over. I tense, but the driver only opens the coach door, the guards staying away from the back where Alice is sliding to the ground.

I hold my breath as her boots touch down. She pauses there, listening before silently scampering off.

Good girl.

One of the guards moves forward to help a young woman from the coach. She steps out and looks around, confused.

"Sir?" she says to the man still in the coach.

"I need to take care of business," his half-muffled voice replies. "There's a room where you can wait, with tea and biscuits."

The girl smiles. "All right."

She lets the guards lead her off as Alice darts in the other direction. The coach door shuts. The asshole inside doesn't even bother to step out. The driver hops back up . . . and spots Alice making a break for it.

The driver scrambles down as the man in the coach bangs on the roof and shouts, "Get that girl!"

*Shit!*

The man shouts something about how the girl is a spy and she can't be allowed to get away. I wheel to Bren.

"Take Nancy and Mae," I say. "Get out of here. I'll help Alice."

Bren turns to Mae. "You stay and help Catriona."

"Me?" Mae squawks.

"It's your sister who's in trouble."

"And how is that my fault?"

Bren's face darkens, but I say, "Take her, please. She won't be of any help to me."

"Useless chit," Bren mutters, but she herds the two off as I whisper for her to move as fast as she can and take advantage of the distraction.

The distraction I am about to provide.

I tear past the three as they set out, and I keep running as fast as these damn boots will allow. When I'm at the far end, down by the docks, I run out and head straight for the nearest conveniently wooden surface, allowing my boots to clatter across it.

The coach driver has taken off after Alice, along with one guard, while the other prods the young woman into one of those tiny stock rooms. It's the young woman who hears my boots—or my feigned loud gasps, as if I'm struggling to breathe.

"Wait," she says, her voice carrying to me. "Is that not Catriona Mitchell? She was selected earlier."

I glance over, just to be sure the guard sees my face. He shoves the young woman into her cell, ignoring her squeaks of surprise, and locks the door as fast as he can while he shouts, "The blond one has escaped!"

I let out a shriek of terror and flail my arms as I make a piss-poor attempt to flee. Even Mae wouldn't be so inept, but the guard doesn't hesitate. He runs for me, still shouting for the others, and I continue my shrieking half-assed run until the second guard appears, zooming in to cut me off. Then I let them get close enough for me to see their faces, count to five and take off running properly, zigzagging until I can crouch behind a pile of crates.

I wait as the two men draw near. They're trying to sneak up on me, but their attempts are as loud as my escape efforts. I wait until I hear their labored breathing—not many joggers among average Victorians—and then I shove the piled crates onto them and take off.

I dodge and dart around every obstacle. When I see a tugboat tied close enough to the dock, I clamber onto the bow, run around the cabin, pretending to hide again, and then I slip off the stern end and keep going.

The ruse works. Behind me, the guards split up to trap me on that tug . . . after I'm long gone.

Alice has two choices. She can run toward the noise of the dock workers or into the quiet warren of warehouses beyond. I'd advise option one. Get to a more public spot where there are enough people that one is bound to take pity on a fleeing girl. But Alice isn't me. Her experience isn't mine. She steers clear of those voices and heads into the warehouses, with the coach driver in hot pursuit.

It's not entirely the wrong choice. She manages to duck somewhere that he doesn't see, and when I draw near, he's searching for her. Then he hears something and strides along the gap between two buildings.

He's bearing down on her hiding spot. So I run into the gap myself, panting and wheezing like I've run a triathlon. When I stop with a yelp, the driver turns and recognizes me. His brows knit.

"Oh!" I say, my hands flying to my mouth. "P-please, sir."

He pivots and comes my way. I back into the building wall. My hands fly up as if I'm trapped.

"Oh, please, sir. You must help me. They're going to . . . They're going to . . ."

I sniff and cower. As he draws closer, I pretend to steel myself, throwing my hair back and thrusting out my chest even as I feign shivering.

"Please, sir," I say. "If you would pretend you did not see me, I would be ever so grateful." I meet his eyes and inhale to better display my cleavage. "*Ever* so grateful."

He smirks and keeps coming my way, as I snap open the knife behind my back.

I'm waiting for him to get two more steps and then—

Small running feet thump behind him. He turns . . . just as Alice swings a board at his head. It hits with a *crack*, and he starts to fall, scrabbling for his footing. I leap and knock him to the ground.

I'm on his back, pinning him. He makes no move to call for help, just keeps struggling, as if confident he can easily get out of this without anyone knowing he was felled by two girls. I have Alice remove the laces from my boots—doing it myself while wearing a corset would require more maneuvering than I have time for. I use the laces to tie his hands and feet while giving Alice my kerchief to stuff into his mouth.

"Nicely done," I say, nodding at the plank.

"I cannot believe he actually fell for your ridiculousness."

I bat my lashes. "What ever do you mean?"

She rolls her eyes. We finish securing the driver. It's not a perfect job, neither of us being a professional kidnapper. He'll get free—or summon help—soon enough, so once finished, we run to another hiding spot before speaking.

"Mae is fine," I say once we're safely away from the driver. "Another of the captive girls helped me get her and a third girl out, and they fled to safety while . . ." I see the problem with finishing that sentence and trail off.

"While *you* came to help me," she says. "And she did not."

"I was standing watch. I spotted you on the coach."

"If you are implying that Mae did not see me, do not bother. She did, and that didn't keep her from escaping while she could."

I open my mouth to argue, but a look from her stops me.

She sets her jaw and shakes her head. "I endangered us both

helping someone who would not have done the same for us. Who *did* not do the same for us."

"*You* didn't put me in danger. I'm quite capable of doing that myself, thank you. Also the other two girls wouldn't have escaped without our intervention. As for your sister, sometimes we help people *knowing* they wouldn't do the same. We help because it's the right thing to do. And we help because we could not rest easy if we didn't."

She eyes me and then gives a slow nod. "Mrs. Wallace is wrong. You are not the Catriona we knew."

"I'm not sure anyone really knew that Catriona," I murmur. "But yes, I'm not her. Now, we need to figure out a way back to the city so I can tell Dr. Gray and Detective McCreadie what's going on here."

"What *is* going on?"

I hesitate. Damn it, I'm heading for another landmine there. But again, her expression says she isn't letting me sidestep it. I explain what we presume—that the girls were being shipped off to work in the sex trade elsewhere. I insinuate that her brother wouldn't have known the truth, and this time, she thankfully doesn't hear the lie in my voice.

"There was another girl in the coach," Alice says. "They were bringing her to join the others. I overheard that and thought it odd that they were all being taken to the same place. That is why I came." She pauses. "I am sorry if I caused more trouble."

I resist the urge to hug her. Instead, I only smile and say, "I'm rather in the habit of causing more trouble when I am trying to do a good thing, and it hasn't stopped me. We are both fine. Mae should also be fine, but we ought to hang about just a little longer to be sure we do not hear anything to suggest she has been captured."

Alice nods, and we make our careful way through the warehouses until we are close enough to hear the guards calling for the driver.

"Good," I say. "She has not been returned."

"There is that other girl," Alice says. "The one that came in the coach I rode on."

I hesitate.

"We should leave her for now, I think," Alice says. "It would be a great risk to rescue her."

"Sadly, yes. However, as she is the only one, I do not think she is in immediate danger. They will want to find the others."

And as I say that, a sound comes again, one that has my head jerking up. Hooves and wheels on stone. The man in the coach must have found someone else to drive it. Still, I can't make that assumption. It could also be another coach bringing more young women.

"Let me see what that is," I say. "I'll be right back."

Alice grabs the back of my bodice.

She doesn't say a word. She doesn't need to.

I sigh. "Fine. Stay with me."

We continue on at a slow jog, both of us in our stocking feet now.

As we move, I realize the wheels sound different from those of the coach. Creakier and rougher. Also, the noise is getting louder instead of receding. A second vehicle is joining the first.

When we reach the edge of the warehouses, I peek out and see an old horse pulling a rickety open cart.

It's just someone visiting the docks to pick up or drop off supplies. I'm about to say that to Alice when two men approach the cart. The same two who'd been guarding us.

"What's going on here?" the cart driver says in a loud whisper. He jerks his chin toward the coach. "The gent having a bit of fun with the lasses?"

The taller of the two guards shakes his head. "Waiting for his driver, who ran off after a wee stowaway. He thought she'd come from the hall, but I think she was just catching a ride."

The cart driver grunts. "None of my concern. I'm only delivering this fellow."

The guards peer toward the cart, frowning.

"The lads want him taken straight aboard the ship. They also said to tell you it's time to put the lasses onboard. The lads will be here shortly."

The guards look at one another.

The cart driver lifts his hands. "I'm only the messenger."

"That's not the problem," the taller guard says. "The thing is . . ."

"The lasses are gone," the other guard says. "All but the last one."

"What?" the driver says.

"It's not our fault. I said there was a hatch in the ceiling, but they didn't reckon the lasses would be able to see it."

The cart driver shakes his head. "Take this fellow and get him on that boat. The lads can figure out what to do about the rest."

The guards walk to the back of the cart. They pull out a body-shaped object wrapped in a horse blanket. One arm falls free, and I can make out brown skin against the white shirtsleeve, and my heart stops.

"Is he dead?" one of the guards says.

"Of course not," the driver snaps. "We didn't sign on for that sort of thing. Now get him on the ship."

The men struggle with the body, and the smaller one fumbles his end. The blanket slips enough for me to get a look at the unconscious man's face, erasing all doubt.

"Is that Dr. Gray?" Alice says.

# CHAPTER TEN

The two guards carry Gray's unconscious body to the boat. It's the one near the building where they'd held us captive. I'd wondered whether that was the one they planned to put us on. At the time, I'd already mapped out our escape route, so I'd been no more than idly interested in the ship.

It's not some massive seagoing vessel. If there are any of those here, I don't see them. I suspect they're moored farther out. This one is roughly the size of a small yacht, though clearly a utilitarian vehicle, and an old one at that. It's the boating equivalent of my dress—patched together to get a few more years out of it.

As Alice and I slip along the nearest building, she says, "I cannot believe you dragged poor Dr. Gray into this."

I swallow a yelp of protest and say evenly, "I would not do that. He was heading home from his day, spotted me and followed. He insisted on joining me. I couldn't stop him."

Her look is dubious.

"If you honestly think I can dissuade Dr. Gray from doing anything, you don't know him very well. He is as stubborn as his sister."

"I think it is a good thing to be stubborn."

"That's obvious," I mutter, "as I cannot seem to dissuade *you*, either. However, this time, I am serious, Alice. I need you to get to safety and allow me to help Dr. Gray."

Her jaw sets in that way I know so well.

"I need to get on that boat," I whisper. "It's going to be tricky enough for one person. Two just doubles the risk."

Her gaze shunts to the side. Then she says, "Fine. But only for Dr. Gray's sake."

I eye her.

She scowls at me. "I am not going to sneak onboard after agreeing to leave. You are correct. I would endanger Dr. Gray's chance for escape. Only remember that he trusts you and that if you do anything to betray that trust . . ."

"You'll hunt me down and make me pay?"

"I will."

---

Alice is gone. I watched her leave as the guards loaded Gray onto the ship. Once that's done, they head back onshore, and I'm glad Alice doesn't see that part or she might have argued to stay, because it makes getting on that ship not nearly as difficult as I expected. The guards secured Gray belowdecks—I saw them come up—and now they're heading back to speak to the cart driver. There is no sign of anyone else on the boat.

As soon as they're out of sight, I sprint down and hurry along the gangplank. Once onboard, I dart around the cabin to catch my breath and peer out.

There's no sign of the guards returning. Even the noise at the farther docks is all but gone, as if the clock struck twelve and the working day ended for dockhands. The silence lets me listen and pick up faint voices from the direction of the coach and cart.

Everyone's occupied. Excellent.

I find my way belowdecks easily enough. At the bottom, the moonlight illuminates an unlit lantern. I take it and find the matchbox nearby. Light the lantern. Shove the matches into my pocket. This room is jam-packed with crates and barrels. I glance in one crate and see old linens, neatly folded. Another holds bottles of cheap whisky. A third contains used clothing.

Fake trade goods. Like drug smugglers packing a plane full of used electronics. If anyone looks, they'll just see a decrepit ship carrying peddler goods.

I'm presuming the men will rearrange these boxes before the boat launches to sea, but for now, there's a clear path to a door. On that door is a padlock. I'm also presuming that when they leave, they'll actually remove the key from that padlock.

I open the lock and start to set it aside. Then I think better of that and hide it. I grab a handful of the old linens and stuff them in the doorjamb to keep it from shutting—or being easily shut— behind me.

Only then do I venture inside, where I find myself in a pitch-black hold. I lift the lantern, shine it around and—

Nothing. There's no sign . . .

I stumble over Gray's leg. He's been shoved aside to leave space for the young women.

As I drop beside him, Gray lifts his head from the floor, blinking. I reach down to help him sit. Then I see the cloth over his mouth . . . and the fact that his hands are behind his back.

"Let me get you free," I whisper.

He nods, still blinking to clear his head. I start by using my knife to slice off the gag. Then I cut his legs free. The rope on his hands is doubled, and my knife isn't big enough to make short work of it. When I finally get it cut enough, he wriggles out. Then he lifts the lantern to peer at me.

"Dear lord, you *are* a sight," he says. "Here I am, fighting for my life, and you've been rolling in the dirt, losing your petticoats and not even bothering to keep your hair tidy."

I snort a laugh. "At least I'm not wearing a paper bag."

His brows rise. I wave him to the door, where we look out as he rubs circulation back into his wrists.

"It was my favorite book as a kid," I say. "About a princess who rescues her prince from a dragon. After the battle, she looks like this. . . ." I wave at my disheveled self. "She lost her dress and had to wear a paper bag. He complained most bitterly."

"So she threw him back to the dragon?"

"Nah, she decided she didn't need a prince after all."

"As she should, and I am glad you knew I was only teasing. Also, possibly, covering up my own embarrassment at needing rescue. I was discovered as I was trying to follow you from the hall, and I made the mistake of thinking I could reason with Detective Broun. Someone jumped me from behind, and before I could throw a single punch, there was a rag over my mouth and nose."

"Goddamn Victorians and their goddamn chloroform."

"It is a relatively recent discovery," he says. "The possibilities for its use are endless and must also be explored and exploited endlessly."

"Yeah, if only people felt the same way about fingerprint analysis and weapon patterns."

We're climbing toward the deck as we whisper. Then Gray stops, and I follow his gaze to hear footsteps on the gangplank. We both go still.

The footsteps pass the hold, and I exhale in relief. I peek out to see the guards untying the gangplank. Then someone onboard hauls it in, just as a loud grinding noise sounds.

"Pulling anchor," Gray whispers.

I look at the side of the boat. We're close enough to dive and swim to shore, but we won't get away without being spotted.

Gray glances around and then motions for me to follow him around the cabin. I wait for him to go first. Then I follow. I get two steps before a hand lands on my shoulder.

My knife starts to fly up just as a blade presses into my throat —and I quickly hide mine back in my pocket. A thunder of footsteps as Gray runs back. Seeing my predicament, he stops short.

"Doctor Gray," my captor says. "They told me it was you, and I did not quite believe it."

On hearing the voice, my heart stutters.

It's Felix.

Alice's older brother.

"Let her go," Gray says.

"Is that an order, sir?"

"No, it is a request. I shall do whatever you ask. Do not hurt her. Please."

There's a tremor in Gray's voice, one that makes the corners of my mouth quirk. Gray raises his hands in surrender, shoulders stooped to make himself a little smaller, his gaze downcast just enough to add a touch of submission.

When Felix doesn't react, Gray says, "Please," with a note of pleading.

I hear the sneer in Felix's voice as he says, "It's true then. Someone told me that Catriona was playing a new game, pretending to have addled her mind while laying out honey to trap the good doctor. I laughed. Alice always bragged about how clever you were, how honorable. Now look at you, sniveling over a girl who's playing you for a fool."

"You are mistaken," Gray says, lifting his chin. "Catriona has changed. For me."

Felix laughs, and I tense, waiting for that blade to ease from my throat. It doesn't.

Gray clearly hoped for the same, and when Felix doesn't relax, his gaze goes distant, brain whirring. Then he straightens.

"Unhand her, you scoundrel, or I shall see you hang."

I wince. It's a bit much, but Felix laughs and *does* relax a fraction, though not enough to ease up on the knife.

Gray continues, "Wherever you are taking us—"

"Australia."

Gray hesitates, "Pardon?"

Felix eases back. "You're getting a trip to the Australian colonies, Doctor. You and your little housemaid. They are in dire need of wives there, and my associates provide them, for a price, of course."

"Wives . . . ?"

"Not you, obviously." Felix relaxes a little more. "But they also have a great need for doctors, and they will not care what they look like, so you will finally be able to practice your trade. Maybe, if you make enough money doctoring, you can even buy back Catriona."

"I . . . do not understand," Gray says, feigning genuine confusion. "You mean to take us to the Australian colonies? But I have a family here. My sisters need me and—"

I knock Felix's knife arm with my elbow. He'd finally relaxed enough for me to do that. I still get a nick on the cheek, but before Felix can recover, Gray is on him.

Gray throws Felix back into the cabin wall and pins his arm. My elbow hits the knife, and it goes skittering across the deck and over the side. Felix wriggles free and punches. Gray dodges the blow and slams him with an uppercut in the jaw. Felix gamely tries to lash out, but he can't regain his balance, and after two more lightning-fast blows from Gray, Felix is on the deck, hands feebly lifted in what might be a fighting stance, but I'll take it as surrender. Gray does, too, backing off and then reaching for me.

We run. We make it to the other side of the cabin before a young man steps out. I vaguely recognize him from Abernathy

Hall, where he'd seemed to be Felix's wingman. Gray lunges at him, but a voice says, "Uh-uh," and a third man steps out.

When I see the young man's face, I freeze. It takes a moment to notice the gun in his hand, but even then, my gaze returns to his face.

It's my defender from the ball. The young man who'd helped me against Felix.

He smiles, gaze fixed on mine. "You *did* believe me, Cat," he says. "I wasn't sure. I expected better of you."

"I knew better than to trust you," I lie. "When you said you wanted in, I knew you were up to something. You feared what-ever I was 'up to' might interfere with your plans. And it did. Seems you're missing a few lasses."

He tries for a smile, but it's tight. "Oh, we'll get them back. We still have one in hand. You and your lover will fetch a better price anyway. A medical doctor and a pretty girl with a head for trouble. Plenty of hard men in Australia from the days of trans-portation, and they'll *love* you. A proper filly to be properly broken."

I glare at him. Then I turn on my heel.

"Where do you think you're going?" he calls after me.

"Down to the hold," I say. "I'm not arguing with a man holding a gun. I'll get my chance later. Come, Doctor Gray." I lift my chin and hike my skirts, using the motion to get hold of my pocket, which contains my switchblade . . . and something even more useful.

Gray protests, but it's only a token, all bluster and "You'll pay for this" nonsense that apparently works well for him.

When he catches up to me, I pretend to slip a little, lean in and whisper, "Distract them at the door, please." Then I touch my cheek and say, louder, "I am bleeding. Might I have your kerchief, dearest?"

"Of course, my love."

Felix—rising from the floor—chuckles. Poor Dr. Gray, duped by the devious Catriona.

I take the handkerchief. Then we reach the door to the hold. Gray ushers me in and uses his body to block the entrance as he calls after me, "Careful, my love! The floor there seems to have glass, and you are barefooted."

He stays where he is, as if hovering anxiously, while I head into the hold and quietly open a crate. Then he wheels and puts his hands on either side of the doorway.

"I am doing as my beloved asks and going quietly," he calls to the men. "But know that I withdraw not out of cowardice but concern."

I uncap the bottle of cheap whisky and stuff Gray's handkerchief into the neck of it.

As I return to stand behind Gray, he's still at the hold door and still going strong with his overwrought performance, and the young men are too entertained to stop him.

"You have already injured Catriona," Gray says, "and I'll not have her hurt again. If any man lays so much as a finger on her, they will regret it. I will not stand idly by—"

I light the handkerchief with the matches I pocketed earlier. Then I hiss, "Move aside!"

He swings to the side, hands up. I stride out, bottle in hand.

"What's that?" Felix says, wiping blood from his cut lip.

"Molotov cocktail," I say as I pull my arm back. "It's Russian."

I throw it at the feet of the trio, now helpfully clustered together. Then I dive as the one with the gun fires. Fortunately, we are not in the era of accurate handguns, and the crash of the bottle startles him enough that his shot goes wild.

Fire whooshes, catching on a coil of old rope . . . and probably the old boat itself. I reach for Gray, but he's already grabbing my hand. We run behind the cabin to avoid gunshots, and then we clamber onto the side of the ship.

"Shit!" I say. "You can swim, right?"

"I am a very fast learner," he says.

My eyes widen. He grins at me and then jumps, pulling me with him.

# CHAPTER ELEVEN

We hit the water, which is freaking freezing for late summer. Behind us, one of the guys is yelling to shoot, and two shots do fire, but they don't even come close.

Gray was joking about not being able to swim, damn him. Well, no, I'd damn him a lot more if he jumped otherwise. I've let go of his hand, but he stays close, swimming with strokes strong enough to pull ahead. When he notices that, he slows, and I wave for him to go on, but he pretends not to see the gesture.

We continue swimming. No more shots are fired. The boat doesn't come after us—it's too slow for that. Also it's on fire.

No one jumps into the water either. I suspect that guys like Felix lack the "holiday at the beach" opportunities Gray would have enjoyed growing up.

The boat had made it a few hundred feet from shore, which is farther than I've swum in years. I can see the glow from the town of Leith, though, and Gray is right beside me, and I am, thankfully, only marginally encumbered by what remains of my clothing.

When we draw near, someone shouts a "hello!" and I start to

back up, remembering the guards. Gray catches my hand and tugs me along, and I soon see why. A figure stands at the end of the dock. It's a man with impressive sideburns and the combination of handsome face and impeccable dress that makes him seem more like a poster boy for police recruitment than an actual officer.

We reach the end, and McCreadie bends down. "Bit cold for a swim, isn't it?"

My response has him laughing. He reaches to grab my arm and hauls me out as Gray climbs from the water and Alice comes running down the dock.

---

I'd worried that Alice had agreed to leave a little too promptly when I insisted on it. That's because she planned to hitch a ride on a passing carriage and fetch McCreadie. Smart girl. Smarter than me, apparently—I should have thought to send her in his direction.

Then McCreadie—being as smart as Alice—did not come alone. He sent officers to Abernathy Hall to break up the evening before additional girls disappeared, and he brought more officers to the docks to arrest the guards and drivers and the gentleman in the coach, who apparently just hung around waiting for his driver when he should have skedaddled. How ever could he have left, with no one to drive the coach?

As for the coach, McCreadie commandeers it for us and has one of the young officers drive us with Alice to Robert Street, where we can recover before any further questioning. Being in the world of early policing means many of the procedures I take for granted aren't in place yet, and if they are, they don't apply to men of Gray's stature. He's not going to be taken to the station and given ill-fitting dry clothing before he makes a statement. He can go home, warm by the fire, dress in his own clothing, have a nice cup of tea—or glass of whisky—and have the police visit whenever he's ready.

Many men in Gray's position would insist the police come by in the morning, after they've had a good night's rest. Or they'd grumble at having to be questioned at all—they're the victims, damn it. Gray knows McCreadie needs as much as we can give, as soon as possible, and so he tells him to come by whenever he's ready.

By the time McCreadie arrives, he has a full update. The gentlemen at the club had dispersed, but the one they caught at the docks seems ready to give up names. Mae, Bren, and Nancy all got to safety, and the officers freed the girl in the storage building. Felix and the other two were caught, and their boat brought in, the fire extinguished. Felix is already wheeling and dealing, promising them the bigger fish of the crew in Glasgow who were running the pipeline of young women to Australia.

When we finish, we're all in the drawing room, Alice and me curled up on opposite ends of the sofa, the men in armchairs, the fire roaring, and the remains of a snack tray on the table. At a movement in the doorway, we all straighten.

Isla walks in, pulling her dressing gown around her. She sees us and stops short. Her gaze travels from sleeping Alice to me to Gray to McCreadie.

She looks back at me. "You haven't been in your room all night, have you?"

"Mmm, possibly not," I say.

She crosses her arms. "There was an adventure, wasn't there?"

"A grand adventure," McCreadie says, "which I also missed until they needed someone to arrest the miscreants. It is most unfair, is it not?"

"Dare I ask what happened?" Isla says.

McCreadie shrugs. "Nothing much. Mallory was nearly shipped to Australia and auctioned off as a homesteader's wife."

Isla glances at me to see whether he's joking. Then she says, "That would be most unfortunate."

"For Mallory?" McCreadie says. "Or Australia?"

Isla shakes her head and moves closer to Alice. Then she stops and pivots toward me. "Is that a whisky glass by my sleeping parlormaid?"

"Don't worry," I say. "I made sure she got the good stuff."

"Alice had a very difficult evening," Gray says. "The poor child's nerves were quite frayed."

Isla rolls her eyes, knowing Alice's nerves are even less easily frayed than her own. She takes the glass, puts it aside and then fills a fresh one for herself before slipping onto the sofa between Alice and me.

"Tell me everything," she says.

It's late the next afternoon. We're in the drawing room again, but this time it's girls only: Isla and me, plus Mae, Nancy, and Bren. The trio spent the night at a house run by an older police officer's wife, the couple often taking in young women needing temporary sanctuary. Now they've come to have tea and discuss their futures, with Isla playing Fairy Godmother.

There is part of Isla that loves being able to do this, and part that is much happier sprinkling her fairy dust from afar. I understand that, and it's one of the many things that makes me admire the hell out of Isla Ballantyne. She lives in a world where charity is becoming a passion for women of means. That's good in the sense that some are truly passionate about it, like Isla. But it also suffers from the same pitfalls as philanthropy in the modern world, where the wealthy see no irony in spending a thousand bucks for a charity dinner . . . and then several times as much on their outfits for it. In the Victorian world, charity is already mired deep in virtue signaling, and Isla despises that. Her greatest fear is coming across as Lady Bountiful, tossing bread crumbs to the poor while she dines on coconut cake.

Here, though, is her favored role: that of benefactor. Giving these young women a hand up rather than a handout.

Isla is here to help them take the first step down the road to independent life. She starts with Nancy, who's very clear about what she wants: to stay in the sex trade. She just doesn't want to keep working for the guy who tried to sell her to Australia. Nancy wants as much independence as she can get, and she knows where to find it: working at a certain New Town brothel. What she needs is finery for the entrance requirements—that young women bring their own attire, suitable for such an upscale establishment. Nancy's plan, which she's been working on for a while, is to borrow the required clothing and then buy her own once she makes enough. She's asking Isla for a loan to either rent or purchase the attire.

At first, Isla doesn't know what to do with this. Wouldn't Nancy rather work in a shop? Or in service to a good family? Or perhaps even train for something like a clerking position?

I take Isla aside and explain that this really is Nancy's choice, and it wouldn't be Isla's—or mine—but we don't have the right to govern what Nancy does with her body. All Isla can do is decide to support it or not . . . and all I can do is escort Nancy to the brothel and check it out for myself, be sure it's as safe as it can be.

Isla might be uncomfortable with this, but she wouldn't think of retracting her offer of help. She'll loan the money to buy dresses, at no interest, and she'll help Nancy find them . . . which means she'll make sure Nancy pays less than retail.

Next up is Bren, and while I'd be thrilled to have her take

over the housemaid job here, she has her sights set on another position in service: that of a lady's maid.

I glance at Isla. "Annis is looking for a lady's maid."

"I'm not sure I'd inflict that on anyone," Isla mutters, but at a look from me, she sighs and says, "Fine. Annis might suit, and if she doesn't, I'll find another position."

"Do you mean your sister?" Bren asks. "Lady Annis Leslie? The one who was accused of poisoning her husband?"

"She didn't do it," I say. "But we can find you someone else."

"Oh, no. I wasn't complaining. I have heard of Lady Annis. She sounds most interesting."

"My sister is nothing if not interesting," Isla mutters. "But yes, we will let you meet her before you decide. Now, Mae."

"I want to work here," Mae says. "As a housemaid. I have heard you are looking for one."

Isla glances my way, but we've already discussed this, and she clears her throat. "That is very kind of you, and I am certain Alice would love to have you join us, but I fear you heard wrong. Mallory—Catriona—still holds that position, at least until she has trained under Dr. Gray long enough to undertake a proper apprenticeship. However, I know of several fine households in need of a maid. You and I will discuss the options and find one to suit. I will also ensure you have everything you need for your new position, and as you're Alice's sister, I will keep an eye on you, should you need assistance. Does that sound reasonable?"

"It does, ma'am. Thank you."

***

That evening, the others gather in the courtyard for the Molotov party—I mean Alice's science experiment, which involves the incendiary devices that will come to be known as Molotov cocktails.

I'm preparing a tray for refreshments when Alice slips into the kitchen. She glances around for Mrs. Wallace, but Isla made sure to do this on the housekeeper's night off.

"Mrs. Ballantyne says you're the one who asked her not to hire Mae," she says.

I tense and say, carefully, "I thought you would not be comfortable with her here. If I was mistaken . . ."

"You were not. I only wanted to thank you." She fusses with the collar on her dress. "If Mrs. Ballantyne had asked me, I would have felt bound to agree, and you are right that I do not want her here. This is my . . ."

"Safe space."

She frowns up at me and then shakes her head. "You have such an odd way with words. Yes, it's the place where I am safe from . . . all that."

"But not the place where you were safe from Catriona."

She stiffens. "It was fine. I could handle you."

"I know you could. I only hope that you understand that you shouldn't have had to handle me, and that you won't need to again. As I have said before, if I ever do the things I did before, Mrs. Ballantyne will find me a new position. She has sworn it." I meet her gaze. "I have changed."

She ducks the direct look. "I know. I do not think it is a trick, as Mrs. Wallace believes. You have convinced me. Mrs. Wallace, though . . ."

I smile. "Oh, let me handle her. I do enjoy a challenge."

***

Alice has gone back outside while I finish loading up the tray. I don't even make it through the courtyard door before Gray is there, reaching for a biscuit.

"Are you sure you want that?" I ask, and he pauses, fingers grazing it.

I pull a plate from under the tray. On it is the last piece of lemon cake.

He smiles and takes it. "You are too good to me."

"Just buttering up the boss."

He holds open the door while I go through. The others are further in the courtyard, setting up the safety zone for our miniature Molotovs. There's a table for the food, which is suitably far from Isla's poison garden. It's a proper table, with a proper linen cloth and proper china. No folding card tables and paper plates for Victorians. No casual Fridays, either. Even for this demonstration, everyone dresses as if it is indeed a cocktail party, and I have to smile at that. I might be a jeans and tees girl myself, but I can see the appeal in this, suits and dresses and crystal glasses in the courtyard, with a repast of home-baked cookies, fresh fruit, cheeses, and lemonade.

Gray takes the tray from me and sets it out as he pours me a lemonade. "I am sorry that Bren didn't choose a position here."

"She deserved to get whatever she wanted."

"And you deserve a position properly befitting your education and experience."

I shrug. "We'll find a new housemaid."

"Soon. I promise."

"I know."

I look out at the others. Alice and Simon are arguing about whether the safety zone is big enough. Isla is pouring alcohol into the tiny bottles we'll be using. McCreadie holds the bottles as she pours the booze into a funnel, and they're deep in conversation, punctuated with smiles and sidelong glances.

I watch them, their heads together as they work, and I sigh.

"Agreed," Gray says. "I do not know what they are waiting for. They are both too blind and too proud, afraid to mistake the other's regard."

"It's not just pride," I say. "Isla was burned. Badly."

"And Hugh's own romantic experience was . . . difficult."

I don't know the whole of that story, only that he broke off an engagement shortly after Isla married her asshole of a husband, and his wealthy family all but disowned him for it.

"Still . . ." Gray says. "I do wish they would wake up and get on with it."

"Seconded."

"Are you two coming?" Isla calls over. "Or are you going to find a quiet corner where you can continue whispering together?"

"Us?" Gray says.

Isla shakes her head and holds out a bottle. "Mallory? You can go first. Show us how it is done."

I smile and step forward. "Let the games begin."

# SCHEMES & SCANDALS

# AUTHOR'S NOTE

Charles Dickens's farewell tour *did* take him to Edinburgh in 1869. He *did* need to reschedule the first date (February 19) due to a broken foot. However, the rescheduled date was only a week later. I've trusted readers will allow me the creative license of moving the rescheduled appearance to accommodate Mallory's timeline.

# CHAPTER ONE

On the first of December, I walk into the town house library and announce, "I believe it's time to discuss Christmas."

I've been very patient about the whole thing, considering it's my first Victorian Christmas. I spent the last one in Vancouver . . . in 2018. That spring, I ended up in 1869 Edinburgh, which is a very long story, the short version being that I crossed into the body of a nineteen-year-old housemaid working for Dr. Duncan Gray and his widowed chemist sister, Isla. Gray is an undertaker with degrees in both surgery and medicine, and he combines the three through his true passion, which is early forensic science. Having been a police detective in my former life, I landed in exactly the right place, and after seven months here, I have turned in my mop and duster to take my full-time position as Gray's assistant.

My current concern has nothing to do with murder or forensics. It's the first of December, and I am tired of waiting for someone to discuss the upcoming holidays. So I'm taking the initiative, having cornered both Gray and Isla in the library.

Gray is reading the newspaper, and his sister is at the desk, editing the account of our latest adventure. Both look up at my pronouncement.

"It's time to discuss Christmas," I say again.

Gray shakes out the paper. "I cannot believe you would say such a thing, Mallory. You, a representative of the law, suggesting we discuss *Christmas*?"

I arch one brow.

"That is—" He lowers his voice. "—illegal."

I roll my eyes. "It's December first. The official date on which we can start playing Christmas carols, wrapping presents, hanging decorations . . ."

"Illegal. All of it."

I eye him. "Is this your way of saying you don't celebrate? That's fine. Just say so."

"Do we celebrate Christmas, Isla?" Gray asks.

His sister's blue eyes widen in mock horror. "Certainly not. It's illegal."

"Banned," Gray says, folding his paper and setting it aside. "And in this household, we follow the rules."

I snort at that. "Follow the *law*, yes. You most certainly do not follow the rules. Either of you. If you want to pull a prank on the time traveler, please try something more believable than saying Christmas is . . ."

I slow. Even as I say the words, a childhood memory surfaces, my nan saying something about Christmas not being a holiday when she was a child. Her eyes had been sparkling when she said it, which meant I presumed it was one of those "back in my day" tall tales, like my Canadian grandparents who insisted they'd walked five miles to school each day. Uphill. Both ways.

"Wait," I say. "This *is* a joke, right?"

"Hardly. The mere mention of Christmas can still get you hanged in Scotland."

"Duncan . . ." Isla says. "If you expect to convince her you are serious, you cannot make the tale utterly outlandish." She looks at me. "Yes, it *was* banned, at one time. While it no longer is, it is still not commonly celebrated."

"Christmas was . . . banned?"

"In Scotland."

I peer at her, still not sure this isn't a joke. "What happened?"

"The Reformation. Christmas was considered both a pagan celebration and a Catholic one, which was practically the same thing. The Church of Scotland prohibited the celebration of it."

"What about Hogmanay? That's pagan."

Isla shrugs. "Scots always find a way around such things. Christmas was banned, so we simply moved the pagan traditions of the solstice to Hogmanay, which, being a secular holiday, the Church could do nothing about."

"Clever. So despite the ban being lifted, people still don't celebrate Christmas?"

She sets down her pen. "It is not a public holiday, but it *is* growing in popularity. If it is important to you, we will celebrate."

"No, I'll stick with Hogmanay. I used to celebrate that with my nan. My parents and I would stay in Canada for Christmas with my other grandparents and then come over to spend Hogmanay with Nan."

Hogmanay is what the Scots call the last day of the year. In other words, it's New Year's Eve, but a bigger deal than it is in North America. Of all the traditions, my favorite custom was fireball swinging . . . which is exactly what it sounds like. You make a ball of flammable material, attach it to a chain, set it alight and swing it over your head. Like an industrial-strength firework sparkler.

"If you *do* want Christmas . . ." Gray says.

"Nah, I just like the trappings," I say. "The decorations, the parties, the gift giving. I can get that with Hogmanay." I pause. "You guys do celebrate that, right?"

"We most certainly do. And on that note . . ." He glances at his sister. "Isla? Would you reach into the top left drawer there? I believe you'll find an early holiday gift for you and Mallory."

She finds an envelope bearing Gray's impeccable script and holds it out to me. "Would you like to do the honors?"

I wave for her to go ahead. She opens it and gasps as she takes out what looks like calling cards. Then she peers at her brother.

"Please tell me this is not a joke."

His brows shoot up. "I never joke."

"You just told poor Mallory that she could be hanged for mentioning Christmas."

"Perhaps she could be. The ban may no longer be well enforced, but if they wanted to make an example of someone, Mallory would be a fine choice."

I toss my hair. "They'd never hang me. I'm a pretty girl with blond curls and big blue eyes." I bat those eyes at him. "The public would rise up in howls of outrage."

"Not if they knew you were also a thief."

"Former thief. Reformed. And that wasn't even me. It was Catriona."

"Ah, right. You can explain that to them. Tell them that you are actually from the twenty-first century, and they won't hang you for mentioning Christmas. They'll hang you as a witch." He glances at me. "We still do that here."

"Scotland has not hanged witches in a hundred years," Isla says hotly.

"They would make an exception for Mallory."

Isla glares at him and waves the tickets. "So these *are* a prank then?"

Gray sobers and meets her gaze. "Would I honestly do that to you, Isla?"

She inhales sharply. "They're real?"

"Very real."

She stares at him, speechless. I hurry to the desk, read the tickets and let out a squeal of glee.

# CHAPTER TWO

I am going to see Charles Dickens. Right now. I am walking along crowded George Street, heading to the Assembly Rooms music hall to see *the* Charles Dickens. When I was in elementary school, my parents snagged tickets to see the Spice Girls, and as happy as I'd been then, I think I'm even more excited now.

My dad is an English prof. I grew up on Dickens. Landing in an era where he's still alive and writing? I'd hardly been able to fathom it.

Many of my favorite classic novelists are still alive in this time. George Eliot. Wilkie Collins. Mary Elizabeth Braddon. I won't have much chance of seeing them—they're busy doing writerly things—but Charles Dickens tours. Or he did. He's now on his farewell circuit. He'd been due to stop in Edinburgh in February, but by the time Isla heard of it, she wasn't able to get tickets. That stop had to be rescheduled, though, because he injured his foot, which had caused such an outcry that the newspaper had to print his doctor's note to prove it.

The stop was rescheduled for late December, and that's how Gray obtained tickets for the last performance. Because, while

Christmas might not be celebrated in Scotland, some of the wealthy travel to England for the festivities, and he snagged four tickets from an acquaintance who could no longer attend.

Isla and I get two of those tickets. Gray is accompanying us, along with his best friend, Detective Hugh McCreadie.

The music hall is only about a quarter mile from Gray's Robert Street town house, so we are walking. To be honest, we walk most places. I won't say that Victorian Edinburgh is a particularly pleasant place to stroll, given the amount of excrement, not all of it from horses. Add in the amount of precipitation, and you can't even avoid that excrement, because it melts into every puddle. But boots come clean, and these days, I don't even need to scrub them myself. Coach travel might be cleaner, but we can usually get where we want to go faster on foot. Also, being late December, the precipitation is all snow, which blankets the soot-covered city in white and also freezes the puddles, bodily waste and all.

The music hall, like Gray's town house, is in the New Town. Initially, that's where the wealthy moved to escape the poverty of the Old Town. These days, it's home to both the upper class and the upper-middle, like the Gray family.

We are dressed for a night on the town. Gray wears a silk top hat and a long coat over a black wool three-piece suit with a starched white shirt and silk cravat. McCreadie is, as always, more stylish, with his checked jacket slightly shorter and more fitted, as is the incoming style. Isla has moved far enough from mourning that she's able to wear lilac, and her dress is divine, with silver buttons and silver-gray pinstriping plus wider strips of silver-gray along the bottom of the sleeves and skirts. My own dress is the same one I wore to a party last month: turquoise silk with rust-brown embroidery and beadwork, and rust-brown lace trim.

To accommodate the narrow walking path, McCreadie and

Isla are ahead of us. Isla has only to slip, one boot barely sliding, before McCreadie has his elbow out for her to take. It's chivalrous, but also an excuse to have Isla on his arm, one she happily accepts. Just as I happily accept Gray's arm when he notices them and puts out his arm for me. It's an old-fashioned way of walking, the man with his elbow extended, the woman holding it. Very Victorian. Also, a welcome bit of human contact in a world where that is just not done.

In this era, physical intimacy is for couples and, even then, only in the bedroom. Hugs between friends are not a thing, and I find myself missing that and cherishing the moments where I have an excuse to do something like hold Gray's arm.

As we near the theater, we need to merge into a stream of fellow attendees. Though everyone is dressed in their finest, not all of it comes from New Town shops. There are plenty of second- and even third-hand dresses and suits. It's appropriate that a Dickens reading should be accessible to the working class. It would be even better if it were accessible to the *poor*, but that's too much to hope for. Gray said that the stalls are priced at five shillings, which my math skills tell me is about thirty dollars in my own world.

As we draw near the music hall, the jabbering of voices whisks me back to sporting events in Vancouver. It sounds like resellers offering overpriced tickets to a sold-out game, but as I draw close, I realize it's actually the other way around. People are banging on the ticket booth, offering to pay as much as five pounds for those cheap seats, as if the venue might be hiding some in reserve. I also notice that no one is stepping forward to sell *their* tickets for that price.

The commotion, however, means we need to slow with the desperate would-be buyers partly blocking the entrance. McCreadie grumbles about that.

"Someone should have had a few officers assigned for crowd

control," I murmur to him. "Pity we don't know anyone who could help them out now."

"Be my guest," McCreadie says. "If I take on that lot, I won't be seeing the performance."

"And so you will not interfere," Isla says, tightening her grip on his arm.

"I will not," he says. "I can still grumble, though."

Slowing means we're stuck standing outside. Being stuck standing outside means people start gawking around the queue. Gazes swing to Gray. That's understandable. He's just over six feet, with broad shoulders and striking—if severe—features. Admittedly, McCreadie is better looking, remarkably handsome even with fashionably thick whiskers. Yet the gazes fall on Gray, and it's not his height that does it. It's his brown skin. He might have been raised by Frances Gray, but his mother was Irvine Gray's mistress, and obviously a woman of color, though Irvine took any details to his grave.

We're in the days of the British Empire, when travel and immigration is easier, if not exactly easy. I can look down the queue and see several people of color. Most, however, are clearly working class. The one young Black woman in a fashionable gown accompanies an older white woman in a manner that suggests she's a companion or lady's maid. I have to crane my neck and squint to see any person of color who looks middle class.

What gets people's attention isn't that Gray is a person of color; it's that he dresses as if he's wealthy enough to have a tailor, which he does. Admittedly, sometimes they also look because he hasn't bothered to change out of a shirt spattered in blood, but that's thankfully not the case today. These days, though, there's another reason people gawk, and that's what I'm on the watch for.

A few months ago, someone started chronicling Gray's

adventures in crime solving. Those adventures may have coincided with him taking on a certain assistant, but I'm still blaming poor McCreadie. Between the three of us—and Isla, when a case interests her—we've solved a few murders. The person who interested that writer, though, was Gray. Well, Gray and his pretty assistant, but my role in the stories seems mostly window dressing.

*The Mysterious Adventures of the Gray Doctor* has recently changed writers and—thankfully—titles. The previous author has been shut down, by methods known only to the new author, who granted Isla a cut plus editorial oversight. There was no way of getting rid of the stories altogether, so taking control of the narrative was our best bet. For now, they're a niche publication, mostly appealing to mothers and their children. Why are women and children the primary market for tales of murder and mayhem? Because these are Victorians.

Tonight, while I do see one mother and her children gesturing at us and whispering, they don't approach, so we can pretend all is well and we are safe in our bubble of anonymity.

Soon we're inside the music hall. Our tickets are for the balcony. In the modern world, I like seats in the orchestra, where I can truly appreciate live performances. Here, the orchestra seats are the stalls, which are for those who can't afford better. My disappointment evaporates when I *see* those stalls. Most of the seats are on church-like pews, with hundreds of people jammed into an area that defies any sort of safety code. One scream of "Fire!" and dozens would be trampled. I decide I'm fine with the balcony.

We aren't in actual balconies, either. More like having seats in concert stands. McCreadie goes down the aisle first, followed by Isla, followed by me and then Gray. While Isla and I would have chosen to sit beside each other anyway, this arrangement is natural for the time period—the men flanking the women so they don't need to sit beside strangers who might be male.

We settle in, and we all remove our hats, which is expected and even mentioned on the tickets. As we wait, Isla and I discuss Dickens's latest work, *No Thoroughfare*, which he wrote in collaboration with Wilkie Collins. Isla has seen the show. I have not, though I read the novel form in the twenty-first century.

"I hear he is working on a new book," Isla says. "I am hoping he will discuss it tonight." She wags her finger at me. "And no spoilers from you."

Which novel would that be? Admittedly, I'm not great with dates. I know Dickens's work but not the order or years of publication. I think back to the library at the town house. Which book is missing? I'm still working through that when someone steps on the stage to announce the main event.

The music hall venue is appropriate, because this feels much more like a concert than an author reading. I can't hear what the MC is saying, as people keep chattering and others keep shushing them, often louder than the actual talkers. Finally, I catch the tail end of the MC's speech.

"—will begin with a seasonal reading of *A Christmas Carol*."

I look at Gray and arch one brow, and there must be accusation in my eyes because he leans over and whispers, "The poor man will be hanged for certain now. Such a loss to the literary world."

It's the week after Christmas, and while there *were* some shop and house decorations, overall, it was far less than I'd expected. I know from my father that the Victorian era was the time when Christmas was still becoming the spectacle it is in the modern world. Credit—blame?—for that can be laid, at least in part, at the feet of the man about to mount the stage and the story he is about to read.

In North America, a secular Christmas revolves around the

family, especially children. You get together with your nearest and dearest, and you make a magical day for the little ones in your life. You also share your bounty with the less fortunate —'tis the season to be charitable. All that comes from *A Christmas Carol*, which refocused a community-based celebration on the family, especially the children, as well as shining a spotlight on the plight of the poor and the obligations of the wealthy.

Isla had asked whether there was any particular part of Christmas I longed to celebrate. I said no, Hogmanay would do the trick well enough, but I did wake to a plate of sugarplums on Christmas morning. May I also say that, like Turkish delight, sugarplums are not at all what I expected? There's no actual plum involved. It's more like a jawbreaker, with a seed at the center and then layers of sugar. Disappointing, but not nearly on the scale of the Turkish delight debacle. I swear I can still taste the cloying rosewater from *that*.

On the stage, the MC is walking away, and I realize the man standing there now . . .

It's Charles Dickens.

This is the Dickens I know from photos, mostly taken in this era, showing a man with kind eyes, balding hair, and a somewhat unkempt long beard. In those photographs, though, he's always dead somber, and that is not the man I see before me. He is smiling and animated and moves spryly to center stage.

As Dickens begins, I ease back in my seat, prepared for a relaxing literary performance. I've attended readings of *A Christmas Carol* before. I even participated in a group reading for one of my dad's university classes. Being the only child among the actors, you can guess who I played. God bless us every one.

Although that had been a reading rather than a dramatization, I'd treated it like a full-blown performance, limping around the stage and looking pathetic but hopeful as only Tiny Tim can.

I had, in short, hammed it up . . . and as Dickens begins to read on stage, I realize I might have underplayed it.

When Isla said it would be a two-hour performance, I'd been confused. I've been to author readings. The best are short and sweet. Even the longest top out at thirty minutes, which let me tell you, is a long time to be actively listening to someone who is not an actor or a public speaker. No matter how interesting the material, most authors are not meant to read their work.

Dickens is an exception. Possibly because, at one time, he'd entertained thoughts of acting as a career path. As I watch, I'm honestly not sure what I think. My preconceptions are smashed to such splinters that I can only sit there and gape.

In my time, Dickens is classic literature. I know that was very different during his own life. He was considered a populist writer, with all the scorn that can bring. His appeal went far beyond the educated upper—or even middle—class. He told stories about the poor and working classes. Real Victorian life, the sort I see every time I visit the Old Town.

Yet as much as I understood his broad class appeal, I couldn't help but still stick him in the "classic author" box, alongside the other literary greats. Which means I am in no way prepared for what I am witnessing.

This is Dickens's final tour because the performances are getting to be too much for him, physically. Yet the man I see is in his fifties and hardly doddering. The reason these performances exhaust him? Because they're actual performances.

I am treated—if that's the word—to the most gonzo reading of *A Christmas Carol* ever. It's as if seven-year-old Mallory got to play all the parts and played her little unselfconscious heart out. Except the guy doing the performance is Charles Dickens himself.

"What do you think?" Isla whispers. "Are readings like this in your day?"

I try to imagine Margaret Atwood getting up on stage and doing this sort of "reading" from *The Handmaid's Tale.*

Nope.

I can't imagine even the most populist authors of my time giving a performance like this.

And this is Charles freaking Dickens.

"He's very . . . energetic," I say.

"Isn't he? They say his readings bring him more income than his books do."

"I . . . can imagine."

As I watch, I am reminded again how much this world is not what I expected. When I silence my preconceptions, I begin to enjoy it, rather than staring like an elderly aunt at her first rave.

Dickens finishes his reading from *A Christmas Carol.* Then it's on to *Oliver Twist.* Good choice. Definitely a crowd-pleaser. I'm wondering what scene he'll read when—

It's the Nancy and Sikes scene. The brutal murder of Nancy at the hands of her boyfriend, Bill Sikes. I glance around nervously. This is an all-ages crowd, and he's reading what might be the most violent scene of his career. And everyone in the music hall—from children to well-dressed ladies—hangs on his every word.

"This is . . ." I manage to choke out, "an interesting choice."

"He always reads this one," Isla says. "The crowd would rise up in protest if he did not."

I sit there, watching a packed theater of prim Victorians devouring Charles Dickens's reading of a gruesome and tragic murder scene.

"At least a dozen women will faint," Isla whispers. "Loudly and enthusiastically."

I stare at her. Then I stare at the bloodthirsty crowd of ladies and gentlemen, all of them dressed in infinite layers as protection against the horror and shame of revealing a stray bit of bare skin.

I will *never* understand Victorians.

"Not what you expected?" Gray whispers at my ear.

I turn and gesticulate, unable to put my thoughts into words. His lips curve in a smile that grows until he needs to cough in his hand, politely, before he laughs aloud. Then I settle in to watch the reading . . . while Gray settles in for, I suspect, the even more entertaining spectacle of watching *me* watching the reading.

# CHAPTER THREE

The performance is over, and I've realized I'm not getting my book signed. I'd tracked down a first edition of *Our Mutual Friend*, my favorite Dickens novel, and tucked it into my bag. The readings I've attended always culminate in a signing. But, again, the author events I've attended aren't two hours of a performance so energetic that I'm exhausted from just watching.

Isla and McCreadie are gone. McCreadie had scoped out a suitable spot to enjoy a polite tipple after the show, and we'd encouraged them to escape as quickly as possible and snag a table. Any chance Gray and I get to give McCreadie and Isla time together is a chance we take.

Gray and I have lingered, with me clutching my book and looking around hopefully, as if there's a hidden "author signing" for those in the know.

"You brought a book?" Gray says.

My cheeks heat. "I was hoping to get it signed, but I'm guessing that's not a thing."

"I have seen signed books. I even purchased several for Isla. But they came that way at the shop."

I try not to look disappointed. "Got it. And after that performance, I can't imagine he'd want to sign hundreds of books."

"Perhaps . . ." Gray looks about and puts a hand to my back. "Let us go this way. There's a corridor into the back rooms where Mr. Dickens would be."

I dig in my heels against his steering. "I'm not waylaying him while he's resting after his performance."

"No, but if we are down there, and he happens to walk out, and he happens to notice a young woman clutching one of his books and looking very hopeful . . ."

I should refuse. Especially since, if I do catch Dickens's eye, it won't be because of the book. I look like a cross between a milk-maid and a young Marilyn Monroe, all bold curves and blond curls. I've finally begun to accept that this is me now. My body, not that of a cold-blooded thief named Catriona Mitchell. But I still hate using this body to my advantage. Well, unless I'm solving a case. Then all bets are off.

Even as I inwardly balk, though, my knees unlock, and I let Gray steer me. I tell myself I'm giving Isla more time with McCreadie. Am I also giving myself more time with Gray? Of course not. I see him every day. We spend hours working together. Okay, yes, holding cadavers and taking notes isn't the same as a social outing, but still . . .

Our relationship is a professional one with a personal angle, that angle being friendship. If part of me has started hoping for more, well, that's on me. Gray has given no sign that he feels the same. Which is fine. That'd be far too complicated.

Gray leads me through a door and then down a few stairs and along a hall. It feels as if we're about to enter the bowels of the Assembly Rooms, but instead, we come out into a small reception area with at least twenty people milling about chatting and enjoying glasses of wine. Gray straightens, pulling on his upper-crust airs.

He steers me through with that gentle hand, his fingertips barely touching my back. As we pass a table, he deftly plucks two glasses from it. He hands me one, and we settle into a corner, where he positions himself with his back to the other guests and his front blocking me, to keep them from looking at us too closely.

"Let us eavesdrop a bit," he murmurs. "See whether there is any indication that these fine people expect the illustrious author to join us."

I nod, sip at my drink, and try not to make a face. I thought it was wine. It's not.

"Port," Gray says. "Poor Mallory."

Port is not to my taste. It's another thing, like sugarplums, that I only read about in Regency and Victorian novels, where it sounded delightful. Dinner ends, and you all retire with glasses of port. Yes, I know it still exists in my time, but I'd never tried it, so I didn't realize it's just overly sweet wine.

Gray opens his mouth to say something else, when a voice says, "Duncan?"

The familiarity of the address has me looking up sharply. First names are for family and close acquaintances. I'm still working on calling him "Duncan," as if I've absorbed the culture. So hearing someone call him that in public is the first thing that gets my attention. The second is the way his head jerks up. Distress flickers over his face.

"Dr. Duncan Gray." The woman's voice grows closer now, though I still can't see her with Gray blocking my view. Then he slowly turns.

The woman is older than us—maybe in her late thirties. She's gorgeous, with raven-black hair, perfectly cut features, and bright blue eyes. Her brilliant green dress makes me feel as if I'm still wearing my drab day gown.

It might seem as if it'd be wonderful to wake up a decade

younger, but it's awkward in many ways, and this is one of them —where I feel the gaze of someone older sweep past and dismiss me as a mere girl.

"This is not where I expected to find you, Duncan," the woman says as her fingertips tap his jacket sleeve. "You have developed a taste for literary culture?"

"I read," he says, a little tersely. "But I am here with my sister Isla, who is a great admirer of Mr. Dickens's work. As is Miss Mitchell here."

The woman's gaze flicks over me again, and she gives Gray a look I can't quite read. Should I slip away and let them talk? Or is that the last thing Gray wants? I can't tell.

I give him the choice by murmuring, "I'm going to set down this port, Dr. Gray. It is not quite to my taste."

He doesn't argue, and I make my way toward the nearest table. I can still hear them behind me.

"I heard you hired a young woman for an assistant," the woman says. "A former maid. I take it that is her."

"Yes."

The woman sighs. "Oh, Duncan. I ignored the titters and insinuations, and I commended you for being so open minded. I know you had a terrible time finding assistants, and I was glad you had located one. But . . . Really, Duncan? I expected better of you."

"Miss Mitchell *is* my assistant."

He grinds out the words, and I set down my drink.

"My apologies, ma'am," I say when I reach them. "I realized I did not introduce myself. I am Mallory Mitchell, Dr. Gray's assistant."

Her gaze flicks to Gray, waiting for him to introduce her, as is proper. Instead, he stands there, with a look that wonders whether he can skip this part.

*Just introduce us, Gray, and we can make our excuses—*

"This is Lady Patricia Inglis," Gray says, and if I still had the port glass, I might have dropped it.

I school my features fast and give the slightest curtsy, hoping nothing in my face reveals my dismay.

There's a reason Lady Inglis uses Gray's first name and acts as if she knows him well. She does. In the biblical sense even.

When I first arrived in this time period, I found a letter in Catriona's dresser. A letter from Lady Inglis to Gray, one that Catriona had apparently intercepted before he received it. She'd likely been looking for blackmail material, maybe suspecting it was from a lover. What she got was even better. Not a sweet love note from a paramour but a full-on intimate missive, in which Lady Inglis had tried to tempt Gray back to her bed by reminding him how much fun he'd had there. Super awkward, and as soon as I figured out what it was, I'd stopped reading.

Even more awkward? The fact that just last month I confessed to him about the letter. I'd felt honor-bound to tell him Catriona stole it, but it was a very uncomfortable conversation. He'd told me to destroy it, which I had.

So this beautiful and elegant woman is Lady Inglis? Of course she is, because that's what I've pictured as the sort of woman Gray would be with. Mature, possibly even older, but gorgeous and refined, educated and charming. Okay, I haven't seen the charming part yet, but I'm sure she is, when she's not wondering what the hell her former lover is doing messing around with a girl barely out of her teens.

"Did you enjoy the performance, ma'am?" I ask.

"I did." Her gaze goes to the book I'm still clutching. "Is that one of Mr. Dickens's works?"

"*Our Mutual Friend*," I say. "My favorite. I have never been to this sort of event, and I was hoping for a signature, but obviously, that is not done." I give a rueful smile. "Dr. Gray? If you like, I could go join Mrs. Ballantyne and Mr. McCreadie."

"Certainly not," he says. "It is dark outside. I must accompany you." He turns to Lady Inglis. "But Miss Mitchell is correct that my sister is waiting for us." He tips his top hat. "Good evening to you, Lady Inglis."

As we turn away, she says, "I could ask Mr. Dickens to sign that book for you, Miss Mitchell. He knows my parents from years back."

I don't hesitate. I know this for what it is—grabbing back Gray's attention with an underhanded ploy. By the way Gray tenses, he also knows what it is. And yet . . .

The reason it's truly underhanded? She's not offering something *he* wants. She's offering something his companion wants, and she must know Gray well enough to realize he can't walk away from that.

"I'm fine," I murmur under my breath. "I don't need—"

"I am sorry to interfere with your evening out," Lady Inglis says. "But I have been wanting to talk to you, Duncan."

His cheek twitches, but before he can comment, she hurries on with, "A business matter. I was trying to determine how best to bring it to your attention. I suspected a—" She clears her throat softly. "—a letter would not do. Nor a message asking to meet with you. Yet I did not wish to show up at your house."

"If you need something, Lady Inglis," he says coolly, "then I would appreciate you saying so and not tacking on an offer to help Miss Mitchell."

"I *can* help her, though. I can get that signature. As for what I need . . . I wish to hire you as a detective."

A beat pause before Gray straightens. "Then you have come to the wrong person. I am a scientist. Any matter of detection would go to the police. I could ask Hugh to speak to you."

Gray is being disingenuous here. He may not be a police detective, but he has come to call himself, only half-jokingly, a consulting detective. Yes, that's my fault, and I owe Sir Arthur

Conan Doyle for making the offhand reference that Gray liked enough to adopt.

Unlike Sherlock Holmes, though, Gray does not hire out his services. He only works for the police, specifically with McCreadie, and he takes no compensation. I could—and do—grumble at that, but I also know how little Victorian police officers make, and the department needs the money more than Gray does.

"I know you do more than work in your laboratory these days, Duncan," Lady Inglis says.

"Does your case involve a dead body?"

"Heavens, no."

"Then I cannot help you. Farewell, Lady—"

"Duncan, please." She reaches for his arm and then stops herself. "I understand you are suspicious of my motives, which is why I could not determine the best way to bring this to you. I made . . ."

Her gaze darts my way, and she clears her throat. "My previous attempts at communication were rebuffed, and I accepted that you did not wish to see me again. It is not as if I have hounded you, Duncan. I made two attempts, and then I stopped. Please do not insult me by presuming that is what I am doing. I think you know me better than that."

"I do, and I did not mean to insinuate anything. I am stating a fact. I am not a detective for hire. I am a scientist who occasionally works with the police in matters regarding murder."

"Blackmail," she blurts. Then she quickly glances around and lowers her voice. "I am being blackmailed, Duncan, and it is not a matter I can take to the police. Nor is it one I would take to a stranger. I am a respectable widow, and what I am being threatened with . . ." She plucks nervously at her cameo choker. "It is very personal."

Gray's voice lowers, touched with the first hint of compassion. "I understand, Patricia, but this really is not my area of expertise."

"Could you at least hear me out?" Her gaze moves to me. "Both of you. I understand Miss Mitchell is your assistant, and she would therefore be involved in any detection you might do."

I grant her a point for that. She's making it clear that this isn't about getting Gray's attention. Which means she really is being blackmailed.

Gray's gaze cuts to me.

"Our schedule is not overly occupied, sir," I murmur.

"We will hear you out," Gray says to Lady Inglis. "I presume we cannot do that here?"

She shakes her head. "It is very private, as I said. I would invite you both to lunch with me tomorrow if that is amenable."

"It is," Gray says. "Now, as for that signature . . ."

"It's fine," I say quickly.

"I can do better than a signature," Lady Inglis says with a soft smile.

She leads us into a side hall. Partway down it, she stops and knocks.

A man opens the door, but from our angle, I can only hear the voice.

"Patsy!" he says. "I had hoped I might see you while I am in town. I am having dinner with your parents tomorrow."

"And I shall be there," she says. "May we step in? I have a young woman who is most eager to meet you."

Dickens waves us forward, Gray nudges me, and I find myself standing in front of Charles Dickens.

# CHAPTER FOUR

We're quickly ushered inside before anyone hears Dickens speaking. Apparently, that reception room isn't actually a reception. It's a place for the wealthy attendees to sip port while the rabble clears out. Meanwhile, Dickens is staying in his room waiting for *that* rabble to clear out.

Lady Inglis excuses herself with an invitation to join her for lunch the next day. And then I am left standing in front of Charles Dickens, gaping, with Gray tucked in behind, ceding the stage to me.

"Sir," I say, words jumbling as they spill out. "Mr. Dickens. It is an honor. I . . . I am a great admirer of your work, and I . . ."

I babble sentiments he has heard a million times as my brain screams for me to do better. I am meeting *Charles Dickens*. I have the chance to speak to an author whose work helped shape my literary childhood. An author who died a century before I was born.

Say something, damn it.

Say something *meaningful*.

I clutch the book to my chest, as if that will steady my nerves. "I appreciate all you have done to tell the stories of those who do not normally get them, the insight you give into the lives of the poor and working classes."

He blinks. Am I not supposed to say that? I remember that he has been mocked for "plumbing the depths" by contemporaries who only tell the stories of the privileged.

"All lives are worthy of note," I say. "And the lives of the rich fill enough books."

He smiles at that. "They do indeed."

I continue, warming to my subject. "Too often, when we look back, we see only those whom history deemed worthy. When we lose the stories of the majority, we lose history itself. We see our past through such a narrow lens that we cannot truly understand what it was like to live in such a time, and I appreciate what you have done to widen that lens for future readers."

His gaze goes from Gray to me. Do I sound as if I am parroting Gray's words? Do I look as if these thoughts cannot possibly be my own? Sadly, yes, I do.

"Miss Mitchell has many opinions," Gray says. "On many topics."

"So I see." Dickens inclines his head my way. "Thank you. That is very insightful and very satisfying to hear."

"Your stories will provide insight and entertainment for generations to come," I say. "Long after some of your contemporaries are relegated to the dust bin—or to required reading for higher learning—people will continue to read and enjoy your work. I am certain of it."

He smiles. "From your lips to God's ear."

When I fall silent, not wanting to speechify, Gray murmurs, "Miss Mitchell has a book she would like you to sign, if we could impose."

"Certainly." Dickens reaches out, and I hand it to him. When he sees which one it is, his brows rise. "You enjoyed this?"

I manage to find my smile. "It is my favorite. I know, I just spoke of the lives of the poor, and this is not that sort of book, but it has my favorite female character of yours."

"Bella Wilfer?"

"Yes. Also, the story is a mystery, and I am overly fond of mysteries."

His smile grows. "One can never be too fond of mysteries. That is what my next novel will be. An unabashed mystery."

He takes the book to a side table with a pen and ink. "Inscribed to Miss Mitchell?"

"Mallory Mitchell, please." I shift closer. "About your next book. My friend—Dr. Gray's sister—was dearly hoping you'd discuss it during the performance. She will be devastated to have missed meeting you. Is there any chance I might take her a hint or two about the next book, in recompense?"

"Certainly." He finishes signing and leaves the book open to dry. "Beware, though, that I may tell more than you wish to know. No project is as exciting to an author as the one they are currently working on. It is bright and shiny, and no critic has read it to tell them where it is dull and tarnished."

I laugh softly. "I will take whatever you care to provide, Mr. Dickens."

"Then may I offer you both a drink?"

He lifts a bottle of what looks like imported Italian wine. We both accept, and Dickens begins to pour.

"My next book is, as I said, a mystery," he begins. "It tells the tale of a man who disappears, an orphan named . . ."

I know the answer before he gives it, and with that name, my heart thuds into my boots.

"Edwin Drood."

I spend the next hour talking to a dead man.

I know it is wrong to say that, to even think it, but I can't help myself. When Dickens tells me what he's writing, I know what it means.

That within a year, he will be dead.

I said I was no good with dates, and here's the proof. My focus was always on Dickens's work rather than the man himself. If asked, I'd have guessed he died when he was elderly. Certainly not in his fifties. Certainly not after I just saw him tearing up the stage in that performance.

I recall that he dies of a stroke. That is all. And dying of a stroke means it's not as if I could say, "Beware the Ides of March . . . and back-clapping friends." He will die, and there's nothing I can do about that.

I spend an hour listening to Dickens discuss *The Mystery of Edwin Drood*. A book he will never finish. A story the world has been trying to finish for him ever since.

I don't sit there in stunned silence. That would be unforgivably rude. I have a chance to listen to Charles Dickens talk about his work, not from a stage, but in person. Once I am past the shock and those premature stabs of grief, I am the best audience he could want. That is what I can give him . . . and so I do.

---

The next day, Gray and I set off to lunch at Lady Inglis's house. I'm wearing my day dress—much simpler than my gown the night before but still a "going out" dress. To accommodate the winter weather, I have fur-lined boots, a fur-lined muff, a fur-lined hat, and fur-lined gloves. I don't even want to calculate the number of tiny creatures that died to keep me warm. In my world, I'd never have worn any of this, but synthetics aren't a thing, so my options are fur or "wrap my feet in newspaper before putting them in my boots." To be honest, I did try that, and it's as uncomfortable as it sounds, but I might have continued doing it if Gray and Isla hadn't been horrified and tried to buy me velvet to wrap my feet instead. And so this was another point where I had to concede my twenty-first-century ethics really only worked for the twenty-first century. My concession is that all my outerwear is second-hand. The critters were already dead, and I'm extending their afterlife.

For my jacket . . . Well, I don't have one. I have a cloak. While I have seen a few women in winter coats, cloaks work better over dresses, especially now that the bustle is coming into style. And, yes, the cloak has fur, damn it.

Despite all my dress layers and fur-lined outerwear, we aren't walking to lunch. Lady Inglis lives outside town in a country estate, one of those places that will someday be a fancy historic house considered part of Edinburgh . . . if it isn't sold and torn down for a new housing development.

I can be outraged at the thought of losing such historic homes, but I often wonder whether that's the New World citizen in me. I grew up in a city where the oldest surviving building only dates back to the decade I currently inhabit. I want to preserve *everything*. But these old houses don't have any true historic value. They're just homes, and there are cities full of them. Also, they weren't built for twenty-first-century living, and retrofitting them isn't always an option.

Given Lady Inglis's title, presumably her late husband was a viscount, baron or some such. Their house reflects that. It's not the monstrosity Gray's sister Annis lived in with her earl husband. It's more like something I'd picture in a Jane Austen novel. A tidy house in the country with a bit of land.

As we approach, I glance at Gray, ramrod straight on the opposite coach seat.

"If you don't want to do this, we can turn around now," I say. "She won't have spotted us."

"It is fine."

I sigh. "You've been saying that since last night, and it doesn't get any more convincing with practice. I regret getting that signature—"

"Nonsense. I am glad you got it, and I am the one who insisted on meeting Mr. Dickens. You tried to demur."

"But if it feels like you owe her, you don't. I can handle this on my own. I *am* your assistant, after all. I can take the meeting and say you were called away on an emergency."

"An undertaker emergency?"

"Hey, it can happen. Lady Inglis doesn't need an explanation. I can write down the details, and if I want to investigate, I can. On my own. *I'm* the professional detective, after all."

"If I seem out of sorts, it has nothing to do with the possibility of helping Lady Inglis. She is being blackmailed and cannot go to the police, and so she deserves help."

"Does she?" I meet his gaze. "I'm trying not to pry here, Duncan, but I'll admit I've been hoping you'd give me more on your own. I don't need details. I just need to know if she . . ."

*If she hurt you. If she did anything that means I don't want to help her.*

"If I need to be wary," I say.

"Of Patricia?" He stops, and his lips purse, as if he didn't mean to be so informal. "Not at all. She is a good woman, deserving of our help."

Which doesn't really answer my question. Lady Inglis can be a decent person and still have hurt him. Yes, I know *he* ended the relationship, but that doesn't mean she didn't do something to deserve it.

"Fine, I'll drop it," I mutter, less graciously than I'd like. The coach has pulled up to the house anyway. Too late to turn back. When it stops, I move toward the door.

"This is very uncomfortable for me," Gray says.

"Which is why I suggested you stay behind."

According to the dictates of polite society, Gray should disembark first, to help me down. Sometimes he does, but he's just as likely to forget, lost in his own thoughts.

Today, when Simon—our groom—opens the door, Gray waves him back to the driver's seat. Then he pulls the door shut.

"Lady Inglis and I had a . . . somewhat humiliating misunderstanding," he says. "When I . . . am seeing a woman, I expect that I am the only person she is seeing, as she will be the only one I am seeing. I made the mistake of not being explicit about that."

"Ah."

"It was not my finest moment," he says. "The fault was my own, for presuming the relationship was exclusive. I handled it poorly."

"But she *did* try to win you back."

He mumbles something I don't catch, and my heart sinks even as I curse myself for that. I'd been under the impression that he'd lost interest or decided the relationship wasn't working. That's not the case and . . .

Shit.

I was trying to get past the awkwardness of taking a job from Gray's former lover, and now I discover that their breakup wasn't as clear cut as I thought. He hadn't simply moved on. He'd been hurt and retreated and then been too embarrassed to reconcile. I'm caught in between Gray and a former lover he might very well still be interested in.

"I could go," I blurt.

He startles and blinks at me. "What?"

"I could leave. Let you handle this. If you'd . . . prefer."

His brows knit. "Prefer what?"

"To do this on your own. If it is uncomfortable for you, and you are determined to do it, would it be better if I were not there?"

"No, this is fine," he says, and climbs out and walks toward the house without another word.

# CHAPTER FIVE

As the butler leads us through the house, I don't notice any of it. I'm too busy fuming at Gray. I've done backflips to be sensitive and suggest ways to alleviate his discomfort, and in the end, all I got was his wasp sting of annoyance.

Screw that, then. He's an adult, and he can make his own choices and deal with his own discomfort. Whatever's going on here is between him and Lady Inglis. I just happen to be stuck in the middle of it.

As long as I'm there, I'll take my place at that center. I'm the detective, and since there are no dead bodies involved, I'm in charge.

We enter the dining room to find Lady Inglis arranging flowers on the side table. That gives me pause. Oh, flower arranging is a very suitable hobby for a wealthy woman. But this is also the era when people assigned meanings to every flower and color. It was a method of communication, especially between men and women. I know nothing about the language of flowers, though I am aware that there could be some meaning in the arrangement Gray might comprehend.

And then I remind myself that I don't give a shit.

I don't even look Gray's way to see his reaction. I greet Lady Inglis and compliment her on the lovely arrangements and the lovely home. She seems startled, and I presume the impression I gave last night was one of slightly less poise.

The flowers *are* lovely—white honeysuckle and blue corn-flowers. The dining room is also lovely, tastefully appointed in the same colors, white and blue, carried from the carpet to the lampshades to the wallpaper.

Lady Inglis invites us to sit at the table, fully set for lunch. She takes what I presume is her usual spot at one end. Gray gets the other, and I'm in the middle, literally this time.

There is a bit of awkward small talk, which I stay out of. Having decided I don't give a damn also means I don't feel the need to smooth the way for Gray. I spend my time discreetly taking in my surroundings.

Most of the art is landscape, but there's a portrait that seems to be Lady Inglis and her father until I realize she's in a wedding gown and he doesn't quite look old enough to be giving away the bride. Her husband, then. In it, Lady Inglis is about twenty. She's holding her new husband's arm, and she doesn't look frightened or even determined. She looks happy. Genuinely glowing.

The first course arrives. At home, lunch is a fairly simple affair, betraying the Grays' middle-class background. There is rarely a first course, and the meal often makes use of leftovers from the day before. That's not frugality as much as convenience and efficiency. Dinner takes much longer to prepare in this period, and unless you have a dedicated cook, shortcuts are essential. One thing we always have, though, is dessert, because our gorgon housekeeper, Mrs. Wallace, dotes on Gray. God forbid the man miss an opportunity to have a rich pastry or slice of cake.

The first course here is a cream of asparagus soup along with fresh bread. I wait for everyone to take their first sips of the soup, and then I say, "You will forgive my bluntness, Lady Inglis, but I do not wish to take up too much of your time. May we discuss the case over lunch?"

Her gaze shoots to Gray, who scoops another spoonful of soup and says, "Miss Mitchell will take the lead here," without looking up.

"Lacking Dr. Gray's background and position, I am usually forgiven for also lacking his manners." I smile, but it feels a little feral. "I am, as I said, rather blunt. I can get to the heart of the matter where he might need to dance around it, and I can ask questions that might give him pause."

"I see," Lady Inglis murmurs. "All right, then. Let us move directly into discussing the situation. As I said, I am being blackmailed. You are aware that I am a widow?"

"I am."

"You said that your background allows you certain liberties. My status allows me others. One is that I do not need to forsake the company of men."

Her gaze holds mine, as if trying to convey a delicate secret that I might be too young to comprehend. Victorians have a reputation for prudery that is well earned. Sex is not a thing you discuss, at least not if you are female . . . or a male in mixed company. I'm going to presume men talk about it among themselves, but not being a man, I can't comment on that.

I know women—at least those in lower classes—talk about it. But well-to-do ladies do not. This does not mean well-to-do ladies aren't having sex. It doesn't mean that men who turn bright red at the most obtuse mention are not having sex. There is plenty of that going on—and plenty of it is extramarital—but everyone acts as if there isn't, even if they're having it themselves.

I'm sure many widows enjoy their freedom to some extent. God knows, I wish Isla would. But Lady Inglis watches my reaction as if I would be scandalized.

"I understand," I say.

She hesitates. "I am not certain you do. This is a matter of great delicacy, Miss Mitchell."

"You have lovers, and this blackmail is connected to them."

I shouldn't be so blunt. The fact that I am might prove I'm still annoyed with Gray and in a bit of a mood. Her gaze shoots to him, and I notice he gives the barest shake of his head. Telling her that this information did not come from him. Technically true.

I continue, "You forget that I do not share Dr. Gray's background, and certainly not your own, Lady Inglis. These things are much more common—even natural—where I am from."

Catriona actually seemed to be from a middle-class family, but Lady Inglis nods her understanding, even as color touches her cheeks.

The door opens with the second course—lamb cutlets, roasted potatoes, and green beans—and I wait for that to be served and for everyone to take a few bites.

"Can you explain the nature of the blackmail?" I say. "Does it come from a former lover?"

"Certainly not." She sets her fork down with a decisive clink. "I am very careful, Miss Mitchell. I would not associate with any man who might do such a thing."

"And you know that because . . . ?"

She blinks, as if taken aback by the very question. "Because they are men of honor."

"If you mean that they are wealthy—"

"That hardly makes them honorable," she says archly. "In fact, in my experience, most dishonorable men come from my own class. I say they are honorable because they choose the companionship of widows over . . . other options."

"Serving maids and sex workers?"

Lady Inglis chokes on her cutlet, and Gray makes the smallest noise of warning.

"This is why I take charge," I say. "Dr. Gray doesn't even like *hearing* me ask these questions. He certainly wouldn't ask himself. You say your lovers are honorable because they choose mature, unattached women rather than seducing young ones." I pause. "I probably shouldn't include sex workers in that. A fair and respectful exchange is always better than seducing serving maids."

Lady Inglis only stares. Not at me, but at Gray. Rather like Dickens did last night.

"Miss Mitchell has strong opinions," he murmurs, "and no difficulty voicing them."

"If that makes you uncomfortable, I'll stop," I say.

"No, it is just . . . unexpected. You are . . . very young, and I did not expect . . ." She manages a smile. "Although, I suppose, if Duncan hired you as his assistant, I should have known you'd be more than you seemed."

"She is," Gray murmurs.

I decide to set aside the question of honorable men for now. From what I understand, Gray's lovers are usually widows, and I agree that is preferable to other options in this world. Sex work is often the course of desperation—and the source of venereal disease. Unmarried women of his own class likely know nothing about the art of preventing pregnancy. And while sex between men and their household staff is common, it's the most problematic of the options.

Whether choosing widows is "honorable" or not, it has nothing to do with whether a man wouldn't blackmail a past lover. My experience—as both a woman and a cop—tells me to be very careful presuming a lover would never blackmail you because once you've left them, they can become a very different person. At sixteen, I made the boneheaded mistake of sending a risqué picture to a boy. I thought I was being sexy—and clever—sending a shot where I was clearly naked but all the "naughty bits" were hidden. Also, he was the sweetest guy, one who would absolutely *never* send it to his friends when I broke up with him.

Lesson learned.

Still, this is not a point I can argue. I've had friends swear up and down that it's safe to send nude pics to their boyfriends, and I've had boyfriends who were offended that I wouldn't send them nude pics. So I'm not fighting Lady Inglis on this. I just know what I know.

"Can you explain the nature of the blackmail?" I say after a few bites of the cutlet, which is really very good.

"Letters of an intimate nature," she says, and I nearly choke on my mouthful.

I manage to swallow and dab my napkin at my lips to hide my reaction.

"Letters you had sent to a former lover?" I say as evenly as I can.

"No."

I look up at her.

She continues, "I sent them to someone I have been involved with for many years. He was a dear friend of my husband and became my friend as well. After my husband passed . . ." Her cheeks color, just a bit. "Eventually, we grew closer."

"I understand."

"It did not happen while my husband was alive," she says firmly. "Nor even shortly after his death. I did not have such feelings for this friend until significantly later. But since then, our friendship is periodically . . . more intimate."

Friends with benefits, Victorian-style? That actually surprises me. Not the sex part but the friendship part. Friendship between men and women isn't common in this time. It *can't* be common in a world where women are guarded as if any man who is alone with them for five minutes will have them against the nearest wall.

Gray and I fight that battle constantly, dealing with the presumption that he only hired me so we can be alone together, and if we are alone together, it's clearly for sex. What else would he want with me?

If Lady Inglis has found a satisfying friendship-with-benefits relationship, I'm glad of it, for her sake. Although, given that it seems to have been going on for years, this might be the relationship that ended hers with Gray.

But I'm not thinking of that, so I'm not speculating on it. Nor am I glancing his way to gauge his reaction.

"You sent this friend letters of an intimate nature," I say. "And you are being blackmailed with them but not by him."

"They were stolen," she says. "He did not even realize they were missing until I received the threat. I contacted him immediately. He checked the locked box where he keeps them and found it empty."

"You received a threat. A letter?"

"Yes. I still have it, and I will show it to you after lunch. In short, the sender threatens to print my letters unless I pay. They included one letter as proof that they have them, which also told me who I'd written it for. I immediately checked with Lord— my friend, in case that was the only one missing, which would mitigate the threat. It was not."

"The blackmailer is threatening to print the letters . . . where?"

Another flush. "They are threatening to *publish* the letters. There is— That is to say, I have *heard* there is a taste for such things. The letters would be sold to a publisher of ill repute. That person would then print and sell them in a chapbook."

"I understand you would not want them published under any circumstances, but are the letters clearly identifiable as having been written by you?"

"No, but the blackmailer knows I am the writer—and that my friend is the recipient—and this person intends to reveal that."

I eat a few pieces of potato as I think. Then I say, "If we take the case, I will need to see the letter. Also, while I understand your desire for discretion, we will need to speak to your friend. Since he is also under threat—and he lost the letters in the first place—he will understand."

Lady Inglis sips from her wineglass. "Is that necessary?"

It's Gray who answers, "It is. As Miss Mitchell said, he lost the letters. They were taken from his home, I presume."

"Yes, but—"

"That makes this a theft, which we cannot investigate if we cannot see the scene and speak to the person who possessed the missing goods." He looks at her. "As I already know who we speak of, I do not see why you would shelter him." Gray pauses. "Unless he has asked to be sheltered."

"He has not," she says. "He is most distressed by this. I simply did not wish to involve him."

"He's already involved," I say. "He's also responsible. He chose to keep the letters, and his security was lacking. If you ask me, he's the one who should be paying the blackmailer."

"He has offered," Lady Inglis says. "I would not hear of it."

"Why not?"

She stares at me as if I've asked her to read the letters aloud. Yep, good thing I led with the warning about being blunt.

I continue, "This is entirely his fault. He should pay."

"I would agree," Gray says. "He chose to keep the letters and store them in an unsafe location, and yet the one who is truly under threat is you. Yes, the blackmailer might say they will also reveal his name, but you are the one they expect to pay because you are the one who will suffer."

"They are still threatening him," Lady Inglis says.

"With what?" I say. "Telling the world that he's getting—"

Gray coughs, as if knowing whatever I was about to say was both improper and probably not a term currently in use.

"That he has a lover," I say. "A lover whom he inspires to write . . . er, letters of an erotic nature. That's not a threat. That's advertising."

Gray chokes on what might be a laugh. Lady Inglis stares, and then she lets loose a low chuckle.

"I take your meaning," she says. "I can assure you that my friend does not require advertising, but the point is that, as you said, I will suffer, and he will not. That is the way of the world."

"Yes, and highly unfair, but that's nothing we can rectify. So why not let him pay?"

She taps her fingers on the tablecloth, and it seems as if she isn't going to answer. Then she blurts, "Because it would put me in his debt." She pulls back, adding, "He is not the sort of person to use that to his advantage. We truly are friends. But in my experience, no matter how much a woman trusts a man, it is unwise to let him come to her rescue, particularly in matters of honor. If the blackmailer went to him, I would let him pay it. As I am the target, I wish to resolve this myself."

Okay, she's not as naive as she seemed with her earlier comments on honor. She has a point here. A good one.

"Can you pay?" I say.

She bristles. "I do not wish to."

"Let me rephrase that. I'm asking whether you could afford to and how easily."

She pauses and then says, "It is not what I consider pocket

change, but it would hardly put me in the poorhouse. But even if it *were* pocket change, I do not wish to pay."

"I agree. You could pay this person and get the letters back, only to have them threaten you again with copies they have made. The only way to stop this is to uncover the blackmailer's identity." I take one last bite of potato. "How long do you have?"

"Only until Hogmanay. I received the demand a week ago, but I have been dithering, trying to determine what to do about it."

"May we see the blackmail letter now?" I ask.

"Certainly."

# CHAPTER SIX

L ady Inglis brings us the letter over dessert. I note that it is coconut cake, one of Gray's favorites.

The letter has been pasted together from words in a newspaper. I'm impressed by that. I've only seen such things in movies, with ransom demands and the like, and it seems like a Hollywood invention, but I realize now it would date to a time before you could easily print off—or even type up—a letter.

We've had two cases now where handwriting played a role. If notes must be written by hand, even disguising penmanship is a tricky business. This person has been clever, cutting words from a newspaper.

Lady Inglis

Enclosed you will find a letter of yours that has come into my possession, along with others. I will return them for £500. I require the fee by Hogmanay, or I shall have them printed and sold. I do not think you or the recipient wish that.

On the morn of December 31, I will send along instructions for payment.

I read it again, and I must have grumbled under my breath because Gray says, "Something is wrong?"

I point at the last line. "This. The trickiest part about demanding a ransom is that you need to get the money somehow. You can specify a location to drop it off or a person to leave it with. Either provides a possible way to catch the blackmailer."

"Drop off the money and then wait to see who fetches it. If it is to be left with a person, question them."

"Because even if they've only been hired as an intermediary, *they* need to get the money to the blackmailer somehow."

Lady Inglis asks, "Is that the way to catch them, then? Wait for instructions?"

I shake my head. "Too risky, except as a last resort. They didn't leave much time between receiving instructions and following them. You'd need to pay and hope we catch the blackmailer." I cut off a mouthful-sized piece of my cake. "Instead of treating this as blackmail, we need to treat it as theft."

"Find out who stole the letters," Gray says.

"Yes. If we decide to take the case, I will need the name of your friend and his consent to be both interviewed and have the location of the theft examined."

"I will speak to him. I do not expect a problem. He is most distraught about this. Any reluctance to share his name is simply discretion, at least as much for my benefit as for his."

"I understand," I say. "If we take this case, you can be assured of *our* discretion. I'm not going to help a woman avoid exposure only to expose her myself. Before we agree to the case, Dr. Gray and I need to discuss the matter. We'll have an answer for you by this evening."

"Thank you. Now, we should discuss payment."

"Unnecessary," Gray says. "Consider it a favor between friends."

She fixes him with a steady look. "First, I believe I already clarified my feelings on owing men a debt for defending my honor. Second, as Miss Mitchell seems to be the one handling my case thus far, ought you to be turning down payment on her behalf?"

Gray had the grace to color at that. "Of course not. You may pay Miss Mitchell."

She turns to me. "I will do that. Your fee, miss?"

I resist the urge to demur. Taking wages from Gray still feels a bit like taking money from my host. I landed in his world—in the body of his housemaid—and he's stuck with me. Except I'm not a layabout guest, leeching off my hosts. I do my job, and I do it well. If Lady Inglis is offering to pay—and *wants* to pay—I should take her up on it. I also shouldn't insult either of us by undervaluing my services.

"Ten percent of the blackmail demand," I say. "If I identify the person responsible, I'll take ten percent. However, what you do with that information is up to you. I would suggest it goes to the police after that. Or, if it turns out to be someone you know, you can decide how to handle it."

"That is reasonable," Lady Inglis says. "Ten percent, then, for identifying the person behind this before I need to pay the ransom. You will decide whether to take this case and let me know by this evening."

"I will."

———

We leave as soon as lunch is finished. I barely touched my cake. At home, that would have had Gray eyeing it, and I'd slide it over for him to finish. Even if I were in that sort of mood—which I am not—he doesn't even glance at my plate, and I notice his own cake is only half gone.

Lady Inglis accompanies us down the hall. Simon has the

coach at the stable, and we'll walk to it rather than have a member of the staff run and fetch him. When we step out, Lady Inglis murmurs, "A word, please, Duncan?"

"I'll be at the stables," I say, not glancing to see his reaction.

"Wait," he says. "I will walk with you. The path can be uneven."

Uneven cobblestones are a fact of life in Victorian times, which makes it an odd excuse, but I don't argue. I pull my cloak tighter against the cold and step aside to wait as they talk.

"I really must be going," Gray says to Lady Inglis. "I do not want Miss Mitchell to take a tumble."

I shake my head. Really? That's the best he can come up with?

"This will only take a moment," Lady Inglis says.

Not wanting to eavesdrop, I walk around the corner of the house, only for Gray to call, "Mallory? Please do not wander."

Do not wander? Am I a sheep now?

I return to where Gray can see me, but unfortunately, I can still hear them, though I look the other way and pretend I can't.

"I wished to apologize," Lady Inglis says. "I was unspeakably churlish last night when I spoke of your relationship with Miss Mitchell."

"She is my assistant—"

"Yes. I see that now, which is why I am apologizing for insinuating anything else."

"I would not hire a young woman with the intention of being dishonorable."

She sighs. "I know, and I was wrong to suggest otherwise. I *do* know you better than that. Even if she were not your assistant, the mistake would have been an insult."

"An insult to . . . ?" he says carefully.

She laughs softly. "To you, obviously, Duncan. While she is

clearly intelligent, she is very young and . . . very much not to your taste. She is a peony. You prefer pansies."

Something in me bristles at that. Yes, Catriona has a very showy sort of beauty. There is nothing subtle or refined about it. But how she looks is a matter of genetics, and her personal style didn't take advantage of that any more than mine does. I'm dressed very primly, with more of my bosom hidden than is fashionable.

Gray's voice cools. "I would like to end this conversation now, Patricia."

"I am not insulting Miss Mitchell, Duncan. She is a spectacularly lovely girl, with a keen intelligence. Were she a decade older, I would be jealous."

"Which you have no reason to be, as you and I are no longer together."

Another deep sigh. "That is not what I meant. I know you are no longer interested in me, and I respect that. I only mean that I would find myself envying any woman who caught your eye. It reminds me that I caught it once upon a time, and I was careless, which I regret very much."

"I do not see the point of this conversation," Gray says. "I would suggest we end it."

"I never say the right thing to you, do I?" she murmurs, and there's something in her voice that makes me feel sorry for Lady Inglis. What happened to end her relationship with Gray wasn't her fault—he hadn't made it clear he expected monogamy. It was a misunderstanding that led to hurt pride, which cost her someone she obviously cared for.

"It is fine," Gray murmurs, and his tone is conciliatory, but he adds a firm, "I really must be going. I will send you a message this evening with our decision."

# CHAPTER SEVEN

We're in the coach. Gray hasn't said a word since he caught up with me, and now he's staring silently out the window as we pull away.

I clear my throat. "I'm going to take the case. You are free to stay out of it, as I'm not really a hapless twenty-year-old in need of guidance."

"No," he says, looking back at me sharply. "I said if you did this, I would, too, and—"

"And I'm sick of circling, so let's skip this shit, okay?"

The profanity startles him out of an answer.

I continue, "Working with Lady Inglis makes you uncomfortable, and it's not necessary. That's my point, Duncan. You don't need to do this. I can handle it on my own."

His tone chills. "If you do not wish my assistance, say so."

I slam back in my seat with a profanity that has him blinking.

"I give up," I say. "You're upset about this whole thing, and you're taking it out on me. I'm doing backflips to accommodate you, and you're determined to see insult in anything I say." I meet his gaze. "You're right, Duncan. I don't want your assistance. Because you're being an ass, and I did nothing to deserve it."

"I—"

"You insisted on accepting Lady Inglis's offer to introduce me to Mr. Dickens, knowing it could put you in her debt. I'm accepting that debt as the person who benefited from it. But I still wouldn't feel obligated to take the case. I'm choosing to do so because no woman deserves what this person is doing to her. She's an unattached woman engaging in consensual affairs and having some fun writing risqué letters to her partners. This person is threatening to brand her with a scarlet letter, and that's wrong."

When he says nothing, I add, "Scarlet letter means—"

"Yes, I have read the book. I understand the reference. You are correct, of course. Lady Inglis's affairs are no one's business but her own, as are any letters she might write."

He leans back in his seat. "You are also correct that I am uncomfortable with the situation and taking it out on you, which I am wont to do."

"Yep."

He gives me a sidelong glance.

"Oh, I'm sorry," I say. "Am I supposed to say that you *don't* do that? Or that you hardly *ever* do it?"

He doesn't answer, but I know that I *am* supposed to say that. He is a Victorian male, head of the household in which I reside, and if he deigns to admit to a failing, I should fall over myself to reassure him it's fine. Okay, maybe "fall over myself" is an exaggeration, but even someone as progressive as Gray has certain expectations. Or certain hopes, at least, because there is not a woman in his household who'd tell him he's fine when he's screwing up. Except maybe Mrs. Wallace.

Gray sighs, and it is such a deeply chagrined sigh that I have to fight against falling for it. I should be annoyed that he expects reassurances—or at least praise—when he admits to a failing, but he's a man of his time, and I find it oddly charming. Of course, it's charming because I know he genuinely tries to do better.

Growing up, I hated it when people told me I was lucky to have loving parents who supported me and my choices. How was it "lucky" to have parents who did what decent parents should do? Yet I do consider myself lucky to have landed in Gray's household, where even before he knew I wasn't Catriona, he'd been happy to take me on as his assistant. What mattered was that I was capable, regardless of my sex. That's how it should be, of course, but how a thing should be is not the same as how it is.

I'd had a much greater chance of landing in a house where I'd be stuck cleaning chamber pots and fending off my boss's wandering hands, because that's what happened to girls like Catriona.

I *am* lucky that Gray is as forward-thinking as he is. I *am* fortunate that he accepts criticism from me. But I can still roll my eyes when he expects a cookie for admitting to a failing. These things are not incompatible.

"May I join your investigation, Miss Mitchell?" he says.

I straighten. "Oooh, I like the sounds of that. Polite and contrite. Say it again."

He only sighs.

"Fine," I say. "You may join it on the understanding that if you get pissy again, I can kick you out."

"Even if I get 'pissy' over something you do?"

"Impossible. I am perfection personified."

Now I get the eye roll. Deservedly.

"Also, you're joining in a volunteer capacity," I say. "All the money is mine."

He sobers. "As it should be. However, if you are taking the case for the money, I can always increase—"

"I said I'm taking the case on principle. I'm just letting her pay because she can afford it. My salary is more than sufficient. So we'll drop that." I rearrange my skirts as the December chill creeps up from the carriage floor. "On an equally serious note, though, the reason I didn't take the job right away is that I do want to discuss it with you."

"All right."

"And if discussing it with you touches on any personal matters that make you uncomfortable, you need to acknowledge that I'm asking because of the case. I'm not trying to make you uncomfortable or pry into your personal life."

He shifts, and I inwardly sigh. This is exactly what I'm afraid of. That every time the case brushes up against his past with Lady Inglis, there's going to be resistance and friction.

"This first question is actually not about the case directly, but I have to bring it up." I clear my throat. "I know Lady Inglis sent you a letter after you ended things. Did she send others before that?"

"No. We did not . . . That is to say . . ." He plucks at his collar. "If this is a habit of hers, she must have decided I was not the properly receptive audience for it."

"Or, more likely, she only does it with this one longtime friend. The reason I'm asking is to be sure you're not at risk yourself."

"I am not. Any other correspondence I received was not of that nature, and I destroyed it shortly after receipt. I realize that may seem cold, not keeping such letters for sentimental reasons, but I do it out of an abundance of caution. As you said at lunch, I would not be faulted for such entanglements, but the women would be. Destroying their letters seems wise."

"Agreed," I say. "And I was going to say that if she did send you any more intimate ones, you should destroy them."

He glances over. "The one she did send, you burned, yes?"

"I did." I adjust the muff keeping my hands warm. "You said you think you know the man involved. The one whose letters were stolen."

I expect his tone to chill—or at least his gaze to—but he only nods. "I am certain I know him. They have been longtime friends, as Lady Inglis said, and I knew they'd been lovers. Because you will likely not ask, yes, he is the one I discovered she'd been seeing while we were together."

"Is that going to be a problem?" I hear myself and rephrase. "I'm sure that'll make the interview uncomfortable. I can conduct that part."

"Hmm?" He looks genuinely surprised. "No, it isn't . . . That is to say, it's not like that. I have no issue with Lord— With the person involved. The mistake was honestly mine. I knew they had been involved, and I did not necessarily think the affair had ended, but he was living abroad while I was seeing Lady Inglis. When he returned, I heard that she had gone to see him. I did not want to presume anything, so I asked and . . ."

He gives a rueful smile. "I discovered that their relationship was ongoing. That was it. I did not walk in on them together. Even her visit to his house was purely platonic, a luncheon with others. But she made it clear that he was still intimately part of her life, and I took it poorly and left. No dramatic encounter. Merely a misunderstanding."

"Still upsetting."

He looks out the window a moment before turning to me. "And still a misunderstanding for which no one else is to blame. If I do blame him for anything, it is only *this* unfortunate incident with the letter. Even then, I doubt that he was careless with them. It is understandable to keep them, and he seems to have locked them away."

"How well do you know him?"

"Not terribly well," Gray says. "I did meet Lady Inglis through him, though. We attend the same club, and he has an interest in medical science and asked me to accompany him to the surgical theater. We did that a few times, and I met Lady Inglis at a party he hosted before he went to Europe on an extended trip. I have seen him since, at the club, and we have been cordial."

"Cordial but cool?"

The corners of Gray's mouth twitch upward. "I am always cool, Mallory. It is my natural demeanor. If you are asking whether I was cooler because of the misunderstanding, I do not think so. I am not even certain he knew I was seeing Lady Inglis in his absence."

I tap my fingers inside my muff as I think. "Whoever stole the letters had access to this man's home."

"Yes."

"What kind of home does he keep? He's a lord, which might mean he has multiple residences."

"As I understand it, he has only one. A town house perhaps a mile from ours, where he lives with his younger brother. As for Lord . . ." He trails off.

"Joe," I say. "Until Lady Inglis releases his name, let's go with Lord Joe."

Another twitch of the lips. "All right. Lord Joe is a widower himself. Only a few years older than Lady Inglis. He lost his wife a year before Lady Inglis lost her husband."

"And the younger brother?"

Gray's expression at that has me leaning forward.

"You do not like the brother?"

"I do not know him well, but he does attend our club, and he is a sanctimonious— I find him unpleasant. Lord Joe is very convivial, but he clearly inherited all the charm in the family."

"Lord Joe is convivial. Can I assume that means he entertains regularly? Has a steady stream of guests who could have stolen the letters?"

"He has a great many friends. He does not entertain in the usual way, having no lady of the house to organize such events, but he would have guests. Yes, I fear, the list of suspects might not be as small as we hope."

"But it's still a constrained number. Whoever stole the letters had access to the house."

"Yes."

# CHAPTER EIGHT

I usher Jack into the library, where Isla waits. Jack is our new housemaid. She's also the writer of our chronicles, as part of her double life as an anonymous chronicler of Edinburgh crime. Double life? Make that triple life or even quadruple. Jack has endless irons in the fire, and when she says her chosen moniker comes from "Jack of all trades," I'm not sure she's joking, but I always follow up with "master of none," because she's just asking for that one.

The choice of a masculine moniker isn't accidental, either. In public, she usually wears male attire. I wouldn't call it a disguise as much as a choice. She goes by female pronouns and keeps her hair long enough that she needs to put it up in a cap for the male persona. In our world, she'd be considered gender fluid.

During work hours at the town house, Jack wears a dress. Isla has made it clear that isn't necessary, and certainly, *I'd* have much rather cleaned in trousers. Easier to move in and *much* easier to bend in. I think Jack makes the choice to present as a female maid because it's easier for Gray and Isla, saving them from adding to the heap of eccentricities that already puts them on the fringe of their social class. If I'd told Isla I wanted to clean in trousers, she'd have let me. I didn't for this exact reason.

Jack's work dress is like my old one, simple and blue. Victorian households haven't yet adopted uniforms, but Isla provides work clothing so her employees don't need to buy it themselves, and she sticks to a blue-and-white color scheme and well-made attire.

Before Isla hired Jack—or, more accurately, accepted Jack's work proposal—I'd only ever seen Jack present as male, so I'm still getting used to her feminine persona. As male, she looks in her late teens, very slender and fine featured. As a woman, she's obviously in her early twenties, with gorgeous red-brown hair that answers the question of why she doesn't cut it to better suit her male persona.

I wave Jack to a chair and shut the door.

"I have called you both here today to discuss something of great import." I look from one to the other. "Pornography."

Isla stares at me.

Jack bursts into snickers and says, "Please tell me you actually meant to say 'pornography,' Mallory, and you haven't simply misused a word again."

Jack doesn't know my real identity. She's been given the cover story—that a blow to Catriona's head changed her personality and she now goes by Mallory. Also, the blow affected Catriona's memory, and she sometimes gets confused, especially with vocabulary, misusing words or making up new ones altogether.

"Yes, I meant 'pornography.' We have a case that involves it, and I need opinions."

"On . . . pornography?" Jack says.

"Mallory is having fun with us," Isla says. "This is not the first time she's managed to connect a case to illicit material of a pornographic nature."

"Managed to connect?" I say. "The connection was there. We had a suspect who moonlighted as a nude model."

"Moonlighted?" Jack says.

"Whatever the word is. She worked a secret job. This is different. We now have a case where a woman . . ." I curse under my breath as I see Jack lean forward. I forgot how *she* moonlights.

"A case?" Jack says, eyes gleaming.

"Not a case for public consumption. Certainly not for your chronicles of our cases. It is a woman being threatened with exposure for writings . . . of an erotic nature."

Jack's brows climb.

I continue, "She wrote it for an audience of one, but the work has been stolen, and she is being blackmailed by the thief."

"Sadly, I could not use this in our chronicles," Jack says. She quickly adds, "Not that I would. It'd be wrong. But even if I could, it is not the sort of case your audience wants."

"Our audience being women who can read murder mysteries to their children under the guise of providing didactic tales to prove that no crime goes unpunished."

Isla sniffs. "In this case, the crime *some* would see is that a woman dared pen such things and was, in their minds, rightfully threatened with punishment."

"Either way," Jack says, "it would be inappropriate. Depictions of gruesome murder, yes. The mention of writings exploring sexuality?" She shudders. "Think of the children."

I want to roll my eyes at the very Victorian-ness of this. And then I remember the childhood friend who was allowed to rent any action or horror movie, however violent, as long as it didn't contain nudity.

I can still blame the Victorians, right? They started it.

Okay, it was probably the Puritans, who passed it on to the Victorians, but still . . .

Isla says, "I presume the blackmailer is threatening to expose this poor woman as a pornographer?"

"Worse," I say. "They're threatening to *make* her a pornographer. To have her writings published and sold, with her name attached."

"Published and sold?" Isla's brows knit. "Is that profitable?"

Both Jack and I turn to stare at her.

"Is pornography profitable?" Jack says slowly. "If that is your question, Mrs. Ballantyne, I fear you are more sheltered than I thought."

Isla glares at both of us. "I know pornographic sketches and photography are profitable. I mean this sort. Writing that is purely intimate in nature, rather than part of a larger narrative, such as *Fanny Hill*."

"You've read *Fanny Hill*, Mrs. Ballantyne?" Jack says.

Isla's glare locks on her. "I read everything, and if you expect me to sputter and flush, I will not."

"Actually," I say, "your question is the reason I called you both in here. I don't know whether things like this are popular or easily sold. I could ask Dr. Gray, but he really *would* sputter, as well as turn a very unhealthy shade of red and, ultimately, not answer the question."

"But you thought *I* could?" Isla says.

"Hey, you just said you read everything."

"Having not known this sort of writing existed, I have not read it."

I grin at her. "Good. Then I know what to get you for Hogmanay."

She does sputter and flush at that, then skewers me with a glare that says *I will pay for this.*

I turn to Jack. "How about you? As a writer, would you say there's a market for letters like this?"

Jack stretches her legs and then remembers she's wearing a

skirt and retracts them. "There is certainly an audience for such work. Putting it into a larger narrative—particularly if one can pass it off as proper literature—is one way to do it, but there is a very avid market for those who do not want story interfering with the risqué bits. It can pay exceedingly well. I tried it myself but . . ." She shrugs. "I am better at writing about murder. That problem, to be honest, seems to be a lack of experience."

"You have more experience with murder than sex?" I say.

She sighs. "I strode into that one, didn't I? No, it's not even a lack of experience with sexual congress so much as a lack of experience with *good* sexual congress. No one wants to read about the bad stuff, even if it's embellished by imagination."

"I feel I should offer my condolences," I say. "I would also suggest you stop bothering with the bad stuff."

"And how would you suggest I do that? Ask men whether they're any good first? They all think they're incredible because *they* finish every time. This is one place where I truly envy men."

"For being able to finish every time?"

"Well, yes, but beyond that, men can easily obtain good sex by paying for it. Go to a brothel and lay down money for a woman of craft and experience. Women do not have that option. We have to take what we can get and hope for the best, which is *never* the best, no matter what the men claim."

I glance at Isla, who is sitting perfectly still, with the expression of a twelve-year-old hearing teen girls talk about sex, trying to look casual, as if she hears this all the time, as if she's not inwardly shocked that they're openly discussing *it* the way one discusses the weather.

As I've said, women in this time do discuss sex, but only among themselves and, from what I can tell, primarily among the lower classes. Jack would have no problem with it, and she'd presume I wouldn't, either.

I also note that Isla doesn't stop us or even give us a scandalized look. Like that preteen girl, she's soaking it up.

"So there is an audience for this," I say, bringing the conversation back around. "How profitable would it be?"

"How much is the blackmail for?" Jack asks.

"Five hundred pounds."

Jack whistles. "It would *never* be that profitable. The primary audience for such writing, from a woman's perspective, would likely be women themselves. In written work, that audience is larger."

"Men prefer pictures?"

She laughs softly. "They do. Women prefer narrative where they may fill in their own imagination. Probably because they have so much experience doing that while lying under a heaving, grunting, sweaty man."

"You really need to cultivate a better class of partners," I say.

She sighs. "I know. But while the audience for such things is largely women, it still is smaller than the audience for visual pornography, and even that would not come close to the price the blackmailer is demanding."

"Meaning they really are counting on our client paying the ransom."

"Yes. The blackmailer is not necessarily bluffing about publishing them. Such things could be sold for a nice bit of income. But that also requires knowing *where* to sell it, which the average person would not."

"But you do?"

"I do, and if it comes to that, we could attempt to avoid publication by paying the printer for the return of the materials. But that would not be easily done."

"So we should presume the threat is serious and try to find the blackmailer before those letters reach a printer."

"I fear so."

# CHAPTER NINE

Gray has told Lady Inglis that we're taking her case. By morning, we have an invitation from "Lord Charles Simpson" to join him at his home. We accept, and at ten, Simon drops us outside Lord Simpson's town house.

The town house is similar to Gray's. Maybe a bit smaller. We're entering an era where it's not uncommon for the middle class to have more money than the nobility. It's the rise of the industrial era, where investing in a trade can earn you more than having a title and a bit of land.

Simpson certainly still lives very well. Cross into the Old Town, and his place would house multiple families on each of its four levels. My impression is that he is averagely well-to-do for a viscount, which is what I expected.

Lord Simpson himself, however, is not what I expected. I've met Lady Inglis—beautiful, cultured, and wealthy. Her lover will be her male equivalent. I know he's a few years older than her, so I picture a dashing and distinguished silver fox. A bon vivant who can capture and hold a woman like Lady Inglis.

When the butler leads us into the parlor, I see a man and remember that Lord Simpson lives with his younger brother. I presume that's who I'm seeing. The man is rotund, with jet-black hair and equally dark whiskers. When he turns, I see he's older than I thought, and the very dark hair likely comes from a bottle.

"Lord Charles Simpson," the butler says. "May I present Dr. Duncan Gray and Miss Mallory Mitchell."

Okay, this was not what I expected, but that's on me, isn't it? Lady Inglis is an intelligent and discerning woman who will expect more than a handsome face in her lovers, and the sparkle in Simpson's eye suggests the bon vivant I imagined.

"Dr. Gray," he says, taking Gray's hand. "It has been too long. So good to see you. And Miss Mitchell. Welcome. I am so pleased to hear that Dr. Gray has found a proper assistant. The last time we spoke, he was having a terrible time with that."

Simpson engages in a few moments of small talk, striking the perfect balance between being a convivial host and recognizing that we're here on business. When he asks after our health, it's in that way some people have of making you feel they actually care about the answer. Then it's a quick exchange on the weather and how the cold is a nuisance but the snow is lovely, and there seems to be actual sunshine today, yes?

By the time that's done, a maid arrives with a tea tray. He tells her to shut the door behind her and warns that this is business and he'd rather not be disturbed unless it is urgent. Once she's gone, he pours the tea before speaking.

"You are investigating the missing letters," he says.

"We are," Gray says. "Lady Inglis requested my help, and while it is not my area of expertise . . ."

"I have heard you are doing some detective work," Simpson says. "With the police. Consulting on murders and such. You really must let me take you out to dinner, Gray, so I may ask all about that. I am *fascinated*. The idea of using science to solve murders? Brilliant. Can you imagine where such a thing could lead? In a hundred years, if a person is murdered, science could lead us straight to the killer and prove they did it. No need for police to investigate nor for lawyers and judges to try the case. Science will prove guilt beyond a shadow of a doubt."

Gray sneaks a look at me, but I see no point in poking a hole in Simpson's enthusiasm. It's like telling modern people that the idea of flying cars doesn't actually, well, fly. Let them dream.

"That would be lovely, wouldn't it?" I say. "As for this case, we're focusing on it as a theft. Finding who stole the letters will lead us to the blackmailer."

"Miss Mallory will ask most of the questions," Gray says. "This is far more her area than mine."

"An excellent partnership, then," Simpson says. "Before we begin, while it has no bearing on the case, you must forgive me for needing to get it off my chest."

He sets his cup into the saucer. "I am horrified by what has happened. It is entirely my fault. I thought I had properly secured Patricia's letters, and clearly, I had not. I desperately wish that this scoundrel had sent the demand to me instead. I would have paid it with Patricia being none the wiser."

"It went to her because her reputation is the one at risk," I say.

"I know," he says mournfully. "She is in danger because of my mistake. I only wish she would allow me to pay this scoundrel."

"She prefers not to pay at all," I say. "If you wish to make it up to her, then the best way to do that is to help us find the blackmailer."

"Certainly. You have my full cooperation." He pulls a piece of paper from his pocket. "I have recorded all the details here. I kept the letters in my room, in a locked box on my dressing table. I know that it was locked December twentieth, as I also keep some jewelry in there and opened it to retrieve that for a seasonal gala. I returned the items that night and relocked it. I did not realize it was unlocked until Patricia notified me of the theft." He checks his notes. "On the morning of December twenty-third."

"You didn't notice the box had been opened?" I ask.

"The lock is not an obvious one. I will show it to you. It is impossible to tell at a glance whether it is locked or not."

"You said it's kept in your bedroom. Is that door locked?"

He looks confused by the question. I don't blame him. In a world of household staff, a bedroom door is rarely locked. Maids and valets need access to it.

"No," he says. "There is a lock, but I rarely use it."

"So everyone on your staff has access."

He shifts in obvious discomfort. "Yes. I . . ." He coughs. "I am about to say something that distresses me. I am very aware of how quick people are to blame the servants for anything that goes missing, and normally, that infuriates me."

"But . . ." I prod.

"I dismissed my valet on the twenty-first. I am planning another trip abroad in the new year, and he . . . is not properly suited to continental travel. I told him I was happy to keep him on until I left, but he said he would rather spend the holidays with family. I gave him a quarter's wages, and it all seemed very amicable, but then Patricia received this demand two days later . . ."

"Do you know where we might find this valet?"

Another shift of discomfort. "I do, but might I ask that you do not say I sent you?"

"We will say that we required a list of all staff employed at the time of the theft, and that you assured us none of your staff would have done this, but we insisted."

He exhales. "Thank you. I have spoken to all of my staff. I said that private correspondence had disappeared and asked if any of them might have seen it. I was hoping that if one did take the letters, they would quietly return them, and we could be done with the matter. That did not happen."

"You also have a brother, I understand, who lives with you."

Simpson blinks. "Arthur? Of course, but he would not have done this."

"We'll need to speak to him. I'll also need a list of every guest who was in the house between the twentieth and the twenty-third."

"No one," he says. "I went out a fair deal, but Arthur and I did not entertain."

"So no one came to the house? No friends? No business associates?"

"It is not the time of year for business. Lady Inglis visited on the twenty-first, but that was it."

"No one else?" I meet his gaze, my look silently reminding him of his promise to cooperate.

"No one," he says firmly. "You may ask the staff. I had a guest on the nineteenth, but that was before the theft. I hosted a small luncheon on the twenty-fifth, but that was after the letters were taken."

"Your guest on the nineteenth . . ."

"Could not have stolen the letters," he says. "They were there when I opened the box the evening of the twentieth, and she had been gone since that morning."

*She.* A woman who spent the night. A lover who is not Lady Inglis. That would be a promising lead, except that the timing doesn't work.

"Might I see the box and where it is kept?" I ask.

"Certainly."

---

As Simpson said, the box is on his dresser, in plain sight. I inwardly sigh at that. It's a pretty box, inlaid with mother-of-pearl, and it screams "I contain valuables!" It's about six inches by four inches, meaning it could easily be stolen whole and broken open for the contents.

The lock makes me sigh again. It's the sort Victorians are terribly fond of. A puzzle lock. Yet the puzzle is so simple that I get it after a few minutes, to Simpson's astonishment. It seems clever enough, but if you've played with puzzle locks, you'd recognize this one.

I like Simpson. He seems like a lovely man. But he really needs to work on his plan for safeguarding private letters. In his defense, he strikes me as the trusting sort, a fellow who'd make the mistake of presuming that if a box clearly contains something private, his staff and guests would respect that.

Anyone who had access to this room could have stolen the letters. And anyone with access to the house had access to the room.

"May I take the box?" I ask. "For closer inspection?"

Gray frowns my way. Then he understands. I want to dust it for fingerprints. I'm not sure that will do any good, but it's worth a shot. Simpson agrees, and I ask a few more questions. Then we take our leave.

Gray and I head down the street, a light snow falling around us.

"The valet and the brother," I say. "Those are my primary suspects. We have the valet's information, but the brother is trickier. I get the sense that, as cooperative as Lord Simpson wants to be, he'd rather we didn't question his brother."

"Because the man is an insufferable prig," Gray says. He makes a face. "That was rude of me."

"But true?"

"Arthur Simpson is the sort of younger son one expects to

join the clergy. He is insufferably sanctimonious and makes it clear that he finds his brother's lifestyle decadently sinful. However, there's a reason Arthur never joined the clergy—he has a dear love of decadence himself. His simply doesn't extend to what *he* considers sinful."

"Taking lovers."

"Yes, though at the risk of seeming a terrible person, I might suggest that jealousy rather than piety fuels his outrage."

"Ah, he's not half as charming as his brother."

"Not a *tenth* as charming. I can understand why Lord Simpson wouldn't want Arthur knowing about the missing letters, but I agree he's an excellent suspect. Even better than a fired valet. I also think I know a way we might encounter Arthur, quite by accident, of course."

I smile. "Perfect."

# CHAPTER TEN

I t turns out that "perfect" is not quite the word I should have used. The place where we can find the younger Simpson brother? His club, which I may not enter because I am a woman.

I don't think I realized exactly how many Victorian venues were off-limits to middle- and upper-class ladies. There are men's clubs, which I would have guessed. Also, brothels and gambling halls and fight clubs. Gymnasiums, too, so that men might exercise in peace. And pubs, so they might drink in peace. That mostly applies to upper-class pubs, but in that sphere, the restriction carries over to all dining establishments where liquor might be served. Men must be free to drink and conduct business without women around.

I can be shocked by the number of places a woman like Isla can't go, but within my own lifetime, there have been countless modern venues where women were barred, either outright or by practice. Places where men went to relax and drink and socialize and talk business.

Gray will need to conduct this interview alone. I'm fine with that. Okay, "fine" might be an exaggeration, but I accept it . . . as long as he grants me permission to try sneaking in and eavesdropping. I really do need to ask permission for that. Gray might not require the women in his household to seek it, but patriarchies work both ways. If I'm caught, he'll be the one punished for not properly "controlling" me.

He agrees to me sneaking in and provides some tips for where I might be able to enter. In return, I promise that if it seems risky, I'll back out.

I get inside the club easily enough. It's not as if they guard the entrance against women. It *is* guarded, but with an elderly man whose real job is making sure no male riffraff sneak through. Members and their guests only.

I slip in through a side door, where I only catch the curious glance of someone's coach driver resting in a tiny room that seems to be for that purpose. With men staying in the club for hours—and no easy way to resummon their driver—that little room is a necessity. Or, I guess, not a necessity so much as a perk. Otherwise, they'd be expected to hang out in the stable.

The driver only tips his hat to me, presuming I'm staff coming in for a shift. Women *are* allowed in places like this. Just not as members or guests.

From there, it gets trickier because if I meet an actual staff member, they'll know I don't belong. It takes me twenty minutes to get near the main rooms—I have to keep backtracking and ducking to avoid notice. Eventually, I find what I'm looking for, and can I just say that for an upscale gentlemen's club, it's sorely disappointing. It looks like a fancy airport lounge. A few big rooms with chairs and fireplaces . . . and that's about it. The chairs are arranged in pods for conversation, and there's a low murmur of that, but at least half the men are alone, reading newspapers or books with a cup of tea at their elbow.

I've approached through a back hall, where I can sneak peeks through discreet viewing ports, and I'm not sure whether that makes me feel like a voyeur or a visitor to the zoo.

*Here you see the upper-crust Victorian male in his natural habitat, smoking a pipe and reading the newspaper, doing things he could also do at home, but then he might need to . . . I don't know, talk to his wife? Acknowledge his children?*

I presume the viewing ports are so the staff can be ready to refill those teacups or empty those ashtrays as efficiently as possible.

When I hear Gray's voice, I follow it down another corridor. I peek out and see him sitting with a man who, again, surprises me. He's clearly Simpson's brother, given the resemblance, but Arthur looks more like the lover I pictured for Lady Inglis, handsome and polished. As I said, looks aren't everything, and it doesn't take long to understand why Lady Inglis would prefer the elder Simpson.

"Don't beat about the bush, Gray," Arthur snaps. "I am not a fool. I know what happens in my own home. Charles keeps a secret as well as a boy in short pants. Someone has stolen private letters from his room. Letters that ought to have been burned the moment he realized what they were. Ladies these days are not what they used to be. They are not *ladies* at all."

"Yes, your brother is missing letters of an intimate nature—"

"Intimate? Pornographic, that is what they are."

Gray pauses, and I try to see him, but the angle is wrong, and I doubt I'd see anything but a studiously blank expression.

"You have read them?" Gray says mildly.

That gets a satisfying spate of apoplectic sputtering from Arthur Simpson.

Gray says, "You seem to know what the letters contain—"

"Because he accidentally left one lying about and I picked it up, innocently thinking it a simple bit of correspondence, only to read . . ." He sputters some more. "Filth one should never find outside a brothel. And the most deviant of brothels at that."

*Read the whole thing, didn't you, Arthur?*

"Do they have such letters in brothels?" Gray says, his tone still so delightfully mild. "Are they intended for reading while you wait for one of the ladies to be available?"

More sputtering as Arthur insists he has no idea what is in brothels, and he was merely making a point.

Gray lets him go on a bit before interrupting. "So you are aware of the missing letters."

"Yes, I am aware. I could hardly miss Charles rushing about the house, whispering to all the servants, asking whether they had seen any 'letters' from a box he keeps locked on his dresser. I waited for him to come to me. He did not, because he knows I would never knowingly soil my mind with such things."

"Do you have any idea who might have taken them?"

"No, but if it finally forces my brother to make an honest woman of that tart, then I shall owe them my gratitude."

"That tart being . . ."

Disgust oozes from Arthur's voice. "You know who wrote the letters as well as I do, Gray. Lady Inglis. My brother's mistress. One of them, at least."

"You do not seem fond of Lady Inglis, though you wish her for a sister-in-law?"

"I am not fond of any of his tarts, but at least *she* is respectable. Outwardly respectable, that is. A widow from a fine family. Still attractive. Clever enough. Well-liked and—" He seems to need to force himself to say the words. "—well-mannered. Charles would do well to marry her and stop this . . . behavior. I do not know why she puts up with him, but she obviously does and has for years. He is not a young man anymore, and he should not act like one. It is an embarrassment."

"You think the letters will lead to a marriage proposal?"

"Of course. Whoever has stolen them obviously intends to blackmail Charles. He cannot afford to pay a ransom, so he will be forced to marry her. Finally."

I peek out to see Arthur sipping his tea while Gray steeples his fingers, as if in quiet thought.

After a moment, Arthur says, "I would not be surprised if she stole the letters herself."

"Lady Inglis?"

"Certainly." Arthur leans forward, his tone almost excited, as if he has just solved the mystery. "Now that this new girl has entered the picture, Lady Inglis realizes she is never going to have him to herself without a wedding ring. She steals the letters —easily done, as she has access to my brother's bedchamber. Then she threatens him with a ransom he cannot pay, and he has no choice but to marry her before this thief takes their affair public."

Arthur lowers his voice and says, "Cleverly done, ma'am. Cleverly done indeed." He rubs his hands together. "There. This is settled. He shall need to marry the woman and be done with it."

"I am surprised you are so eager to see Charles wed," Gray murmurs. "After all, as his first marriage was childless, his title would pass to you and your sons, should you have any. If he marries Lady Inglis, he might still have a son."

Arthur laughs. "She is nearly forty, and she did not bear her first husband any heirs. I am hardly worried . . ." He trails off and then says, "I wish to see my brother wed. That is all. If he is fond of Lady Inglis, I see no reason for this mistress nonsense."

"You mentioned a new girl—"

Someone clears their throat right beside me, making me stagger back and miss the rest of what Gray says. A severe-looking woman in a dour brown dress stands there with her arms crossed.

"May I help you, miss?" she says.

"Oh!" I clap my hands to my mouth. "Oh!"

"Do not tell me you are one of the serving girls," she says. "As I am in *charge* of the serving girls, I know you are not."

"N-no," I fake-stammer. "I am not. I am . . . I am so sorry, ma'am." I give an awkward half curtsy. "I . . . I know I should not be here, but I followed that gentleman in." I wave toward the viewing port. "The older one, with the light-brown hair," I say, describing Arthur Simpson.

Her face darkens. "You followed one of our members into his private club?"

"I am so sorry, ma'am. I am ashamed of myself and truly appalled by my boldness, but it comes from desperation. I hoped I might hear someone address him by his name."

"His name?" The woman looks through the hole and then glowers at me. "If you are looking for a wealthy gentleman to keep you in comfort—"

"No!" I round my eyes in shock. "No, ma'am. I am a respectable young woman. I am a shop clerk, over on Princes Street. I would never be a kept woman. It is only that . . . that I made that gentleman's acquaintance, from my shop, and I . . ." I bite my lip. "I found him handsome and let him take me rowing, and now I most desperately need to speak to him about . . ." I let my hands slide to my stomach before pulling them away. "A private matter."

"You do not even know his name?"

I drop my gaze. "He gave me one, ma'am, but I have learned it is false."

She glowers again, but this time, it's aimed at the viewing port. "His name is Arthur Simpson." She turns that hard look my way. "But you did not hear it from me."

I bow and scrape and stammer my thanks, and then I let her lead me to the nearest door.

I meet Gray outside the club about twenty minutes later. I don't tell him I got caught, and I certainly don't tell him how I got out of it. He might not like Arthur Simpson, but he'd still feel guilty knowing that one of the club's staff mistakenly believes Arthur knocked up a shop girl. He'd be wrong, of course. By the end of the day, *all* the club's staff will think that, and I personally don't feel the least bit guilty.

"You managed to get inside, then?" Gray says.

"I did, and I was sorely disappointed by the lack of dancing girls."

He stops midstride. "Dancing girls?"

"Dancing girls, maybe a few dancing boys . . . What kind of gentlemen's club is that?"

He gives me a sidelong look as he resumes walking. "So in your world, a gentlemen's club has . . . dancing girls?"

"Strippers."

"And strippers are dancers who . . . ?"

"Pretty sure it's right there in the name, Gray."

He turns the most adorable shade of mahogany.

I continue, "To be honest, though, while they call themselves gentlemen's clubs, it's not quite the same thing. In my world, that's just a fancy name for a place where you can watch naked women sliding on poles."

He chokes so violently that his eyes water.

"Not sliding on them like that," I say. "Get your mind out of the gutter. If you want that, you need to go to Amsterdam."

"Amster . . ."

"It's a city in—"

"I have visited Amsterdam."

"And you missed the sex shows? What kind of tourist are you?" I continue walking. "As for your club, it was boring. I didn't honestly expect dancing girls, but there wasn't even a heated game of chess. Now I know why you don't let women in. So they don't see how dull you all are. *Ah, yes, let us go to our secret club and drink tea and smoke cigars.* How scandalous!"

He only shakes his head. "As for the case . . ."

"Fine," I say with a deep sigh. "Drag me back on point."

"Yes, I am as dull as my gentlemen's club."

I could go along with it and tease him. But I find myself leaning to tap my winter bonnet against his shoulder and murmuring, "You are never dull, Duncan."

"I know."

I have to laugh. "Do you?"

"Of course. If I were dull, you would not stand my company for one moment longer than necessary. Did you hear my questioning of the younger Simpson?"

"Enough to think him a very fine suspect. I love it when my suspects are assholes. Makes my job a true delight." I glance over, catching his expression. "You disagree?"

"About preferring heinous suspects? Not at all. But while I think Arthur is eager to see his brother wed to Lady Inglis—especially as she is unlikely to provide an heir—stealing the letters will not do that. Lord Simpson likes his current lifestyle. Note that he was quick to offer to pay the ransom but not to marry her. He won't."

"But does Arthur know that?"

"Fair point."

We cross the road, and I pick up my pace to keep up with Gray's long strides. "Tell me about this new mistress. I missed that part."

"She is an actress."

"Ah."

That's all that really needs to be said. Female actors inhabit an odd place in Victorian society. They're independent women pursuing a career that was once entirely the province of men.

Actresses have more freedom than the average Victorian woman. Yet when women move out of their prescribed roles, they risk no longer being seen as "proper women." They become dangerous, and the easiest way to dismiss them is to question their morals.

To many, "actress" means "harlot." They are considered women of easy virtue who make most of their living off the stage. Do some of them engage in sex work? Sure. So do some shop girls and factory workers. Mostly, actresses just enjoy a greater freedom overall, which also extends to their sex lives.

"Did Arthur give you a name for this actress?" I ask.

"He did. I do not recognize it, and he says she's an ingenue."

"Young, then."

"Catriona's age or slightly older."

While a nonmonogamous arrangement wouldn't be my choice, it *is* a valid choice. With Lady Inglis and Lord Simpson, not only are both parties consenting, but both parties apparently pursue other relationships. So maybe it shouldn't bother me that Simpson is hooking up with an actress half Lady Inglis's age. But it does because I can't help but wonder whether it would also bother Lady Inglis.

Sharing him with other mature widows would be one thing. This feels . . . It feels like the stereotypical form of adultery, the guy screwing around with a girl from a lower social strata, one young enough to be his daughter.

If Lady Inglis *is* bothered, might she decide she'd finally had enough of this open relationship and lock him in with marriage? She *did* visit just before the letters went missing.

I'm not sure how I feel about Lady Inglis—and I know any judgment could be marred by her past with Gray—but I'd like her to be what she seems to be: a merry widow, independent, free thinking and free loving, not an aging woman who fears losing her lover to a younger woman and tricks him into marrying her.

I don't say any of that to Gray. Arthur Simpson raised the possibility, and I will let Gray bring it up. If he doesn't, then I trust his judgment.

"Could the actress be a suspect?" I say. "She might be the hot young new fling, but Lady Inglis is the longtime lover who'd stand in the way of the actress winning Lord Simpson." I pause. "Is that even a possibility? Can an actress marry a lord?"

"It has happened," he says. "More likely, though, there would be an arrangement."

Like what the woman earlier thought I'd been seeking with Arthur Simpson. A sugar daddy.

"However," Gray says, "you are forgetting that the actress could not have stolen the letters. She spent the night *before* they disappeared."

"Which only means she could have found them while she was there and then snuck back to steal them."

He sighs. "I did not think of that."

"This is why you're the junior detective. But don't worry. You'll get the hang of it someday."

# CHAPTER ELEVEN

Next on our interview list is the valet. He'd said he wanted to spend the holidays home with his family, but when we knock on his sister's door, she tells us he's working at a pub.

"Poor lad cannot even take the holidays off," she says. "That man let him go without a penny's wages. At this time of year? Can you believe it?"

That certainly isn't the story Lord Simpson gave, and it seems odd that he'd send us after the valet with a lie easily exposed.

She gives us directions to the pub, and then says, "Tell Lewis he need not bring home any money for the rent. I know he feels he must contribute, but I do not begrudge him a few coins in his pocket."

I ask for a description of her brother, and she seems confused —why do we need that when he's working there, easily found? Still, she describes him, and we set off along the snowy streets.

Along the way, we pass a small market, and I slow to eye the wares. It seems to be a little holiday market, full of holiday purchases—a stall of sweets, another of toys, a third of toiletries wrapped in pretty bows.

"Have you finished your Hogmanay shopping yet?" Gray asks.

"Isla and I went out last week, but I couldn't buy for her, obviously." I didn't buy for him, either, as I continue mulling over and rejecting ideas. Gray is fond of giving me gifts— perfect little presents that only I would appreciate, like a poison ring or a tiny derringer. I need to get exactly the right one for him.

"Do you wish to pause here?" he says. "Find something for her?"

My gaze slides over the stalls. I have a few ideas, but like buying for Gray, I won't find the right gift for Isla here. I still take the excuse to wander and browse. I purchase scented hair oil for Simon, and Gray buys a bag of boiled sweets for Alice, mostly so two of the best-dressed customers don't walk away without spending any money.

"Where do you shop for presents in your time?" Gray asks as we continue on.

"Online."

He gives me a look.

I shrug. "I'm not much of a shopper. I know what I want, and I order it online and get it shipped to my door."

"That sounds . . ."

"Soulless?"

"I was going to say wonderfully convenient." He slides a glance my way. "I do not suppose I can hope for such things in my lifetime?"

"It only started in *my* lifetime." I peer in the sooty window of a curiosities shop. "I do like to go out at least once for actual holiday shopping. When I was visiting my nan a few years back, she took me to the Christmas market here."

"A Christmas market in Edinburgh? Sacrilege."

I smile. "They still do a big blowout for Hogmanay. Music,

live theater, and lots of fireworks." I glance at him. "You have fireworks, right?"

One brow shoots up.

"Don't give me that look," I say. "I know they were invented in China centuries ago, but I don't know when they arrived in the UK. I'm not a historian."

"Have you heard of Guy Fawkes?"

"Right! Bonfire night. *Remember, remember, the fifth of November.* Mostly by blowing things up. Including fireworks, in honor of foiling Fawkes's plan to blow up parliament. When did that happen? About fifty years ago?"

"1605."

"Huh. History. Really not my thing."

"Evidently. Yes, we have Gunpowder Treason Day, which can be celebrated with bonfires and fireworks. In fact, until about ten years ago, it was illegal not to celebrate it."

I peer at him.

"The Observance of Fifth November Act," he says. "It was repealed in the past decade."

I can't tell whether he's serious. Before I can ask more, we arrive at the pub. It's a tavern in a middling area of the Old Town. Very small, very dark, very much a local watering hole. At this time of day—early afternoon—it's only about half full.

Using the description Lewis's sister gave, it's easy enough to find the valet, being the only guy under forty. He's deep in conversation with an older man, and unless his "job" involves chatting up customers while downing a pint himself, he is not working.

Here's another interesting thing about Victorian life. When I see depictions of domestic staff, they look very proper, like poor relations of the family they serve. Diffident, polite, starched, even a little stuffy. If I could picture their home lives, I'd see them sitting by the fire stitching Bible verses into tea towels. The truth is, of course, that their work persona is an act. Or, more accurately, it's Victorian code-switching. They act and talk in a manner that reflects well on their employers. Get them away from work, and it's very different.

Gray doesn't have a valet, but I've met a few, and they are very dapper and proper soft-spoken men. That is not the guy downing that pint. He's loud, gesturing wildly, and unshaven in a way that suggests he just hasn't bothered with it in a few days. He's young—maybe midtwenties—and handsome, and I can tell he'd clean up well enough to present the very picture of a fashionable young valet. Right now, though, he's off the clock. Permanently off the clock.

As we move toward Lewis, he glances over. Then he stops midsentence, stares at Gray for a moment, drops his pint and runs.

I look at Gray, who looks at me.

"That was . . . unexpected," Gray says. "I suppose we should go after him."

"Nah, we can just grab a drink. He'll be back soon enough." I smile at Gray's obvious disappointment. "Yes, we're going after him."

---

I let Gray give chase out the back door as I head around front. It's the Old Town, but it's a decent neighborhood and midday. I'm not concerned about being alone—either for safety or propriety.

I slip out the front and look each way. Like many streets in the Old Town, it's so narrow that two coaches can't pass each other. These are medieval roads, meant for walking and riding horses and maybe pulling a cart. At midday, the street is crowded, and I scan for Lewis's light hair. He hadn't bothered to grab his outerwear when he ran, which should make him easier to spot. There's no sign of him, though.

The rear door would likely exit into a close—an even narrower lane between buildings, similar to an alley. I hurry left, spot a close and pick up my pace. I swing into it to find an exceptionally narrow passage. Towering buildings on both sides plunge the alley into darkness. I break into a slow jog as I strain to listen. Somewhere ahead, I catch the pound of running feet.

A rickety wooden staircase blocks easy passage. That's not unusual. Access to many apartment floors requires external stairs so decrepit they make me shudder. I duck past this set and—

A figure grabs me from the shadows. I wheel, fists rising, only to stop when I catch a glimpse of a tall man in a fur-trimmed coat and top hat.

"Goddamn it," I say. "How many times do I need to warn you not to sneak . . ."

I trail off as I squint up into the pale face of a stranger.

"Well, now, you have a tongue on you, don't you, lass?"

The man is about Gray's age and height, but otherwise, there's no way to mistake one for the other. He's missing half his teeth, and a dentist would insist on pulling the remainder. Even his coat only superficially resembles Gray's. It's shabby and tattered, and the smell of it is enough to have me backpedaling even as his grip tightens on my arm.

"What a fine little thing you are," he says, with a wave of breath that smells worse than a week-old corpse. "So fancy. Surely you can spare a few coins for my supper, lass?"

I eye him, thinking fast. When he calls me "fine," he means my clothing, which indicates I have a bit of money. That's what he's interested in. While I'm carrying a derringer in my cloak pocket and a knife in my boot, I'd rather not pull them if I can part with a few coins instead. The last time I stabbed a man who grabbed me in an alley, I spent the night in jail for assault.

"I am sorry, sir," I say with a pretty half curtsy. "I mistook you for another. Yes, I believe I can spare a few pence to help a gentleman down on his luck. God tells us to be charitable."

I cast my gaze up in what I hope is a pious expression as I fish a few coins from my pocket. When I extend my hand, I see I'm offering three pence and two shillings. More than I intended, but not more than I'm willing to give.

"If you will please remove your hand from my arm, sir," I say. "Your grip is very tight."

He tightens it enough to make me inhale sharply.

"Is that better?" he says.

"I am offering you money, sir," I say, struggling to keep my voice sweet and a little confused. "That is what you asked for."

"It's not enough."

I look down at my hand to double-check the coins. Hell, yes, it's enough. From Gray and Isla, I've learned more about charity than I knew in modern-day Vancouver, where I'd walk past panhandlers with an "I don't see you" expression and make a mental note to donate to a shelter instead. Here, a few small coins go a long way. What I'm offering is double what he should expect.

"Forgive me, sir," I say, "but I need my last shilling to get home again."

"You can walk. You'll give me that last shilling . . . and everything else in your pockets, along with that ring on your finger and the necklace—"

"There you are," a voice rumbles behind us. "I wondered where the devil you took off to."

I turn to see Gray and bow my head. "I am sorry, sir. I tried to take a shortcut."

He grunts. "And look where that got you." He lifts his gaze

to the man still holding my arm. "I am going to presume you are holding my assistant's arm because you helped her up from an unfortunate fall."

The man's gaze sweeps up Gray and back down, his eyes narrowing as he assesses. Then he says, "If I did, I believe I am due some recompense. Who knows what could have befallen the child back here."

Gray hands him a shilling. "There. Thank you for your kindness."

The man looks at me, that narrow-eyed gaze telling me I still owe him the money I offered.

"How generous, sir," I say to Gray. "I was about to pay this good man myself, but as you have done so, I will take my leave of him." I look at the fingers gripping on my arm. "I am quite recovered, sir. You may remove your hand."

The man hesitates. Gray tenses, jaw setting, and with another look at him, the man releases my arm, mutters something and disappears into the shadows again.

Gray ushers me along the alley, and I mutter, "Do not do that."

"Do not do what? Rescue you from ruffians twice your size?"

I snort. "He was just a troll, guarding his bridge and demanding a fare for passage."

"Which you had offered, and he was not accepting."

"I was working it out."

Gray looks down at me.

"You need to let me work it out, Duncan," I say, my voice softer. "I do appreciate that you were close enough to intercede. If I hadn't been able to get out of it, I'd also have appreciated actual intercession. But I need to find strategies for all situations in this world."

"What would you have done in yours?"

I consider as we step onto another street. "If he'd just asked,

I'd have given him money. Grabbing my arm changes things. That's a threat. I'd have shown him not to expect women to be easy marks."

"And you would not do that in this world?"

I turn a look on him. "Remember why I spent a night in jail this spring? Also, knocking him down is a whole lot harder in this body and this clothing."

"All right. So I should watch until you need my help? Presumably signaling to you that I am near."

"Mmm. Signaling me means I know I have backup, which changes things, but sure. Signal me and then stand down until the last possible moment."

"The split second between him pulling out a knife and ramming it between your ribs?"

"Pfft. I'm wearing a cloak, dress, corset cover, and corset. He'd better have a sharp knife and a sharper sense of anatomy."

Gray sighs and steers me around a woman passed out drunk.

"I'm guessing we lost Lewis?" I say.

"No."

Gray leads me down another close, this one wider and busier, with people walking in both directions. Then he pauses and points with his chin. Ahead is a recessed doorway, and in it stands Lewis, pressed against the rear as if rendered invisible.

Now it's my turn to sigh. Yes, household staff might not be as prim and proper as they appear on the job, but unless they work for Isla Ballantyne, they're not exactly criminal geniuses, either.

"Head around and come in the other way," I say. "I'll wait here. When I see you, I'll approach him. Be ready in case he runs."

"Is that an order?" he says.

"Of course. I'm the lead detective, remember?"

His headshake says he's humoring me, but he does backtrack the way he came. That means I need a reason for hanging out here that doesn't look like active solicitation. That isn't easy with Catriona's body and a lack of "pause in public place" excuses like cell phones.

I decide to fuss with my glove. Pull it off. Peer inside, scowling slightly, as if something is poking at me. I'm turning each finger inside out when I finally spot Gray. He slips into the end of the close, sees me, and then moves to the side and removes his own glove to examine it.

I laugh softly at that and put my glove on before someone decides we're engaged in an elaborate mating ritual. Or planning a midday heist.

I stroll over to where Lewis still "hides" in the recessed doorway.

"Hello, Lewis," I say.

He frowns at me with zero recognition. Apparently, the only one he saw at the pub was Gray.

"I need to speak to you about Lord Simpson," I say. "We had your sister's address and—"

Lewis flinches, his gaze going over my shoulder. I look to see Gray.

"He's with me," I say.

Lewis looks from Gray to me and says, "Lord Simpson sent you?"

"No, but we're here investigating his missing property."

"This has nothing to do with, er, a young lady I've been seeing?"

"Uh . . . no."

Lewis exhales. "I thought it was about that. She has an older brother, and they are . . . That is to say, he might resemble . . ."

He trails off, but I can figure out the rest. Lewis is seeing a young woman of color, and on seeing a man of color bearing down on him, he bolted.

"This has nothing to do with your social life," I say. "It is entirely about work. Speaking of which, though, your sister seems to think you're employed at that pub."

His eyes open, far too wide to be genuine shock. "What? No. She must have misunderstood."

"She says Lord Simpson let you go without a shilling in payment, when he told us he paid you a quarter's wages."

Lewis colors and tugs at his collar. "She's misunderstood."

In other words, Simpson did pay, but Lewis doesn't want his sister knowing he has money. He's pretending to work at the pub and then giving her a few "hard-earned" coins for his rent, like a good brother.

This puts us in a position of power. If he decides not to cooperate with the interview, we have leverage.

"No matter," I say. "We are here to speak of Lord Simpson's missing property. Would you like to go someplace else?"

"I am a wee bit thirsty," he says, "from all the running."

"Let us return to your pub and buy you a pint."

# CHAPTER TWELVE

Yep, gotta love Victorian detective work, where even McCreadie wouldn't see a problem interviewing a witness over a pint. We get Lewis settled in with a fresh drink, and Gray takes one for himself, to be hospitable. I'm tempted to ask for a glass of water, but . . . there's a reason why beer is so popular in historical times. It's not that everyone was a lush, downing a "small beer" with breakfast, giving beer to children and such. It's that beer—or cider or wine—is safe to drink where water might not be. Boiling it for tea helps, but I won't find tea here, so I settle on a small glass of beer. While the beer itself might be safe, I can't say as much for the smudged glass. Welcome to the time before running hot water and cheap soap.

"I know about the missing letters from Lady Inglis," he says. "Lord Simpson came and spoke to me."

I hesitate. "He told you they were from Lady Inglis?"

"No, but I cannot see his other mistresses penning him letters, and I know he's been receiving them since he hired me, so they must be from Lady Inglis. A fine lady, that one. He really ought to marry her."

"So we've heard," I murmur.

"I can understand him liking the actresses and such, but I do not get the sense Lady Inglis would mind if he continued that, discreetly, of course. She is a very sensible lady. And that house could use a mistress."

"Has Lady Inglis indicated she'd like the position?"

"As lady of the house? No. She teases him about its management, and he says she's welcome to do it for him, but she says she has her own household to manage. The solution, clearly, is to marry. Her house is much nicer, and they could boot out that sodding brother of his."

I press more. I really do want to know whether Lady Inglis has given any sense that she's unhappy with the arrangement or would like to marry Lord Simpson. Lewis has seen none of that.

So why should she want to marry a man of equal rank, with a lesser home, a loutish brother, and multiple mistresses? The question confuses Lewis. She's a woman without a man. Of course she must secretly wish to marry.

This is one of the things that astounds me about the Victorian male. How he can see a woman enjoying an independent life and say, "That poor dear, if only she had a man." It's not just men, either. Older women say the same thing. Of course, the older women who say it are all married and may just not want other women having things they do not.

I conclude that Lady Inglis has given zero indication of wanting to marry Lord Simpson. Lewis just thinks she should, for the convenience of his former employer, who is in need of a good domestic manager.

"You seem fond of Lord Simpson," I say. "It was an amicable parting?"

Lewis shrugs. "I would have preferred *not* to have been sacked, but his lordship assured me I will receive excellent references. Apparently, Lord Simpson did not think I would do well overseas, and while I would have appreciated the chance to prove otherwise, that is his choice, and he paid me well."

I glance at Gray. I'm asking whether he wishes to continue this line of questioning, but he only uses it as an opportunity to swing the interview back to the stolen goods.

"So you knew of the letters," Gray says.

"Yes, sir. And if you are going to ask whether I took them, I almost wish I had."

Gray frowns.

Lewis gives a low laugh and leans back in his chair. "I'd be a wealthy man if I did. Wealthy enough, that is. Seems very unfair, if you ask me. Had I stolen from his lordship, I'd be buying passage on a ship to America with a pocket full of money to make my fortune there. But no, I was an honest chap, and so I have nothing." Lewis shifts in his seat. "All right, his lordship *did* give me a few quid for my honesty, but it's a sad world when a man would have gained more for admitting he was a thief."

"I . . . do not understand," Gray says.

"Lord Simpson says whoever stole the letters wants money for their return. He offered me five *hundred* quid to quietly return the letters. Alas, being an honest man, I could not claim it."

Lewis sips his beer and continues, "I even thought perhaps I could say I stole the letters and burned them, but he required the return of the letters." He shakes his head. "That will teach me to be honest."

I see Lewis's point, even if he is belaboring it. Simpson meant well, but his execution was flawed.

Could Lewis still have stolen the letters? Maybe he knew Simpson had no intention of paying and just wanted a confession so he could put the screws to his former valet and get those letters back for free. Or Lewis could be playing it safe and waiting for the payout. Except the payout isn't actually the safe bet here because if Lady Inglis decides not to give in to the blackmail, he's stuck with the much smaller reward of income from publishing the letters.

Lewis doesn't strike me as a guy who'd think through all the angles. If he stole the letters and Simpson showed up on his doorstep, he'd freak out. If Simpson offered to pay the full amount of the blackmail, he'd jump at it.

Also, Simpson doesn't strike me as someone who'd offer money and then replace it with threats. No, I suspect Simpson really would try to buy back those letters, and if Lewis had them, he'd hand them over.

After we wrap up the interview, I run this all past Gray, who agrees with my logic. Lewis hardly seems like a wily blackmailer. And the Lord Simpson Gray knows isn't going to get a confession and then refuse to pay.

Lewis isn't a vengeful former employee. He's a guy who has been let go but paid well for the inconvenience. He'll spend his holidays drinking and seeing his girlfriend and then, in the new year, he'll take Simpson up on that offer of references to get a new job.

That clears our most obvious suspect.

---

I'm spending the evening alone. Gray is paying a house call to a family too illustrious to make funeral arrangements in an undertaker's office. While I'm technically his assistant, I can't yet pass as a Victorian well enough to be sure I won't say or do something wrong in front of grieving families. It's easy to explain away my peccadilloes in everyday life. Dealing with the griefstricken is another level, one where I want my manners to be perfect.

Isla is out on a social call. She has two sorts of social engagements. One is lunches and teas and such with women whose company she genuinely enjoys. The other is duty, all the various charitable endeavors that women like Isla are expected to engage in.

Those charitable endeavors would seem like a happy duty for Isla, who is genuinely interested in the plight of the poor. Unfortunately, in those settings, she's one of the very few *genuinely* interested women.

We're at a time of shifting views on the poor and charity. My father used to teach this with Dickens in particular, showing how Dickens's own views shifted over the course of his career. He moved from heartily endorsing charity from the rich to questioning whether it can ever *not* be condescending, while advocating for other solutions. That's the dilemma Isla faces—she wants to use her privilege to help, but is it ever possible to do that, however sincerely, without condescension?

With both of them gone, I am alone and reminded that, since I have decided to stay in this world, I really need to make a full life for myself here, including hobbies. Normally, I would see whether Alice wanted to play cards, but she's with Mrs. Wallace, and I don't dare intrude.

Alice and Mrs. Wallace are enjoying a free evening with both Isla and Gray away. Our bosses might be very low maintenance, but as long as they're in the house, the staff is on alert, ready at the sound of footsteps to see whether anything is needed. With both Gray and Isla gone, Alice and Mrs. Wallace can truly relax.

My other option is to pop out to the stables for a chat with Simon, which is always time well spent. He was Catriona's only real friend, and while I can't fill that role, I very much enjoy his company. However, he is with Gray, who can't be seen paying visits to clients on foot.

That leaves me with reading, which would usually be fine, but reading reminds me of Dickens, which reminds me that I met a dead man two days ago.

I'm struggling with that more than I would have expected. Last month, I watched my terminally ill grandmother die, but it's not the same. I met a man who believes himself to be healthy, who is on his last tour before settling into semiretirement. I listened to a man enthuse about a book he will never finish writing. It has unsettled me more than I expected, and I realize some of my earlier pique with Gray might be misdirected emotional fallout from that.

When I first came to this world, I'd felt lonely in a way I didn't even truly recognize as loneliness.

Now Gray, Isla, and McCreadie all know my secret, and with that, I have friends I can be myself around. Yet I have given them a secret *they* must keep, and I don't want to add to that with the uncomfortable sort of prognostication that comes with realizing someone is going to die.

But keeping that secret lets the loneliness creep in again, along with the fear that I'm always going to be an outsider, however much they welcome me. There will always be knowledge—uncomfortable knowledge—that I can't share.

So when Jack swings into the library, I may greet her a wee bit more effusively than normal.

"Bored, are you?" she says, tugging at her trousers as if she just finished changing into her male garb.

I shrug. "A bit out of sorts. What are you up to tonight?"

"And can you join? That is your real question."

Another shrug as I play it cool. "Depends on what it is and whether you want company."

"From the look you gave when I walked in, unless I plan to spend the night digging through rubbish, you'll think it sounds splendid."

"You can find a lot of interesting things in the rubbish."

She laughs. "The situation is desperate, then. Well, I came to see whether you'd care to call on a print shop. To learn whether anyone might be offering letters of an intimate nature for paid public consumption?"

"Ah. That *does* sound more interesting than picking through rubbish."

"We can stop for a pint afterwards," she says. "You can be my lady friend for the evening."

"Which means you'll be paying for the pint? Excellent."

# CHAPTER THIRTEEN

Jack is the sort of person who lets you feel as if you know them, but once you stop to think about it, you realize you don't know a damn thing. She's chatty and open, and gives the impression that she likes you, and that you could be friends . . . or at least friendly acquaintances. But she has perfected the art of talking a great deal without giving away one iota of truly personal information.

I don't know how old she is, where she grew up, what sort of life she's had, what her plans for the future are or her pains of the past. She could come from poverty or royalty. She could have two husbands and a child growing up with relatives. She seems like someone who has waltzed through life, spinning too deftly for anything to leave a scar. Maybe that's true. Maybe it's a persona she adopts, like the masculine one she's inhabiting as we cross the mound into the Old Town.

I am fascinated by Jack, and I'm also learning from her, even if she never realizes it. How she acts is how I must act toward most of the world . . . including her. My past isn't something I can discuss, both because it took place over a century from now and because

I'm inhabiting the body of someone who already has a past. What if I tell Simon that my parents were loving and incredibly supportive, only to have him remember that Catriona's were cold or abusive?

I've never been a private person. Hell, meet me at a party and you'd walk away an hour later knowing my favorite color, the name of my childhood cat, and that I broke my arm in third grade, climbing a tree. Yes, I broke it climbing a tree, not falling from it, which is a certain kind of special.

On the walk, Jack chatters away. She tells me something funny Alice said and how Mrs. Wallace gave her shit for whistling, which she relates in a perfect imitation of the house-keeper. She points out a Princes Street shop that kicked her out last year when she'd been browsing "intimate ladies' apparel" while forgetting she was still dressed masculine. Once we're in the Old Town, she points out a close and tells me a friend swears it's haunted by one of Burke and Hare's victims. All very enter-taining and companionable, and not revealing one scrap of personal insight.

"Did you grow up in Edinburgh?" I say, mostly just to amuse myself because I know how she'll answer.

"Here and there, now and then." She waves a hand. "You know how it is. You?"

"Same."

She shoots me a grin, as if she knows I'm playing her game. She's said many times that she knows something's up with me, some secret she's not privy to. That would make me nervous if I got the sense she was digging for answers. After all, she *is* a jour-nalist, by practice if not by trade. But my sense is that this is a secret she'll let me keep, as long as I let her keep all of hers, which seems fair.

It's a clear night, crisp and decently lit with stars just visible through the smoke of a thousand fires keeping a thousand lodgings warm—or warm enough. We weave through a few neighborhoods before she slows.

"Here we are," she says.

I look around, but I'm not even sure I recognize the area. She leads me to a building with no obvious storefront . . . and no obvious front door. We go to the side entrance, and she raps a few times in a pattern.

"Secret entry code," I say, and then stop myself before adding a period-inappropriate "Cool."

A moment later, there's a snick, and I notice a peephole on the solid door. Another moment passes, and a lock clangs. Then the door opens a few inches, and the unmistakable smell of ink rushes out.

"You have something for me, boy?" a voice rumbles.

"Questions," Jack says cheerfully. "I have questions."

The door slams shut. Jack only sighs and knocks again. When it opens, it's a scant inch, and the voice rumbles, "You come here with a stranger and questions? You're lucky I don't set Blackie on you."

"Have you seen these?" Jack waves one of the pamphlet installments of Gray's adventures. "I have it on good authority that the scribe is looking to change presses."

There's a pause. It's long enough that I'm concerned, but Jack only waits.

"You know the writer?" the voice says.

"Would you like a peek at the next installment to prove it?"

More silence. The peephole snicks open again.

"Miss Mallory?" the voice says.

Thankfully, I don't jump, though I will give Jack shit for not warning me. Or actually, maybe I won't, because she probably thought I'd figure it out as soon as she waved around that pamphlet.

"Yes, the pamphlet is about the adventures of Dr. Gray and his lovely assistant, Miss Mallory," Jack says breezily.

"I mean, is that Miss Mallory with you?"

Jack looks over at me and blinks, as if in surprise. Then she laughs. "Heavens, no. Miss Mallory with me? A pleasant thought. She sounds a right perfect little morsel. This one is a right perfect pain in the arse."

I'm allowed to glare at her for that, and I do, but the door also opens to let us in, as if the person on the other side suspects I'm "Miss Mallory," but they aren't pushing for a positive ID.

The door opens into darkness. We slip inside, and I see the owner of the voice, a stout woman with her arms crossed over her chest. I glance around for the dog, Blackie, and instead see a hulking guy with jet-black hair and an equally black beard, his arms also crossed. The woman leads us past him, and I swear he growls . . . until I look up at him from under my lashes. Then his broad face colors, and he tips his grimy hat with a few mumbled words.

The woman takes us into what is obviously the print room, given the two printing presses. That's where my attention goes: to those presses.

My parents talk of their childhoods, with no computers, just typewriters and mimeograph machines, and that's always been hard for me to fathom. How do you write an essay if you can't just pull up the file and edit it into submission? What if you need more than one copy? You couldn't even go to the library and use the copy machine.

I remember once when they were explaining these concepts to me, and I blurted, "But what about books?" How did you produce a thousand copies of a book without printers? Did they live back in that time I'd seen in old movies, with massive printing presses and movable type? They'd thought that was hilarious . . . and then gently explained all the steps between ancient printing presses and modern ones.

Here, I expect to see one of those massive beasts that would take up an entire room. Instead, there are two presses. Both are much smaller than I expected, maybe double the size of those old library copy machines from my youth.

The room is cavernous, and I see what looks like living quarters to one side. The rest is boxes. Some seem to be finished products, and I squint into one and see flyers for a workers' rights movement. And in the one beside it . . . fancy pamphlets arguing *against* the dangers of granting workers more rights.

"Your friend there should keep her eyes to herself," the woman rumbles.

"Occupational hazard," I say with a smile, mostly to watch her pause to decipher that very modern phrase. When she does, she eyes me. "You really are Miss Mallory, then? Of the stories?"

"Miss Mallory is sweet and gentle," Jack says. "And knows not to poke her nose where it doesn't belong."

It's a credit to her acting ability that she can say that with a straight face.

"I am only fascinated by the presses," I say. "May I ask why there are two?"

The woman sighs, as if I'm being unreasonably curious, but her eyes light with the look of someone who actually likes talking about her work. The smaller machine is a jobbing press meant for simple low-print tasks like letterhead or business cards. It takes about fifteen minutes to set up and can print a thousand copies an hour. The larger one is the proper press and can do about half as many copies an hour. Both are manual presses. Newspapers use steam-powered ones, which can do about ten thousand pages an hour, but her business has no need for that.

I cut my questions short at Jack's obvious impatience, and

then she says, "I come tonight with questions about pornographic literature."

The woman eyes me again. "If you're not Miss Mallory and you're looking for a few extra coins in your pocket, I can suggest an artist or two. Sketches are best. Photographs do not flatter as well."

"And if I *am* Miss Mallory, and I were still looking to make a few extra coins? Would your answer be something different?"

"In that case, it would. I'd suggest your chronicler print a separate set of your adventures . . . for a different but better-paying sort of customer."

I smile and shake my head. "I can imagine the poor mother who picks up the wrong one to share with her children. No, in either case, I am not looking for that sort of extra coin. I merely accompany Jack on his labors tonight."

"His labors being the pursuit of pornographic literature?" she says.

"*Questions* about pornographic literature," Jack says as she lifts a chapbook from a box. "Like this."

The woman sniffs. "You do not want that. It is far too pretty for a young man like you. That sort of thing is written for Miss Not-Mallory over here."

I take the chapbook from Jack. It's only about twenty pages long. On a skim, I can see it's a story about a young woman alone in the city, innocent and sweet. By page five, she's no longer so innocent and sweet.

I wrinkle my nose. "This is written for men."

Jack's and the printer's brows shoot up in unison.

I wave the chapbook. "Innocent girl. Big bad city. Oh, please don't touch me there. No, wait, I like being touched there. There would be a female audience for it, but it's mostly aimed at men."

"We have others," the printer says.

"Such as?"

"Not-so-innocent governess who goes to work for a lord and his longtime friend."

"Is the friend actually just a friend?"

She meets my gaze. "No."

"Huh. That might work. The key is the not-so-innocent part. Women don't want to read about other women being ruined. They want to read about them having fun."

Jack chokes on a laugh.

The printer says, "We also have an entire series called The Merry Widow."

That makes me think of Lady Inglis, but I hide my reaction. "Even better."

"The Merry Widow, you say?" Jack murmurs, moving forward. "So there is an appetite for such things?"

"The fellow who has them printed up certainly seems to think so."

"And if someone came by asking about printing intimate letters written by an actual widow, you'd send them to him?"

She waves a hand. "No, it's not that sort of thing. This fellow has a writer already. And they aren't letters. They're stories."

"So if I had such letters . . . ?" Jack says.

She snorts. "Keep them." Her eyes glitter. "Unless they were written by that most illustrious of widows. Adventures between her illustrious self and a certain Scottish servant?"

It takes a moment to realize she means Queen Victoria, and even I flush at that. I do recall the widowed queen was rumored to have an affair with a Scotsman who worked on her estate.

Jack rolls her eyes. "If I had those, I'd be a rich man. One such letter from Her Royal Highness, and my coffers would fill in the blink of an eye."

"Or you'd wind up in the dungeons," the printer says. "Never to be seen or heard from again."

"True enough. But what if the letters were from a less illustrious personage?"

The printer shrugs. "If she has money and you took the letters without permission, you'd make far more by asking her to pay to *prevent* them from being printed."

That gives me pause. "Do such things happen?" I ask.

"I'm certain they do. It does not involve me, though."

"So if I brought you such letters, you would not print them?"

She meets my gaze. "I would not."

"Would you know anyone who would?"

She shrugs. "A shop or two, but they'd only buy them for a few pounds, and then probably turn around and see if they could 'sell' them back to the writer. Why print such things written by amateurs when you can have them written by experts?"

"Experts using the full scope of their imaginations," I say. "Rather than relying on fact."

The printer points an ink-blackened finger at me. "Just so. I do not think you are going to find many merry widows with the temerity and the skill to write of their intimate adventures, and even if they did, they would not sell as well as the made-up sort."

Jack asks a few more questions, but it's clear that the printer hasn't heard of anyone trying to sell such letters. From what I gather, this shop would be their first stop, as it's well known for its underground publications. But the printer is correct, too, that no one is likely to print such a thing when the real money would be made in blackmailing the letter writer.

As we prepare to leave, I say, "You mentioned a Merry Widow series. Might I purchase those?"

The printer gives a low, rumbling laugh. "Caught your fancy, did they?"

"They did."

"Well, I am only the printer, but I have some samples I'd be willing to part with for a few shillings. Do you want the governess one as well?"

I imagine Isla reading that story, with the governess, the lord, and his more-than-a-friend. "No, the Merry Widow ones will suffice."

"Well, I shall throw that one in as an extra." She winks. "You might find it more to your taste than you would expect."

I make my purchase, and we leave. We don't get more than a few feet from the shop before Jack says to me, in her more natural voice, "Getting a little lonely in that attic bedroom, is it?"

I make a noncommittal noise. I'm certainly not telling her who they're for. Also, I probably *will* need to read them to make sure I'm not giving Isla anything so far out of her comfort zone that she might never recover.

"You do know there is an easy fix for that," she says. "A mere two flights down. A very fine doctor who would happily provide whatever examination you require."

I can feel her gaze on me in the dark, waiting for a reaction. I only shake my head. "If you mean our shared employer, that is inappropriate."

She makes a rude noise. "Not unless you only agree because he *is* your employer. Otherwise, it is a perfectly fine arrangement." She glances over. "It adds quite an exciting dynamic, as I say from experience."

"I thought all your experiences were neither exciting nor dynamic."

"Mmm, I will not say that one was excellent, but it was the best of the bunch. He was my first employer. First *legitimate* employer, that is." She grins my way. "I had taken the position posing as a boy, which only added to the illicit allure. He enjoyed knowing my little secret and being the only one to see me in a dress." She purses her lips. "Though there was that one time when he did not want me to change into a dress first."

She peers at me and sighs. "You are quite impossible to shock, Miss Mallory."

"Not really. You just need to tell me something shocking. Like that he invited three of his friends along for the ride."

Her cheeks redden, and I laugh.

She scowls at me. "You enjoyed that."

"You started it. Do not try to shock me in such regards, my dear, or I shall turn the tables faster than you like. Now, you promised me a pint, did you not?"

"I just helped you with your case. And helped you find reading material. I think you owe *me* a pint."

"True, however, if you choose to dress as a lad, you must behave as a lad. It would not do for people to see a young lady paying for your pint. What would they think?"

She shakes her head and grumbles under her breath as she leads me to a pub.

# CHAPTER FOURTEEN

When we get back to the town house, the coach has returned, and we pop into the stable to speak to Simon, who's putting Folly to bed for the night. Simon has been wary around Jack. It isn't that he has an issue with cross-dressing. That's actually why Isla hired him. Simon was part of the molly subculture, as a gay man who sometimes socialized while dressed as a woman. He'd been young, and with youth can come the confidence that people won't care what you do as long as it doesn't hurt them. A lovely sentiment, but sadly false.

While being a gay man isn't illegal in Scotland, as it is elsewhere in Britain, it's still not something you want to flaunt, which is what got Simon into trouble. If he's cautious around Jack, it's because she's cross-dressing for a different reason. Tonight, though, they strike up a conversation, and I use the opportunity to slip off and give them a chance to chat.

I'm just inside the door and sitting to change into my indoor footwear when boots clomp on the stairs. I look up to see Gray coming down.

"You were out," he says.

I lift the winter boot I just removed. "Yes."

"It is late."

"It is." I finish lacing my indoor boots. While I'm going to need to take them off again upstairs in my room, walking around in my stocking feet would be like walking around half dressed. It is simply not done.

I stand. "I did leave a note."

"Yes, I got it."

I lean against the wall and look up at him still halfway down the stairs. "You know, this feels familiar. Like when I was a teenager and I'd come home past curfew and my dad would wait up to give me hell."

"I did not wait up. I was *still* up."

I don't answer that. I know from Simon that Gray has been home for the past hour, and given how late it is, he'd normally have gone straight to his room.

"But you *are* giving me hell?" I say.

"I am expressing mild concern. I know you were with Jack, and I know you are fond of her, but I am not convinced . . ."

"She wouldn't leave me to my fate if we got jumped in an alley?"

"Exactly so."

"I had my gun and my knife."

He considers this. Not considering whether this is enough—I suspect I could roll through the Old Town in a tank and he still wouldn't be convinced it was safe enough. What he's considering is whether he would be justified in pursuing the complaint.

"How was *your* evening?" I ask.

He still pauses, as if debating whether he's ready to drop this. Then he sighs. "It went much later than I expected. I thought I would have been done hours ago, but I was not even granted an audience until nearly nine."

"Damned nobility."

"I considered leaving. Unfortunately, they were good clients of my father's, and they are also well connected enough that being rude to them might cost me half my clientele. Which sometimes I think would not be the worst thing . . ." He scratches his chin and sighs again. "Perhaps someday."

I used to wonder why Gray keeps the undertaking business when he clearly does not care for it . . . and doesn't need the money. I understand better now. It's duty and pride. Duty to his family, because his father built the business and Gray inherited it. It's also pride because his forensic work doesn't pay the bills, and he wouldn't be comfortable living off passive income from money his father made and invested.

"Dare I hope your evening went better?" he says.

I head up the stairs to join him. "Pour me a drink, and I'll tell you all about it."

"It smells as if you've already had a few."

"Is that judgment of my drinking habits, Gray?"

"No, it's knowledge of your drinking habits, which suggests you may regret another."

"It was a few sips of a pint to be polite," I say.

"The glass was dirty?"

I sigh. "It always is."

"Poor Mallory. Let me get you a proper drink, then, clean glass and all."

---

From what my visit to the print shop suggested, we're not looking for someone who seriously intends to sell the letters. If they had thought they could, they don't seem to have made any inquiries to that effect. So we're most likely dealing with someone who fully expects Lady Inglis to pay. This is useful because it suggests some knowledge of her finances. As she said, five hundred pounds certainly isn't pocket change. It seems to be about as much as someone could expect to pay. Otherwise, they'd be left with letters they can't actually sell.

Of course, that could all be pure luck—they just happened to pick the right figure—which is why our first stop the next day is to the suspect least likely to know Lady Inglis's finances.

It seems early to be calling on an actress. They're not known for being morning people, especially in this era, when an ingenue like Miss Howell might be picking up some cash on the side. Not the sex trade per se, but entertaining—providing a pretty bit of scenery for a late-night party.

However, what kept Gray out late last night wasn't only inconsiderate clients. It was the stop he made afterward, to what seems to have been a far less staid sort of gentlemen's club than the one I got a peek at earlier.

It can be hard to remember that Gray is only my age. He seems older, with the weight of his era and his responsibilities. But he is a young man and a bachelor at that, and so I don't doubt he knows where to go for late-night entertainment, the sort with gaming tables and actresses on their off nights.

From there, he learned that Miss Howell was not known to frequent such establishments . . . or any other sorts of establishments that might be popular with pretty young women whose acting careers don't pay the bills. Miss Howell actually has a day job working in a dress shop.

That is where I find her, and not even in the front, where I'd expect to find a pretty and poised young actress. She's in the back, working with several seamstresses. Even when the shop girl calls her forward, I think there's been a mistake. The young woman presented to me is small and plain looking, with the sort of red hair that isn't quite as flattering as Isla's.

When the clerk summons her, I say, "Miss Mary Howell?"

"Yes?"

"I am terribly sorry to bother you. It is about Lord Simpson. Might I speak with you outside? I *am* very sorry for the interruption."

She gives no sign of confusion or consternation and only smiles. "I will not refuse the excuse for a break. Yes, let us walk."

We head outside. Gray has stayed on the street for this interview. It makes more sense for me to speak to Miss Howell alone. I still spot him dressed in a shabby jacket and cap to blend in as well as he can. He'll tail us, but he's been warned to keep his distance. It's midday, and I doubt I need protection from Miss Howell.

"I wish to say in advance that Lord Simpson did not send me," I say. "I was given your name by another, and Lord Simpson will be piqued to hear we have spoken."

She frowns at me. "I have trouble even imagining Charlie in a state of pique, and if this would upset him, I am not certain we should speak."

"He has had an item go missing," I say. "My employer and I have been hired to find it."

She brightens at that. "Are you Pinkertons?"

There'd been a time when I'd have been flattered by the question. To young Mallory, the Pinkertons were swashbuckling American Wild West detectives. Sherlock Holmes on horseback, with a pair of six guns at his side. I know better after having chosen the Pinkertons for a high school history report. While I'm sure there were real detectives among them, they were union breakers and corporate thugs, hired to protect the wealthy, not the innocent.

I laugh softly. "Not quite. We are private investigators of a much more discreet nature."

Her eyes still glimmer. "Detectives? Oh, please tell me you

are a detective. I am an actress, and my company is putting on a murder play, with a woman detective, and I wanted the part, but the director says the only women detectives are elderly spinsters."

"You can tell him he is wrong. Anyone may be a detective, and the best are the ones no one expects, which may be elderly spinsters or . . ." I gesture at myself.

"Oh, this is terribly exciting. You say Charlie has lost something?" Her eyes round. "No, you said it had been stolen. And he did not wish to give my name because that would imply I could have stolen it. That is very sweet of him, but most short-sighted. In a proper mystery, one cannot rule out suspects simply because one does not wish to accuse them."

"Quite so. It is a delicate situation, and I understand why he did not wish to give your name, but I hope you recognize why we needed to find and speak to you."

"Of course."

"It is even more delicate because the item stolen belonged to another woman of Lord Simpson's acquaintance."

"Lady Inglis?" At my expression, she laughs. "That is the only other woman of his acquaintance at the moment, at least in the manner in which I presume you mean. I can certainly see why you would need to speak to me, though. If a man's . . . womanly friend loses an object at his home, his other womanly friend would be the primary suspect."

"Whoever this other woman is, she did not give your name, either."

A soft, trilling laugh. "You do not need to be quite so discreet, lass, but I understand why you feel the need. I am glad to hear that this other lady did not name me as a suspect. She is truly lovely, is she not?"

The genuine warmth in her voice gives me pause.

"Oh, apologies," she says with a sidelong grin. "Should I hiss and show my claws at the mention of the other woman in Charlie's life? I am sorry to disappoint you, but the situation is far less dramatic. This other lady being in Charlie's life is a blessing. It means I can rest confident that I am getting exactly what I want, a companion for when I wish companionship. Nothing more."

When I don't respond immediately, she says, "That is not what you expect, either, is it? After all, I am an actress, only on the stage in hopes of securing a wealthy man to whisk me off it."

She grins. "If that were the case, I have chosen very poorly. No, I realize that is what people expect of actresses, but sadly, it is also what men expect. They fall in love with us on the stage, but to them, it is like seeing a pretty doll in a window. They do not wish us to stay on the stage. That is only the display case. Once they choose us, we are to give it up and live tucked away in comfort." She glances at me. "Comfort and abject boredom."

I smile. "It does sound rather dull."

"It would be. I will admit, I do not always intend to be a seamstress, but only because I aspire to make a proper career as an actress, which will not happen if I am a kept woman."

"Or a wife."

Another trilled laugh. "Heavens, no. Fortunately, I do not need to worry about either of those things with Charlie. If he wanted a wife, he'd marry the woman whose name we are not saying." She purses her lips. "If she'd have him, which she will not. But he would not marry me, and he cannot afford to keep me, so I am free to enjoy what he does offer."

I consider which avenue to pursue first. "You said his other lady friend will not have him?"

"Sadly, no. Sadly for poor Charlie, that is. Not sadly for the lady in question, as I do not blame her for not wanting another husband. If I were a widow with money, I would never marry again. I would simply take lovers."

"You are under the impression that Lord Simpson would like to marry her?"

Here, Miss Howell loses a little of her sparkle, retreating into a solemn, "That is not for me to say, miss, and as I cannot see how it relates to any missing item, I should not speculate."

"Understood and, as you say, inconsequential. You also said he cannot afford to keep you." I smile at her. "I presume you would be expensive."

Her good nature returns at that. "*Dreadfully* expensive. I would require oranges and strawberries year round."

"Which is more than Lord Simpson could afford?"

She sighs. "The poor fellow. I am only glad that he is still able to go abroad, as he planned. I had begun to worry he would need to cancel the trip. But the situation seems not as dire as he feared."

"Are you going abroad with him?"

"Heavens, no. That he could *certainly* not afford. Nor could I afford the time away from either of my jobs. No, I will travel one day, lass, but it will be to step on the stages of the world."

"Sounds lovely," I say. "Where would you most like to visit?"

She answers, and we finish our walk in amicable discussion of the places we'd love to travel.

---

"I do not like the sound of that," Gray says morosely as I tell him about the interview.

"Yep."

"We had contradictory accounts of Lord Simpson's finances from his brother and the valet. I was inclined to believe his brother was mistaken."

"That Lord Simpson was just crying poor to keep his money from Arthur? That's what I hoped."

"You will want me to investigate his financial situation, then?"

"Yes, and I'll let you set that ball in motion before we pursue a bit of science."

He glances at me.

"It's time to check that ransom note for fingerprints," I say.

# CHAPTER FIFTEEN

It's teatime when Jack—dressed in her maid clothes—comes into the laboratory to tell us our guest has arrived. Our other guest, that is. Our first guest joined us earlier this afternoon for the fingerprint analysis, as he has requested—possibly demanded—to be present anytime we need to do such a thing.

We leave him behind and meet Lord Simpson just inside the front door.

"What's this about, Gray?" Simpson says, and Miss Howell might not have been able to imagine him piqued, but he definitely seems piqued right now.

I step forward. "Thank you so much for joining us. We do appreciate you coming on such short notice, sir." I pause and then say, "I fear it is about your valet, and we wished you to hear this in person."

"My *former* valet?" Simpson exhales. "He stole the letters, didn't he? You could have just said that, instead of summoning me to speak on a 'delicate matter' in regards to your investigation."

"It *is* delicate," I say. "Now, if you will permit our maid to take your coat, we shall have tea upstairs and explain the situation fully."

---

Gray, Simpson, and I have settled in the drawing room, where Jack has served tea. I wait until we've started to eat, then I exclaim, "Oh! Lord Simpson, that plate is not supposed to be used. It has a crack." I rise and put out my hand. "Can you pass it to me, please?"

He does, with some confusion, and I give him a fresh plate from a stack on the sideboard. Then I sit back down.

Gray clears his throat. "About your valet . . ."

"Yes," Simpson says. "You believe he is responsible for this, but I assure you, I cannot see it."

"Because you offered to pay the blackmail if he was."

Simpson pauses. "Yes."

"That is what we wished to speak to you about. The fact that you offered to pay—and did not tell us—meant we went into the interview missing vital information. We need everything, Charles."

Simpson sighs. "So you have summoned me to rap my knuckles? Fine. I deserved that. I could not help myself. Lewis was the obvious suspect, and so I had to be sure."

"And how did you intend to pay him, should he have been the culprit?"

Simpson stops with his teacup raised. "Hmm?"

"This is the other delicate part of this meeting," Gray says. "We had several accounts that your finances are in disorder, and so I investigated, because it seemed odd that you would attempt to pay your valet five hundred pounds if you did not have such funds at hand."

"You investigated my—"

"Yes." Gray meets his gaze. "We are investigators. That is what we do. It appears you have recently defaulted on a loan. It also appears that you have planned a trip to Europe but have not paid for it."

"How the devil—?"

A knock at the door. Gray calls a greeting. It opens, and McCreadie walks in, having only come from downstairs, though he rubs his hands, as if still warming them from the winter cold.

"Hugh," Gray says. "How good of you to join us. Hugh, this is Lord Simpson. Lord Simpson, this is my good friend, Detective McCreadie, criminal officer of the Edinburgh Police."

Simpson visibly blanches before daubing his lips with his napkin and rising to shake McCreadie's hand.

"It seems you have another guest, Duncan," Simpson says. "I shall take my leave—"

"No, Detective McCreadie is here on business. And has shown up just in time for tea." Gray waves to the fourth spot, which Simpson obviously hadn't noticed was set.

"Have you heard of finger marks?" Gray says. "And their applications to criminal science?"

Simpson looks at McCreadie, as if this question is clearly intended for him.

"I am asking you, Charles," Gray says.

"Me? I know nothing of criminal science."

"But you said the other day that you wished to know more about my cases and the application of science in them, and so I thought you might find this interesting. If you look at your fingertips, you'll see tiny ridges in fascinating patterns. No two people's patterns are alike."

Simpson's brows rise as he looks at his fingertips. "They are unique?"

"Yes. In fact, for well over a century, China has used finger marks as an acceptable substitute for contractual signatures.

Japan has used them. India has also used them. We are slower here, but European scientists have been studying finger marks for over a century."

"That is fascinating," Simpson says, in a tone that suggests he's simply being polite.

"Finger marks are everywhere," I say. "Every time we touch something, we leave our mark, quite literally. Like this plate." I gesture at the one I took from him. "You touched one side, so your prints are there. I touched the other. Mine are there."

"And the maid's are all over it," Simpson says, with an easy smile. "The maid's, the cook's . . . I can only imagine how many of these finger marks are on it."

"Only the two sets," I say. "It was cleaned before we ate." I look at Simpson. "Would you like a demonstration? I can show you the marks."

"That's hardly necessary. While this is all very interesting, we are in the midst of tea—"

"Detective McCreadie? Would you assist me?"

I produce four blank cards and a stamp pad that Gray helped me devise. With McCreadie's help, I roll my fingertips in the ink and press them onto the cards. Then I do the same to take Gray and McCreadie's prints. Simpson hesitates, but then he decides to be a good sport and lets me take his prints, which saves me from needing to use the ones on the plate.

"So these are your fingerprints," I say, holding up the card. "Earlier, we conducted the same experiment on the ransom note Lady Inglis received."

Now Simpson stops short. "What?"

"Detective McCreadie? May I have that card?"

He produces an envelope, and I open it with all due drama. "We lifted two sets of prints. One belonged to Lady Inglis, who provided an exemplar so we could exclude hers. The other . . ." I lay it down beside the card with Simpson's print.

"Hmm . . . Am I correct, Detective McCreadie? Do these match?"

I knew they would. I'd memorized a part of the pattern from the letter and noted the match as soon as I took Simpson's prints. If it hadn't been a match, I'd have just pretended this was a very peculiar piece of teatime entertainment.

"It is indeed a match," McCreadie says, his gaze rising to Simpson.

Simpson blusters. "Because I touched it. When Patricia showed me. I held the note."

"No, you didn't," I say. "We asked about that before we took it. Only Lady Inglis handled it. She read it to you aloud and then returned it to the envelope, which she immediately put into her safe, along with the letter."

There are several ways Simpson could play this. The most obvious is to call bullshit on the science. Most people would— it's not even admissible in court yet. But there's a reason Gray liked Simpson. The viscount is a curious and intelligent man, interested in science. He is a believer, and so it never occurs to him to call this bullshit. He knows it isn't.

Instead, his gaze goes straight to McCreadie. "I stole nothing. The letter from Lady Inglis was my own property, and therefore, I cannot be charged with theft."

"Hugh was only here to witness the fingermark identifica-tion," Gray says. "Unless you wish to press the point—and have him agree it was not theft, but it *was* blackmail, which is also illegal."

"The situation is not as it seems," Simpson says.

Gray simply nods, but some offenders need only the vaguest hint of empathy to unburden themselves. As a detective, I inter-viewed suspects where I couldn't bring myself to fake empathy, but sometimes, even a nod was enough.

"I am not a bad person," Simpson says. "You know that,

Duncan. I care very much for Patricia. The problem is . . . Blast it, this was never supposed to go so far."

I open my mouth, but he's not looking at me. Not looking at McCreadie. His confession is for Gray alone.

"You expected her to pay," Gray says.

"Yes, blast it. She has the money. I was very careful about that. I would not have asked for more than she could afford. I never thought she'd bring someone else into it. It wasn't as if she would take such a case to the police."

Because she'd be too ashamed. It wasn't only the amount he'd been careful about. He'd chosen a method of blackmail designed to shame Lady Inglis—his lover, his friend—into paying.

It's probably a good thing Simpson only has eyes for Gray right now, because if he looked my way, I'm not sure I could hide my disgust and outrage well enough to keep him confessing.

"You offered to pay the ransom because you knew she would never allow that," Gray says, still calm, his expression blank. "You also offered to pay your valet because you knew he didn't have the letters. And, if Lady Inglis accused him, as the obvious culprit, you could say you'd attempted to buy them back. That would stall any further investigation until it was too late."

Simpson had let the valet go at exactly the right time for Lewis to be the obvious culprit. Offering to buy back the letters would deliberately muddy the waters. Lady Inglis would think Lewis stole the letters, yet Simpson's offer seemed to prove otherwise, and the date for payment would arrive too quickly for her to make a decision. She'd be forced to pay.

"I would have repaid her," Simpson says.

"Then why not simply ask for a loan?" Gray says.

Frustration darkens Simpson's face. "Because I do not wish to be treated as a child. If I told Patricia that I needed money for my

trip, she would say I do not need the trip. She does not understand that I *do* need it. My mind must be stimulated by travel, or
I grow bored." His lips jut in something dangerously close to a
pout. "I am poor company if I am bored."

I try not to stare at Simpson. Is this what it's like to be born
into the nobility? To never need to work for a living? To not even
understand the difference between a want and a need? It all
blurs together into your unalienable rights.

"I would have repaid it," he says, that lip jutting a little more.
"So it *would* have been a loan."

"For which you threatened her with public humiliation,"
Gray says, his tone still deceptively mild.

"I'd never do such a thing. Not to Patricia. Not to any
woman. I am not that sort of man."

Gray says nothing. I inwardly seethe with all the things I
want to say, all the things I can't say. Gray's silence speaks
enough, and under it, Simpson squirms.

"I would never have exposed her," Simpson mutters. "The
letters are all safe. No one has seen them."

"Good," Gray murmurs. "Then you shall return them to
Lady Inglis."

Simpson perks up. "Yes, of course. I will quietly return them,
and she need never know that I was the one—"

"No."

"I can still credit your investigation. Whoever stole them realized you were on the case and returned them to me in the
post—"

"No."

"But you cannot tell her the truth," Simpson protests. "She
will be hurt, and there is no need—"

"Yes, there is." Gray meets his gaze. "The only question is
*who* tells her the truth. You or me?"

# CHAPTER SIXTEEN

We're at Lady Inglis's house. Simpson never answered Gray's question. He'd gotten up and walked out.

Gray had given him twelve hours. He did ask me about that, and I can grumble that his "consultation" came after he'd made up his mind, but I'll give him this on the grounds that the parties involved are his casual friend and his former lover. They are also members of the nobility. Gray must take care where he places each step to avoid landmines.

Gray and Isla might choose to step on some of those social landmines, but it's a calculated decision with equally calculated efforts to avoid stomping on enough of them to make life in this world untenable.

The next morning, we go to see Lady Inglis. If I'm to cut Gray a break in not consulting me on the timeline, I suspect that if it weren't for me, he'd have given Simpson a full day, possibly even waited until after tomorrow, which is Hogmanay. Yes, that's the deadline for the ransom, but I've already notified Lady Inglis that she doesn't need to pay. Waiting until after the holiday would be the more socially correct thing to do, but in moving sooner, Gray is acknowledging that this is my investigation. And, maybe, he's also acknowledging that while letting Lady Inglis enjoy Hogmanay in blissful ignorance may seem a mercy, I don't think she's the kind of person who would appreciate that. I know I wouldn't.

I suggest Gray go alone. It may be my investigation, but this is still a personal-adjacent matter that might be easier without me there. He asks me to attend, though, and I can tell that's not just Gray being polite. He's uncomfortable visiting Lady Inglis on his own.

I do suggest he tell her in private. We don't know whether Simpson has confessed. I suspect not. Either way, it will be easier for Lady Inglis to hear it from Gray alone.

I sit in the parlor while they go into another room. This time, I make sure the doors are shut and I can't hear any of their conversation. When the clock strikes the half hour, Gray emerges. He shoots me the smallest shake of his head, which means no, Simpson did not confess. Coward.

Lady Inglis appears a moment later, smiling with false brightness, her eyes red rimmed from tears.

"Miss Mitchell," she says. "If I might speak to you, we may conclude our business."

"That isn't necessary, ma'am. We can finish this up in the new year. I will leave you to your day."

"I insist." She tries for that smile again. "I would like to thank you. Duncan? Would you please have someone fetch your coat?"

Gray hesitates. He realizes he's being dismissed, and his gaze shoots to me. I nod, and he leaves with obvious reluctance.

"Miss Mitchell?" Lady Inglis says, and leads me into the adjoining room, which is . . .

Look, I can't tell one Victorian sitting area from another. Sitting room. Parlor. Drawing room. Unless it has books and I can clearly identify it as a library, I know it probably has a specific purpose—Victorian rooms always do—but to me, it's just another place where people sit and talk.

Oh, wait. Scratch that. This one has a piano. That makes it a music room. Of course, it also has chairs, which means it's probably mostly used for sitting and talking. Although, having been in a few of these while someone is playing the piano, I've discovered that just because there's live music doesn't mean people *don't* also sit and talk. It's like going to a piano bar . . . except the player is probably your poor spinster sister-in-law, whose job is to provide pleasant background music.

Lady Inglis walks to the piano, and for a second, I think she's going to sit down and play, but she only runs her fingers along the top of it. Then she looks up abruptly, as if having forgotten I'm there.

"I do appreciate you resolving this matter, Miss Mitchell," she says. "I realize it is an awkward conclusion, and there may have been some temptation to resolve it quietly, with me never knowing the truth, but I appreciate the honesty. I would not have wanted to be coddled with lies."

"Dr. Gray thought you deserved to know." I don't add that I agree—there's no need to insert myself here.

She smiles a little wistfully. "Of course he did. He is a good man."

"He is."

She looks toward the window. "I suppose you think me foolish."

"Not at all. Lord Simpson is very charming, and everyone we spoke to had nothing but praise for him."

"Oh, I do not mean that." Her smile turns my way, rueful now. "I am disappointed in Charles but, perhaps, not as shocked as I should be. I recognize his flaws, and I always thought they did not affect me unless I married him, which I had no intention of doing. I misjudged. That is my fault."

She sighs as she walks to the window. "I have known for a while that the affair ought to end. I may retain him as a friend, if that is possible, but otherwise . . ." She shrugs. "While I loved my husband very much, I was young when we married, and after his death, I wanted to experience a different sort of life. That whim is passing, and I fear in a few years, I shall be much too dull for Charlie's tastes, an aging widow with more interest in her charities and foundations than the latest gossip and balls."

She gazes out the window long enough that I eye the door, wondering whether I'm supposed to leave.

"When I said you must think me foolish, I was referring to Duncan," she says finally, still looking out. "You are aware I had a past with him?"

She glances over and then nods before I can say anything, as if my expression answered for me. "I thought as much. That is where I was foolish."

She turns fully my way. "Shortly after I met Duncan, I made the mistake of saying I knew French. What I meant is that I know enough French to give instructions to a maid in a Paris hotel. He bought me a book in French—about Renaissance art, which is an area of interest for me. I could barely decipher five words per page. That book reminds me of Duncan himself. He is a story written in another language, one I do not know. One I pretended to know."

She walks across the room. "I never knew where I stood with Duncan, what he truly thought of me, and so I made mistakes. Silly mistakes more becoming an infatuated girl than a grown woman. I am not certain why I did what I did. To make him jealous and force some admission of caring? Or to pretend I did not feel any depth of emotion for him myself?"

She makes a face and waves her hand. "You have no idea what I mean, and I'm prattling. My point is that I *was* foolish. I hurt him, and I lost him, and I know I am not getting him back."

She meets my gaze. "Do not make the same mistake, Miss Mitchell."

"Dr. Gray and I are not—"

"Not currently involved. I know, and if I ever thought otherwise, that was my jealousy speaking. Duncan would not employ a young woman with any other intentions. But you are more than that pretty face, and he is clearly fond of you. Consider me a soothsayer peering into the future and offering you a warning. Do not mistake his seeming lack of emotion for an actual lack of it. He does feel, and he can be hurt."

*Yes, I know that.* I could say so, but there's no point. This is advice offered genuinely, and it applies even to friendship, so I can take it as that, with only a solemn nod and a "Thank you, ma'am."

"Good." She brightens, but it's still forced, the look in her eyes a little lost before she finds purpose with, "Let us get you paid. Best to settle my accounts before the year's end."

# CHAPTER SEVENTEEN

It's the last day of the year, and Gray and I are enjoying a day of rest. Okay, "enjoying" might be an exaggeration. Possibly even sarcasm. It isn't even noon yet, and we're already at loose ends.

Any festivities won't begin until this evening, which means we have the whole day to do whatever we want. Except . . . Well, we can't do what we want because before Isla left on last-minute errands with Mrs. Wallace, she made us promise not to do any work. At all. We can't crack open a jar from Gray's collection of pickled body parts. We aren't even supposed to set foot in the laboratory. Gray can't work on his latest paper for publication. I can't catch up on reading his past publications. If it is even tangentially related to the triumvirate of work—undertaking, forensic science, or detection—we are forbidden to engage in it, which seems more like a punishment than a gift.

As for gifts, I'm still short one for Isla, which means I need to go shopping, but Isla also made me promise to keep an eye on her brother and make sure he doesn't work. I have a feeling that's supposed to go both ways. If I need to watch him, then I also can't sneak in any work. But if he's supposed to be relaxing, then last-minute holiday shopping with me isn't what she had in mind.

While we've been reading, there's really a limit to how long either of us can do that without getting antsy. So when the doorbell rings, we practically bowl each other over in our haste to answer. Jack is running last-minute errands while Alice is with Isla and Mrs. Wallace, meaning we are left to answer the door . . . or fight over who gets the privilege. I manage to throw it open first, with Gray right at my heels.

It's a young man with a thick envelope. "Package for Miss Mallory Mitchell."

"That is me. Thank you." I take it and turn to Gray. "Pay the lad, sir."

"For *your* package?"

He doesn't hesitate, though, and gives the young man enough to set the boy grinning. After the door is shut, Gray whisks the envelope from my hand.

"Fine," I say. "I will repay you."

"That is not my concern. My concern is that this almost certainly contains work, and we are not to work today."

I reach for the envelope. "Let me open it and find out."

He holds it aloft. "I cannot allow you to take that chance. In merely opening it, you might lay eyes on correspondence of a work nature and thus break your vow to Isla. I will save you from that. You may have this the day after tomorrow."

I glare and grab for it, but he easily holds it above my head.

"Pity you are not taller," he says. "If only you could reach — Ow!"

He dances back, lifting his knee. "Did you just kick your employer in the shin?"

"Certainly not." I pluck the envelope from his hand. "I am forbidden to work today, so you cannot be my employer."

"That isn't how it works."

I peer up at him. "Is it not? So you are always my employer? Always in a position of authority, ready to wield it over me even on a rare full day off? How very Victorian of you."

"That . . ." He fixes me with a look. "That is unfair."

"Nope." I walk off, holding the envelope. "See, now if you'd accused me of kicking a *friend* in the shins, I'd have felt bad. But an employer who insists on being treated as an employer even when I am not working? *He* deserves a kick in the shins."

"Who is the package from?" he says as I head for the stairs.

"Such an employer also does not deserve to share in the temporary distraction of *my* unexpected mail."

I'm halfway up the stairs when Gray snatches the envelope from my hands. I wheel and nearly stumble straight into his arms. He manages to catch me.

"Trying to trip me on the stairs now?" I say.

"I just saved your life. You could have fallen and broken your neck."

"Only because you—" I shake my head. "The envelope, please."

"Am I allowed to witness the opening?"

"If you can be quiet and patient. Which means no."

He shakes his head and hands it over. We continue up and back into the library, where I sit. Then I open the envelope to find a sheaf of papers. I flip through the sheets and frown.

"It seems to be a manuscript," I say. "How odd. Who would . . . ?"

I trail off as I see the letter on top.

Dear Miss Mitchell,

I very much enjoyed meeting you and Dr. Gray, and I would love to learn more about your joint efforts in the science of detection. Might I

take you both to dinner next year, when I visit
Edinburgh in the summer?

In the meantime, here are the first chapters of
my new book. I have even signed it. I thought it
might be an appropriate Hogmanay gift for Dr.
Gray's sister.

All the brightest blessings in the new year.
May 1870 be wonderful for you both.

Faithfully yours,
Charles Dickens

I stare at the letter as my eyes fill. Then I hand the papers to
Gray and go to look out the window over the rear gardens.

"Mallory?" Gray says, his voice soft. "Are you all right?"

"I am overcome by his kindness, that is all."

His hand closes on my elbow, making me jump, but I don't
turn.

"That is not all," he murmurs.

I shake my head.

"Mr. Dickens will not be taking us to dinner next year, will
he?" Gray's voice is so soft that it breaks the dam, tears flowing
even as I wipe them away.

"I wondered if that was it," Gray says. "You were very kind
when we spoke to him, but I could tell something was wrong.
When he spoke about his new book, you . . . seemed distressed. I
did not know whether to speak of it again later. I realize there are
things you know that . . . we should not."

I nod, still looking out the window.

"Might we talk of it?" he murmurs. "Since I have figured it
out for myself?"

I hesitate, and then I turn. "I didn't know until he mentioned what he was writing, and then I realized what it was and that he'll never finish it and . . ."

Gray pulls me into a hug. It's a careful movement, gently tugging me and checking for any resistance. I let myself fall onto his shoulder, and he pats my back, a little awkwardly.

"I'm overreacting," I say.

"Not at all."

"I don't know Mr. Dickens beyond his work. I shouldn't be so rattled by knowing he's going to die soon. I just . . ." I take a deep breath and blurt, "It reminds me of watching the hanging."

I expect him to ask how, but he only nods and says, "You see a living person and know they're going to die."

"Which happened with my nan, too. I knew she was dying. I was there when she did. But it felt different. I helped put someone on the gallows and watched her die. Saw her speak, knowing she would be dead in a few minutes. She was a horrible person, but still . . ."

"Yes."

After I'd gone to the execution, Gray told me that he'd accompanied McCreadie to a couple, when McCreadie had to stand as witness. Like me, he thought he'd been prepared, and then discovered he wasn't.

"And Mr. Dickens *isn't* a horrible person," I say. "He didn't kill anyone. But somehow, because I know he's dying soon, I feel as if I'm responsible. It wasn't like that with my nan."

"Because in Mr. Dickens's case, you possess knowledge no one else does."

"I can't stop his death," I say. "In case you're wondering."

"I would never wonder that," he says softly.

"It's a stroke. Maybe he already feels poorly and that's why he's retiring from the performances." I glance at the letter. "So, yes, that has been weighing on my mind, and I apologize if I've been testy."

His lips quirk. "If you were, I presumed I gave you cause, as usual."

He sobers and steps back. "In this case, I *did* give you cause, and I would like to apologize for that. I insisted on hearing Lady Inglis out regarding the case, and then I snapped at your every attempt to make the situation easier for me."

"Yes," I say, but then add, "I understand it was difficult for you."

"Which is why you tried to mitigate that." He walks across the library and lowers himself to a chair with a sigh. "I thought I could emotionally detach myself from it, but I could not."

I know what I should say, and I don't want to. But if I really am his friend, then I need to.

I settle into the seat next to his and turn to him. "If you regret how things ended . . ."

"I do."

I tamp down the blaze of disappointment.

"You could reverse that," I say.

He frowns over at me, brows creasing. "Reverse . . . ?"

"If you still have feelings for Lady Inglis, I strongly suspect they would be reciprocated."

He lets out a deep sigh and slumps into his chair. "Which is both the problem and *not* the problem. The opposite of the problem, in fact."

"Okay . . ."

He slants a look my way. "I am going to make a confession that will not reflect well on me. I was not entirely honest about how things ended. Yes, I made the mistake of thinking it was an exclusive relationship. Yes, I found out otherwise. Yes, that would have ended the relationship for me. However . . ."

He fusses in his seat before saying, "I may have given the

impression I was angry, even hurt. I certainly behaved that way to Lady Inglis. But that is a lie. I was relieved."

"Relieved?"

His hands move on his lap, as if he's not sure what to do with them. "When it happened, I discovered I was relieved to have a reason to end the affair. I enjoyed her company, but we did not suit, and instead of politely disengaging, I leapt on an excuse."

He glances my way. "An excuse that could be seen as her fault. Which was not my intention at the time. I took full responsibility for the misunderstanding. I thought that would be the end of things. However, the problem with blaming a misunderstanding is that it leaves the other party thinking that the problem can be rectified."

"Ah," I say. "Lady Inglis wanted to fix things. That's why she sent the letter and such."

A slight flush touches his cheeks. "Yes, and the more she tried to reunite, the worse I felt." He takes a deep breath. "I treated her poorly."

"Not as poorly as Lord Simpson did."

A humorless smile. "That is not much consolation, given how horrified I am by his actions. It also compounds the matter. She deserves better."

"She does," I say. "And I hope she finds it. What you did . . ."

I consider before I continue, "I understand that you feel bad for misleading her, but I also understand why you did. Is it ever possible to break up with someone and *not* hurt their feelings? There's a breakup cliché in my world. The person ending things often says 'It's not you, it's me' in hopes of making it easier. Because how do you tell someone you just don't fancy them enough?"

"Yes. I was fond of her. I enjoyed our time together, and she was a good person who did nothing wrong." He exhales. "So that is my confession. If I was uncomfortable during this case, it was because I had done wrong by her. I could fix that by confessing . . . but it feels as if it would only make things worse."

"Yeah, going back and saying you just weren't that into her definitely *isn't* going to make her feel better. We solved her case, and from what I understand, that pushed her to make a choice she already knew she had to make." I glance at him. "Like discovering she was still seeing Lord Simpson pushed you to make a choice you knew you had to make. Sometimes we need the push. Now I hope she finds someone who treats her as she deserves to be treated."

"As do I."

I rise and take the envelope from the table. "Circling back to this, Mr. Dickens wanted me to give the first chapters to Isla, but I don't feel right doing that."

"Because he'll never finish the book."

I nod. "I think, after his death, I can give this to her and explain."

"She would like that very much."

I pass him a wry smile. "I still need to get her a gift, though."

His brows shoot up. "You have not—" He winces. "Of course you haven't. You have been busy on the case I dragged you into."

"You didn't drag, and thanks to that case, I can get her something nice. I just . . ." I glance at the window, the light already fading. "I need to do it fast."

"Let us go out together, then."

# CHAPTER EIGHTEEN

That evening is a true delight. I might not have gotten the Victorian Christmas I envisioned, but this is even better. It resurrects wonderful memories of my nan and our Hogmanay celebrations together, while building new memories for this new life.

We start with a feast that's half Scottish and half Dickens's Christmas Carol, with haggis and roast goose and mincemeat and black buns. Even Jack decides to stay for this part, though she'll leave later to meet up with friends. McCreadie comes to dinner, as does Annis.

Once the meal is eaten, we all help with the cleanup, over Mrs. Wallace's protests—I get the sense this is an annual mini-drama, with everyone knowing their lines. Once the dishes are done and the kitchen is clean, Isla presents all the staff with the traditional Hogmanay gift of new clothes, which we wear that night to symbolize a new year and new beginnings. As I put on my dress, I discovered a pound note in each pocket, which is apparently another tradition to ward off misfortune, presumably of the financial sort.

From there, we go into the streets where the party is heating up . . . quite literally. There are endless torches and bonfires, and the others indulge my love of fireballs by joining a parade. The evening proceeds up to Calton Hill, where we watch boats below, which have been, yep, set on fire.

We end the celebrations at midnight with Molotov cocktails —yes, that's my fault, too. Then Simon, Alice, and Mrs. Wallace stay behind at the town house, and Annis returns home, while Gray, Isla, McCreadie, and I go to McCreadie's apartment so Gray can be first over the threshold.

According to Scottish custom, the first foot over the door sets the luck for the year, and the most lucky guest of all is a tall and dark-haired man. My nan said this hearkened back to Viking days, when finding a blond dude on your doorstep was really bad luck. Gray does the first-footing every year for McCreadie, taking his friend a gift of salt and a black bun. Then we all go inside to exchange gifts.

It's nearly three when we get home, a little tipsy and a little giddy. Gray stays to share a drink with Simon, which also lets him serve as the first-footer for Simon's apartment.

"I have another gift for you," I say to Isla once we're inside.

"More? You were overly generous already."

I wave that off. "This is just a little extra. It's in my room."

We make our way up, and I pass her a package wrapped in brown paper. "Jack and I visited a print shop during the investigation, and I bought you some samples."

She slowly takes the package. "Given what you were there to investigate, do I want to know what sort of 'samples' you bought me?"

"Warming material."

She arches an eyebrow. "Warming material?"

"Scottish winters are very long, very dark, and very cold. That might make them a little more tolerable."

Her cheeks go bright red, and she feigns a scowl.

"You just like to see me blush, don't you?" she says.

"You blush very prettily."

Her eyes narrow. "And you are a very poor liar."

"Happy Hogmanay, Isla."

She looks at me. Then she puts her arms out, and I fall into her hug.

"Happy Hogmanay, Mallory."

I am in the kitchen by dawn, having entreated Alice to get me up, no matter how tired or hungover I am. I still have one gift left to give, and while I convinced Mrs. Wallace to lend me her kitchen for it, I can't rely on her to wake me.

Mrs. Wallace may have granted me the kitchen—or a piece of countertop and a burner on the stove—but that doesn't keep her from grumbling about my "nonsense." I ignore her and spend the next two hours working, past the time when Alice rushes in to say, "They are awake, ma'am!" and Mrs. Wallace kicks into high gear preparing the first breakfast of the new year.

Once I'm ready, I race upstairs to change as quickly as I can. Luckily, I already put on all my undergarments and only need to switch out my dress, wash my face and adjust my hair. Then it's back down to the kitchen to get the gift.

I walk into the dining room just as Gray is saying to Isla, "Is Mallory not joining us?"

"Mallory is right here," I say. "Mallory had to get up at an ungodly hour to make your gift."

I set the platter in front of him. On it are a half dozen still-warm pastries.

"Doughnuts," I say. "I can't tell whether they're a thing yet, but if they are, they're an American thing."

Isla leans forward and inhales. "They smell delicious."

"They're for you, too," I say. "Duncan gets first pick. Those two are dusted with cinnamon sugar." I point. "Those two are jam filled, and the other two are my attempt at a chocolate glaze, which is tricky here."

I take my seat. "They're basically fried dough. I went through a phase of making them as a teen, and I remember the recipe. *And* I can get all the ingredients here and make them without an electric oven."

Isla sighs. "Do not tease me again with talk of electric ovens and electric ice boxes."

I could ask when's the last time she actually used the oven here, but I hold my tongue and turn to Gray. "If you don't like them, please feel free to say so. I have a couple more recipes I could try."

"And if I do like them?" he says.

"Then I'll make you a batch every month. One plateful wouldn't be a proper gift. Although, you might need to speak to Mrs. Wallace if you want that—the biggest problem making these was getting her to give up part of her kitchen this morning."

He takes his fork and cuts off a piece, and I don't correct his process. One bite, and then another, and then another.

I try not to hold my breath awaiting the verdict. Of course I do. This isn't the fanciest gift I could get him, but I put more thought and effort into it than I care to admit.

"There is one problem," he says as he takes a bite of the next one.

My heart thuds. "Okay."

"I will tell Mrs. Wallace that you need to commandeer her kitchen once a month, but you are going to need to explain why I do not eat her carefully prepared breakfast this morning."

He glances at Isla. "You will need to wait and try next month's batch. *These* are all mine."

She rolls her eyes, reaches over and snatches one, and I relax and settle in to watch them eat as they chatter and laugh.

1869 has been a hell of a year, and I'm still reeling, as much as I try to pretend otherwise. But it's no longer 1869. Today is the first day of 1870, and I'm still here, no longer a guest but a citizen.

While I've never been one to make resolutions, this year, I will. It's time to make this my world. Find my place and settle in, because I'm not going anywhere.

I snake a hand out to grab a doughnut from Gray's plate. He tries to grab it back, but I take a quick bite before holding it out.

"Still want it?" I say.

He eyes the bitten doughnut. "I ought to say no but . . ."

I laugh, cut it in half and give him the piece without the bite. Then I settle in with my pastry and my coffee and listen to Isla and Gray making plans for the day. Plans for *our* day, together.

## Thank You For Reading!

Death at a Highland Wedding is the next novel after the *Schemes & Scandals* novella. In it, I whisk Mallory, Duncan, Isla and Hugh off to the highlands for the wedding of Hugh's little sister. Death at a Highland Wedding is now available, and you can turn the page for the first chapter.

# CHAPTER ONE

There's nothing quite like a Highland wedding. I say this as if I've been to dozens. I've gone to two, both times as my grandmother's plus-one, attending the weddings of happy couples I'd never actually met and had to keep checking a note on my phone to remember who they were.

This time it's different. Okay, I'm still a plus-one. And I still don't know the happy couple. But instead of keeping notes on my phone, I have them written on a piece of paper, stuffed deep into the voluminous pockets of my equally voluminous layers of Victorian dress.

The last wedding I went to in the Scottish Highlands was June 2016. This one is also taking place in June . . . 1870.

There's a story there. A long one. The short version is that I passed through time at the fickle whim of some unknown cosmic force. My nan named that force Fate and said I am exactly where I was always supposed to be. Which is apparently in the body of a buxom blond twenty-year-old housemaid instead of an athletic brunette thirty-one-year-old police detective.

I have yet to appreciate *that* part of the switch, but I must appreciate where else I landed—in the household of a chemist and her doctor-turned-undertaker brother, who works in early forensic science. Along with their police-detective friend, they know my story, so I'm no longer scrubbing chamber pots. I'm the assistant to that forensic scientist, Dr. Duncan Gray. I'm also, apparently, his plus-one for this wedding, which is for Detective Hugh McCreadie's younger sister . . . Iona? Fiona? It's in my notes.

At the moment, we're in a coach, heading into the countryside. For propriety's sake, Gray should sit beside his sister, but since no one can see us in here, we've maneuvered McCreadie to sit beside Isla instead. He's across from me—to make room for both Isla's skirts and mine—and Gray is beside me, separated by a decorous handspan gap between my skirts and his thighs.

I'm wearing a traveling dress, which means shorter skirts and extra petticoats for warmth. My bustle pad makes the jostling journey more comfortable. I'm warm and snug, and it would be lovely, if not for the atmosphere.

Any other time, we'd be chattering away, excited about a rare country holiday. Instead, it feels as if we're going to a funeral, everyone somber and staring out windows, with Isla occasionally casting anxious glances at McCreadie.

This is not four friends off to a rousing Highland wedding. It's three friends going along to support the fourth—McCreadie —who looks like he'd rather be at work.

I don't know why McCreadie is estranged from his family. Now that we've all become friends, I think I could get that information easily, but they seem to have forgotten that I don't know, and it's awkward to ask. So I've been playing detective, putting together the puzzle pieces.

I know McCreadie's family is well-to-do. Upper middle class, like the Grays. That's how the boys became friends—they attended the same school. Despite the estrangement, McCreadie is still well-off for a police detective—criminal officer, as they're called in Victorian Scotland. I suspect he receives some family money. I know the break happened when he'd been in his early twenties, around the time he became a police officer, which is also around the time he'd broken off an engagement. I don't know how these three things—the law-enforcement career, the broken engagement, and the familial estrangement—are connected, but I suspect they are.

As for his family, he has one sibling—the sister getting married, who is significantly younger. Like Gray, McCreadie is thirty-one, and his sister seems to be about twenty-one. In the modern world, we sometimes get the impression that Victorian women were all married off at eighteen. In reality, McCreadie's sister is marrying at what's considered the perfect age, as it was for most of the twentieth century.

Any ill blood between McCreadie and his family doesn't extend to his sister, which is why we're here. She asked—begged —him to come, and so he has, for her.

Now we're rumbling along in this coach, with our groom— Simon—driving and the thirteen-year-old parlormaid, Alice, riding beside him, having been invited ostensibly as Isla's lady's maid, but really to give the girl a holiday in the countryside.

When Isla casts yet another anxious glance McCreadie's way, I decide it's up to me to break this ice, which I do in the most time-honored of road-trip ways.

"Are we there yet?" I say, peering through the dusty window. "It's so much faster with the bridge."

That gets McCreadie's attention. There are people who are good at long, morose silences—such as the guy sitting beside me —but McCreadie fairly leaps on this excuse, his handsome face lightening in a smile.

"Bridge?" he says. "Over the Forth?"

"Yep."

"How is that even possible?"

"I'm not an engineer," I say. "But there's also a railroad bridge that I'm pretty sure gets built in this century."

"They are starting one next year," rumbles a voice beside me.

I glance over to see Gray, relaxing with his eyes still shut.

I elbow him. "Tell us more."

He sighs. "I do not know more. I only heard that they are beginning a suspended bridge for trains."

I frown. "Are you sure? I don't think they start construction until near the end of this century." I pause, thinking hard. "No, they did build another one, but it coll—" I snap my mouth shut. "Never mind."

Isla's brows rise. "Are you suggesting that if another bridge is built first, we should not use it?"

"Er, probably not."

"Well, I for one might be willing to play the odds, if such a thing comes about," McCreadie says. "Taking the ferry really does make this an interminable trip. Dare I ask how long it would take in your day, Mallory?"

"With bridges and motor cars? An hour to Stirling Castle. So probably two hours to where we're going."

Isla sighs. "I was born in the wrong century."

"What is going on out there?" McCreadie says, opening his window to poke his head through. "I swear we have slowed."

"See what you have done?" Gray says to me. "A few moments ago, we were all perfectly content with our eight-hour coach ride, and now everyone is complaining."

"*You* spent all of yesterday moaning about spending all of today in a coach."

His eyes narrow. "I mentioned it once."

"Once at breakfast, once while we were dissecting that liver, once while—"

"I had resigned myself to the journey," he says. "And now you have spoiled it. Remember whose coach this is. It will be a much longer trip if you walk."

"Can I walk?" I say. "Please?" I lean toward McCreadie's open window. "I'm sure I can move faster than this."

"There does appear to be some sort of slowdown," McCreadie says, still looking out the window.

"See what you did?" Gray aims a mock glare my way. "You complain about our speed, and the universe takes umbrage."

"Can you tell what's going on up there?" I ask McCreadie.

His smile sparks. "No, which means we ought to investigate."

McCreadie raps on the roof for Simon to stop the carriage. As I gather my skirts, Gray rises and reaches for the door handle.

"Opening the door for us?" McCreadie says. "Very kind, but unnecessary. Stay right there and nap—"

Gray is already out of the coach. Then McCreadie holds the door as I descend.

"Not joining us?" I say to Isla.

"I deem this particular mystery too minor to deserve my attention. I will stay here, and absolutely will not stretch my legs onto the other seat in a most unladylike fashion. Nor will I sneak anything from the picnic basket in your absence."

Gray slowly turns around.

She rolls her eyes. "Do not worry, Duncan. If I open the basket, I shall take only a sandwich. Sometimes I think I would *prefer* a brother who worried instead about me behaving in an unladylike fashion. Now go. Your beloved pastries are safe."

As soon as we're out of the coach, the problem is evident: it's a traffic jam. The road curves ahead, but there are three coaches between us and that curve. Simon had discussed the route with Gray, and they'd decided to avoid the major road and take a side one. Seems everyone else did the same, and now it's like leaving modern-day Vancouver on a Friday, heading up to the lakes and mountains and fresh air of the Okanagan.

I'm guessing it will get better the farther we travel from Edinburgh, but for now, this really is like those weekend traffic snarls —city folk trying to get a bit of time away on a gorgeous June day.

It's *not* the weekend here. In fact, it's Monday. Weekends aren't a thing yet, at least not in the sense of getting time off. If you're nobility, you have all the time off you want. Middle class? Depends on where you fall on that scale. Gray runs his family's lucrative business and can take time off whenever he pleases. McCreadie cannot.

As for the people who *really* need time off to rest? Those working in factories and shops and domestic service? A good employer will give you Sunday morning for church, and there's been a move toward making it a full day, but two entire days off? How would the world function?

In modern times, we look back at that with equal parts horror and superiority. Horror at the long hours, and superiority at the thought that no one realized people are more productive with time off to rest and enjoy themselves. And yet the forty-hour work week has been a thing for a century, despite studies proving that employees can do as much by working less. Don't tell that to corporations, though. A four-day work week? How would the world function?

The people in the coaches ahead will *not* be working class. The carriages are all as fine as—if not finer than—Gray's. While the "less fortunate" might get into the Highlands to visit relatives, they'll take the train. The well-to-do want the privacy and convenience of their own conveyances. Like private jets that move really, really slowly.

I don't grumble for long. It's too nice a day, and walking under the shade of oaks and willows, I'm reminded of how much I love country getaways. Oh, I'm a city girl. No doubt about that. But there is much to be said for walking along a sun-dappled dirt road, a light breeze smelling of grass and loam and lifting the heat, birdsong filling the air. No stink of coal fires. No clatter of hooves. The only familiar smell is . . .

Gray takes my elbow to sidestep me past a pile of steaming horse dung. Yep, there's always that.

As we walk, coach doors and windows open, with people calling out to ask what's going on, as if we can see better than their high-perched drivers. We keep walking. When we reach the corner, I let out a groan.

It's not a "volume of traffic"–style jam. It's the kind caused by a disabled vehicle. Just around the corner, a single coach has stopped. Two well-dressed men stand back, eyeing the coach as if waiting for it to levitate, lifted by a hand from the heavens above.

McCreadie sighs. "Looks as if we will get our jackets dirty, Duncan. These fellows are going to need some help."

Gray only grunts. If the problem is a stuck coach or broken wheel—which happens as often as flat tires—neither of them will stand by waiting for divine intervention. They'll take off their coats, roll up their sleeves, and get to work.

"Trouble with the coach?" McCreadie calls as we draw near.

The two men turn, and McCreadie's gait slows. They're about our age. Both are dressed as if heading to a formal event, wearing silk cravats and top hats. Even McCreadie—usually a total fashion plate—is dressed for travel.

One of the men is tall and broad-shouldered, with light

brown hair. The other has medium brown hair and is more compact. When they see us, the darker-haired one's frown lifts in a welcoming grin. He opens his mouth to speak, but before he can, his companion steps forward.

"Duncan Gray," the bigger man says. "Thank God you are here. We are in most urgent need of your very special skills."

Something in his tone grates down my spine, and I find myself hoping he's in need of a doctor . . . to treat some terribly embarrassing rash.

"Cranston," Gray says, his tone managing to be both cool and cordial at the same time. "What seems to be the trouble?"

"I have lost my lapel pin." He motions to his cravat. "We stopped to take . . . a brief jaunt into the woods, and when I climbed back into the carriage, I realized it was gone."

McCreadie's eyes narrow. "You are holding up an entire line of coaches because you lost a stickpin, Archie?"

"It is a very expensive pin."

The darker-haired man murmurs, "I did mention that we ought to pull over up ahead and walk back."

"Nonsense, Sinclair." Cranston claps the other man on the back. "They can wait. We shall be moving soon, now that we have Detective Duncan Gray on the job."

"Hugh is the—" Gray begins.

"Yes, yes, but Hugh is a *police* detective." Cranston gives the word a derisive twist that has my hackles practically vibrating. "Gray here is the celebrity. Even has books written about his adventures. Well, children's books, but still."

Yes, someone is chronicling Gray's investigations. No, they are not children's books—they are detective serials. Victorians may be a prudish lot, but they make up for it with a thirst for blood and guts, and a good mystery provides that.

We are seeing the start of the detective novel, with Sherlock Holmes still nearly twenty years away. The primary market for such work, especially true crime, is women, just as it is in the modern world. Such an interest, though, could be concerning in a woman, and so these stories are shared with children, as cautionary tales.

*Crime doesn't pay, lass.*

*The detective will find you out, lad.*

Seeing a market, someone leapt on Gray's adventures. Since then, they've been shut down and replaced with our own scribe —and new housemaid—Jack, who is far less inclined to make me look like a simpering magician's assistant and McCreadie look like a bumbling police detective.

But it's still Gray who gets the limelight. People prefer heroes to ensemble casts, and that's fine for McCreadie and me, who like to stay out of the limelight. Not quite so fine for Gray, who would really rather join us in the shadows.

"Dr. Gray's specialty is forensic pathology," I say.

Both men turn my way, as if the trees spoke.

"My assistant, Miss Mitchell," Gray says. "Who is correct. Unless you have a body that requires dissection, I cannot help solve your mystery."

"As for the stickpin," I say. "It's right there. Caught on your pocket."

Cranston looks down, and McCreadie barely suppresses a snicker as he sees the jeweled pin, half caught on the edge of Cranston's pocket.

"The mystery is solved," McCreadie says, "we will take our leave. Good day, gentlemen."

"Wait. You cannot leave before saying hello to Violet. She would be most offended."

Something spasms in McCreadie's face, but he quickly schools his features and gives a stiff nod of his head.

"Violet!" Cranston bellows, as if the coach isn't six inches away. He throws open the door. "Look who we have met on the road. Hugh McCreadie. You remember Hugh. Your former fiancé."

I tense, and my gaze swings to that open door. A small hand grasps it. Then a woman looks out. She's tiny, with perfect features, milky skin, and raven-black hair. Her gaze is shuttered until it falls on Gray, and then she smiles.

"Duncan," she says. "It is good to see you."

She visibly braces as she turns to look past the door. She doesn't try to keep the smile, just fixes on a placidly empty look as she turns to McCreadie.

"Hugh," she says.

He dips his chin. "Violet. I hope you are well."

"Oh!" Violet says, as her gaze lands on me. "Miss Mitchell?"

I nod and smile as I move away from McCreadie, and Violet gratefully follows me with her gaze.

"Our housekeeper adores the stories of your adventures with Duncan," she says. "She is most enamored with your character." Her cheeks pink. "With you, I mean."

I smile. "It's half me and half a character. I'm glad your housekeeper is enjoying the stories."

"She truly is. I shall have to read them. I keep meaning to but . . ." She trails off, and I can imagine why she doesn't read them. I'm not sure what I expected of McCreadie's ex-fiancée, but it wasn't a woman who—a decade later—still needed to brace herself before looking his way.

Violet clears her throat. "I *will* read them. They sound most delightful. And I am pleased to make your acquaintance. I am sorry for the delay. My brother . . ." Her gaze slants his way, with the faintest eye roll. "I do apologize, and we will not delay you any longer. It is good to see you, Duncan. And . . ." That hitch, as she braces. "Hugh."

They both tip their hats as Violet withdraws into the coach.

"We will see you all again soon enough," Cranston says as Sinclair climbs in after Violet. "A race to the castle."

"You are attending the wedding?" I say, in what I hope is a neutral tone.

Cranston grins over at me. "I should certainly hope so," he says as he swings into the coach. "They would have a hard time holding the wedding without the groom."

# ABOUT THE AUTHOR

Kelley Armstrong believes experience is the best teacher, though she's been told this shouldn't apply to writing her murder scenes. To craft her books, she has studied aikido, archery and fencing. She sucks at all of them. She has also crawled through very shallow cave systems and climbed half a mountain before chickening out. She is however an expert coffee drinker and a true connoisseur of chocolate-chip cookies.

*Visit her online:*

www.KelleyArmstrong.com
mail@kelleyarmstrong.com

 facebook.com/KelleyArmstrongAuthor
 x.com/KelleyArmstrong
 instagram.com/KelleyArmstrongAuthor

www.ingramcontent.com/pod-product-compliance
Lightning Source LLC
Chambersburg PA
CBHW021146310726
48971CB00002B/511

* 9 7 8 1 9 8 9 0 4 6 9 6 8 *